Beneath the Western Slopes

Beneath the Western Slopes

Stoddart

First published in 1987 by
Stoddart Publishing Co. Limited,
34 Lesmill Road,
Toronto, Canada M3B 2T6

Canadian Cataloguing in Publication Data

Roscoe, Patrick, 1962-
  Beneath the western slopes

ISBN 0-7737-2113-4

I. Title.

PS8585.082B46 1987   C813'.54   C86-094937-0
PR9199.3.R657B46 1987

An Ontario Arts Council grant is here gratefully
acknowledged.

Printed and bound in Canada

*For you, Rickie Lee, and for the day
we meet again upon the western slopes.*

Contents

Some of the stories in this book first appeared in the following publications, sometimes in slightly different forms:

"Ingrita and the Governor's Daughter" in *The Malahat Review*; "Never Tears for California" in *The Malahat Review* and the *New Press Anthology: Best Canadian Short Fiction #1*; "The National Circus of Argentina" in *The Malahat Review* and the *New Press Anthology: Best Stories #2*; "There Must Be More to Life Than Kissing Boys" in *dandelion*; The Scent of Young Girls Dying" in *The Canadian Fiction Magazine*; "The Boat in the Stars" in *The Malahat Review*; "Poppies Always Fall" in the *Canadian Forum*; "Heaven, Hell, and Some Points In-between" in *The Canadian Fiction Magazine*; "Beneath the Western Slopes" in *The Canadian Fiction Magazine*.

Ingrita and the Governor's Daughter

The daughter of the state governor was coming to town and
no one knew why.

Señor Ramirez, the owner of the Swingtime Café and the
town's leading citizen, received the news in an oddly worded
letter. It was stamped heavily with the official state seal and
the scent of a disturbing perfume. The café's dim lighting did
not make the vague contents of the letter clearer, and the scent
swimming about his mind made Señor Ramirez uneasy. He
enjoyed thinking precisely.

Señor Ramirez heard a sound behind him and turned to see
two ladies sitting at his best table. One was the town's crazy
old woman, Chonita. Although silent, her moving lips implied
that she was communicating with the floor. The other woman
was young, foreign, and named Ingrita. She was tall and thin,
with long stringy hair and a complexion that did not darken
in the tropical sun. For several months she had been staying
in the town, neither holidaying nor working, but only staring at the townspeople when not asking them many and often
personal questions. Ingrita looked at Señor Ramirez with fixed
eyes. He turned abruptly and walked from the shadows of
his café into the bright sunlight.

He called the townspeople to action. "We have been letting things slip," he announced. "What if the governor is
thinking about constructing his summer residence or some

large government building here in our little town? What if he wishes to know if we are worthy of the long-promised paved road from the capital city? What if he is sending his daughter to see what is what? We must be prepared. Things must change. For instance, all the garbage in our streets must be swept away. And these cows and pigs! These cows and pigs must not be allowed to roam freely. They are dirtying everything and eating the flowers in the plaza. Do we wish to be the laughing stock of our state?"

Before this question could be answered, an unorderly procession burst through the gathering of townspeople. Chonita ran skipping by, surrounded by a ring of loudly laughing and singing children. The parade party careened through the plaza, plucking blossoms and throwing them into the air, knocking into the citizens and forcing them to scatter. "No skipping!" Señor Ramirez shouted. "No skipping and no playing in the graveyard!" The severe expression on his face clouded as he looked around at his friends and neighbours. They were watching the gay parade stream toward the cemetery at the edge of town, where Chonita and the children would pass the afternoon singing to the sun and dancing rings around the headstones. On each adult face there was a look of longing. Then the parade disappeared around a corner, and the citizens turned their faces down to the blossoms scattered about their feet. "It will not be easy," thought Señor Ramirez.

Nevertheless, the townspeople bustled about for several days. They were truly shocked to see the sloth in which they had been living with such ease. Fences were mended and houses repaired. The men curbed their habit of spitting on the sidewalks, the women sewed new clothes for their families, and the children were taught some manners. They were also put to work sweeping the streets, and could be seen standing in the centre of great dusty clouds they conjured with their wands of brooms. Daily customs were thrown on fires to burn with the garbage, and flames of excitement and speculation raged through the town. Everyone felt that some kind of good fortune would befall them as a result of the governor's daughter's visit, but they were not sure what form this luck would take.

During this time the town's prominent citizens, the owners of five small stores, lunched every day at the Swingtime Café, as was their habit. They were the only ones who could afford the prices. Normally the five men sat at separate tables, stealing occasional glances at one another like guilty schoolboys while, under the close scrutiny of Señor Ramirez, they made some show of nibbling at the fancy dishes. They really desired rice and beans, but Señor Ramirez would not allow it. "If you, the leading citizens, began eating peasant fare, where would it all end?" was his typical comment. So the prominent citizens were forced to look at their plates until a suitable period of time passed and they could escape the Swingtime with empty or upset stomachs.

But in the week before the state governor's daughter arrived for her visit the prominent citizens sat together at one large table and ate the food heartily while holding serious discussions. They considered honouring the governor's daughter with banners, parades, musical bands, and displays of native dancing. In the end, however, they decided to create no special to-do. Señor Ramirez put it best: "We are simple, honest, hardworking people. Such qualities are worth more than a million brass bands. Our plain virtues are good enough show for a Spanish Princess."

Late one night, when the town was sleeping beneath the moon, the visitor arrived in a car driven by a minor government official. Only the town's two disreputable citizens, idle unmarried men, witnessed her entrance. The next morning they told stories of a car that flew like a bird and shone like a star, and of the shadow riding in the back seat.

The townspeople were horrified by the news. It was a scandal. Such a long, wearing journey had the governor's daughter made from the capital to be met with what kind of a welcome? What was worse, her exact whereabouts were unknown. The driver was discovered drinking with the town's two disreputable citizens in the cantina. But when the name of the governor's daughter was mentioned he only seemed to become alarmed, muttering incoherently before throwing a fit and falling unconscious into his pool of vomit.

Señor Ramirez was incensed. "In what kind of position are

we being placed? Is the governor's daughter here on state business or on a holiday? How long will she remain? This entire matter is a disgrace to our town." He sent a group of men to look for the missing guest.

They found her several hours later at the river that ran beside the town on its way to the sea. She was not alone. Sitting very near to her on a large, flat rock was Ingrita. The two girls were watching some women wash clothes in the middle of the stream. Both girls were dressed in shameless, revealing bathing costumes. The governor's daughter was especially ill-clad because her suit, borrowed from Ingrita, did not fit her very well. It was too small. The young women splashed their feet in the water and laughed in English, and they did not appear to notice the throng of little children who from a certain distance watched them wide-eyed and open-mouthed.

The prominent citizens did not know what to do. They could hardly speak with dignity to their visitor while she was dressed as she was, yet it would be equally improper to ignore her presence altogether. Señor Ramirez was elected to speak some words in his best politic manner. "Honourable Miss, we have taken the liberty of preparing a delicate luncheon in honour of your gracious visit to our humble town. We beg of you to partake." While waiting for a reply, Señor Ramirez kept his eyes fixed on the mountains which ranged above the town. Ingrita and the governor's daughter laughed and splashed as before, and they accidentally succeeded in soaking Señor Ramirez's fine clothes. He had no choice but to withdraw, and the special luncheon was served to the pigs.

For two days the situation did not improve. The governor's daughter made no attempt to speak with any of the townspeople. Ingrita and she were constant companions and passed the mornings walking around the town, arms wrapped about each other's waists and dressed always in their little bathing costumes. They whispered together, giggled together, and shared secrets no one else could hear. Often they would point to some object or person, then burst into laughter that could be heard all through the town. Each afternoon they took a picnic basket to the graveyard and were seen sitting or chasing butterflies in the long waving grass there. Though Chonita and the children played around them, the two women did not join in their games, and seemed as though alone. At night they shut themselves in Ingrita's room, which the governor's daughter was sharing. It was the room in Chonita's house that was rented to the odd tourist who happened to stray into town. A light burned in the window through all the hours until morning.

Then, on the third day, Ingrita and the governor's daughter approached Señor Ramirez with several requests. Ingrita did the talking while glancing scornfully around the Swingtime Café. They wanted: a typewriter, a typist, pens and paper, and a cool room to work in. The time of play was finished, Ingrita said, but she ignored Señor Ramirez's subtle inquiries into the nature of the work. What she did do was order much food for herself and the governor's daughter, which they ate very quickly. Señor Ramirez did not see how he could ask the only daughter of the state governor to pay for her or her guest's meals.

He speedily made all the arrangements. For the next week Ingrita and the governor's daughter marched around with an official air. They made the habit of striding uninvited and unannounced into the church, school, stores, and houses. As they observed their surroundings, the young women conferred in inaudible tones, with Ingrita writing rapidly all the while. At the end of the afternoon they gave the day's notes to the young girl selected by Señor Ramirez to do the typing. Because her skills were wanting, the girl was forced to work far into the night turning Ingrita's messy handwriting into neat clean pages of English which neither she nor anyone else in town could decipher. Even then, upon checking over the typed pages on the following morning, Ingrita and the governor's daughter often rejected certain sheets as being faulty for reasons only they could see, and ordered them retyped. When not working the two women spent their time eating freely and heartily in the Swingtime Café. They liked to start at the top of the menu in the morning and make their way to its bottom through the day.

The whole town was upset. At the sight of the two women the townspeople took to stealing away like thieves through their own streets. They would not, they told one another, be surprised if one day soon everyone in town were charged with fines, carried off to jail, or executed for unpatriotic thoughts.

Señor Ramirez was the most nervous of all. It was he who was bearing the expense of the typist, her machine and workroom, and the pens and paper. This was not to mention the considerable cost of all the food and beverages consumed by the two young women in his café. Under this strain his finances would surely break soon, but Señor Ramirez did not like to think of a day when the needs of the young women could not be satisfied.

He began to stay up all night, and this served to increase his anxieties. He suffered from cricks in his neck caused by glancing nervously behind him. When all the town should have been sleeping, Señor Ramirez would slip down the back streets and knock softly upon doors until he succeeded in rousing the people behind them. He begged money from the sleepy citizens to help provide for the demands placed upon him. He felt trouble coming, and felt also that he would be the most harmed by it. There was a saying in the town that the biggest boat sinks fastest and deepest. Señor Ramirez whispered about the two figures he often saw creeping through shadows and around corners late at night. He saw other things, too, things too strange to speak about. Lights bobbing in the graveyard and flames flying in the wind. And children awake when no children should be, their faces pressed against the windows of their houses, looking out into the moonlit streets. Soon all the townspeople stayed up through the nights, waiting in darkness behind locked doors for Señor Ramirez and his fears to visit.

One afternoon Señor Ramirez paced up and down the back of his café. Ingrita, the governor's daughter, the minor government official, and the town's two disreputable citizens had been eating, drinking, and smoking for hours. They showed no signs of leaving in the near future. "More cigarettes!" shouted the governor's daughter. "Ten more beer!" called Ingrita. "And make it snappy." Their table was already crowded with empty bottles and plates, and Señor Ramirez's heart fell into his shoes as he counted how much of his money was being consumed so quickly and carelessly. His hands trembled as he placed the full bottles on the table, and he clumsily knocked one onto the floor. Looking down, he could see cigarette butts, ashes, and matches scattered amid the glass. The party did not care to use ashtrays.

Señor Ramirez looked pleadingly at the governor's daughter, appealing with his eyes as a citizen of her father's state. Though the café was dimly lit, the governor's daughter, like Ingrita, wore dark glasses from behind which she stared at the proprietor of the place. She had gained not a little weight during her visit, especially around the belly, and now her body spilled more completely from the small bathing suit. "More matches!" she suddenly shouted in a voice which, considering that Señor Ramirez stood close before her, need not have been so very loud.

The party remained in the Swingtime for several more hours. The minor government official and the two disreputable citizens drank quickly and quietly, as though afraid that at any moment their free drinks and good fortune would be snatched away. Ignoring them, the two women leaned together across the table, whispering in English.

At last Señor Ramirez heard the governor's daughter shout at him. "I want some things. I want more paper, more pens, more typewriters, more typists. I want a camera and I want film. I want these things by tomorrow morning at eight o'clock. Sharp." With that the party left the café.

Señor Ramirez worked all night acquiring what the governor's daughter demanded. The next day the two women moved unhurriedly around the town, followed by the two disreputable citizens, the minor government official, and a man known from neither the town nor any neighbouring village. Whenever the two women stopped to examine or discuss, their followers stopped also, and patiently waited.

Their sleepless nights had left the townspeople dazed, and whomever the party neared started suddenly, as though feeling footsteps treading upon their graves. Men looked fearfully down at their feet or made vague motions that held no meaning. Women looked on, horrified and helpless, as their children fixed bright eyes on the swelling belly of the governor's daughter; and when a child darted up to rest a hand on this stomach, its mother would feel a cold voice touch her heart and tell of the day this child would wade across the River and into California, to vanish forever. The governor's daughter only swatted at the children as she would at flies, and like Ingrita took no notice of their parents, or of the babies that cried and dogs that ran yelping into the cover of bushes at their approach. The two young women seemed able to see only the town's crazy old lady, Chonita, who smiled and waved and called out sociably to the passing group. The day grew more humid than was usual during that season, and no breeze stirred through the flowers in the plaza.

Ingrita and the governor's daughter continued to discuss and take notes as before. Now they also photographed. They took pictures of: an empty wall, a pair of shoes, a stone on the road, a sleeping dog's tail. Before noon they asked Señor Ramirez for more film.

Late that night the people of the town stole from their houses and up into the hills. They wasted no time gathering up blankets or food or clothes. They walked only by the light of the moon and the eyes in their feet. Children, balking like stubborn donkeys, were dragged by their parents. The old were carried on the backs of the young and strong. Half-asleep in their mothers' arms, babies looked in wonderment at the stars above.

"Go, go, and go quickly," urged Señor Ramirez. "But I shall stay behind. Someone must. I shall remain behind with the typists." He looked after the long line of people filing quickly and noiselessly from the town. Then he crept through the empty streets. The only signs of life were the four lighted rooms wherein the typists worked, and the clicking of their machines sounded strangely through the night where once birds called and children cried.

Señor Ramirez jumped. He heard his name called again and turned to see crazy Chonita sitting alone on a bench in the plaza, partly obscured by the black flowered trees. "Sit down and take a load off your feet, Ramirez." Her hands were lying easily upon her lap and she was looking appreciatively at the pretty gardens glowing beneath the fancy street lamps scattered here and there around the plaza. She darted a look at Señor Ramirez, who was sitting stiffly and at some distance beside her on the bench, and said, "Want a shot?" Pulling a nearly full bottle of brandy from her big black bag, she motioned it toward him. When he shook his head she took a long pull herself, then sat humming with a smile upon her face.

"Peaceful, ain't it?" she remarked conversationally. "I do miss those kids, though. I miss them already. The fact is that since my two young friends are busy tonight I'm at a bit of a loose end. In any case, it's pleasant sitting here in the plaza with my reflections and the fresh air for company."

"What are those two doing?" interrupted Señor Ramirez.

"Oh, heavens, don't ask me. Some foolishness or other, I would guess. They call it work, but I call it craziness. What is it but crazy when two healthy young girls, both unattached, sit inside a room over papers when outside there is the fine night, the moonlight, the boys, et cetera. You see, Ramirez, my friends are normal, healthy girls, but also unhappy. What they need is some kissing and some babies. That or travel. Go up to California, I tell them. Things hop up there. I know all about it, I'm almost Californian myself."

"I beg to differ," replied Señor Ramirez. "Tell me something, what street do you live on?"

"Ramirez, you're tense, your sense is frozen. You know perfectly well I live on the street where old Mama Lupe fell and broke her hip that time."

"Precisely. But how would strangers to our town know about old Mama Lupe and her hip? Strangers — say important businessmen, developers, and so forth — like to see signs on the street so they can know exactly where they are. We have no street signs, there is no map of our town. I suspect that these two ladies are collecting facts and data on our town in preparation for some large government development scheme. I think it is all very clear."

"What's clear is that you need a drink, Ramirez." When her companion ignored the offered bottle and departed impolitely, Chonita smiled, then drank.

Señor Ramirez stalked the dark streets. Rounding a corner,

he very nearly bumped into Ingrita and the governor's daughter. For a moment he stood face to face with them, block-ing their path. Then they pushed him aside and rushed onward in the direction of the graveyard at the town's edge. A fairly large sack bumped against Ingrita's legs as she ran, and Señor Ramirez noticed that in her other hand she carried some kind of tool.

He slumped upon the dusty street without regard for his costly white linen suit. For the remainder of the night he huddled there, deep in thought, while waiting for the two women to return from their mission. When the sky began to pale in the east and the two women did not appear, Señor Ramirez walked quickly to the graveyard.

He had not visited it often. Among the headstones, the sunken mounds, the crosses, and the rings of plastic flowers Señor Ramirez wandered, seeking the places where his parents, and their parents, hid beneath the earth. Nearly everyone in the town was in some way related to everyone else, and during this time before dawn Señor Ramirez roamed past countless cousins, uncles, and aunts. A number of graves were unmarked, and it was possible only to imagine who in-habited them. From the filled earth the grass stretched toward the rising sun; wet with dew, it brushed against Señor Ramirez, washing his clothes clean of the road's dust. When the new day arrived he stopped searching and stood beside a small patch of freshly broken ground.

That morning the work of the two women continued as before. They made no mention of the deserted houses and streets, but only commissioned from Señor Ramirez a portable tape recorder. To obtain this article he was forced to search through all the neighbouring villages, and to purchase it he had to sell a large interest in his café. Ingrita and the gover-nor's daughter captured ten hours of sound. They recorded the voices of the river rushing over its bed of stones, the waves breaking against the shore, the wind speaking into the salias, the palm fronds crashing onto the ground.

Several days later Señor Ramirez stood in his café, unsure whether he was sleeping or awake. "It is time." He blinked, then saw Ingrita and the governor's daughter before him. "It is time," repeated Ingrita. "Go now. Go and bring back the people of the town. Walk three hours up into the hills and one half hour south of the river. Walk quickly because we wish to make an announcement immediately. They are waiting for you."

Señor Ramirez struggled up the hills that sloped toward the west. He followed the path that wound now beside the stream and now some distance to the north or south of it. The roar of rushing water, however, stayed inside his ears. The path ended, plantations of bananas and papayas and oranges gave way to jungle, and the air became thinner. Señor Ramirez rose above the places he had been before. He walked slowly, peering through wide green leaves and past vines which twisted themselves around trees. Butterflies appeared before his eyes and fainted onto bright blossoms. Señor Ramirez searched for his townspeople, and he listened for them, too. But all he could hear were calls of birds crying back and forth across the stream, and the sound of the stream itself.

He fell over an unseen stone and lay with his face pressed into the damp leaves and dirt. He could not yet feel the pain in his ankle. Hands lifted him by his shoulders and stood him up again. He saw several of his fellow townspeople. "This way," they motioned to him, then stepped quickly through the thick undergrowth without looking back to see if he was following.

When they reached a large clearing they halted. Señor Ramirez wiped at the dirt that had caked with sweat upon his face. He looked around at the people scattered over the clearing. Usually talkative and sociable, they were now silent and each alone. Some were lying with faces turned up to the sky or down to the earth. Others were rocking themselves back and forth to the rhythm of some song which Señor Ramirez could not hear. Little children dug with sticks into the wet leaves but without seeming to look for anything. It was only after several minutes that Señor Ramirez noticed those of his fellow townspeople who were wrapped in leaves or coiled around trunks of trees. Still others hung by their feet from branches. He thought he recognized one or two of them as neighbours who lived just down the street, and several as men who owed him money. However, none of his fellow citizens appeared to perceive him. They did not look at or speak to him.

"Dear friends, neighbours, and business associates," began Señor Ramirez. "The time has come when we must all return to our beloved village. It waits for us. Already dust forms in our rooms and spider webs hang from our ceilings. We have all had a nice holiday and we have enjoyed it very much, but now it is over. Let us return to work with glad hearts and thanks to God."

The people did not seem to hear his words. They turned their heads as though listening for some sound from the west and looking at some point in the air. They seemed to be waiting for something, but what it was Señor Ramirez did not know. As minutes passed and the silent suspense grew, he only knew that it was not him they waited for.

He turned and staggered from the clearing. He was very tired. No sound of following footsteps could be heard. Señor Ramirez headed toward the river, but as he approached it the sound of water seemed to come from farther away. This sound mixed together with the words of the wind moving through the top of the jungle. But below where Señor Ramirez walked there was no breeze to shake the leaves. It was very still. And as the sun soared higher and higher around the sky, the jungle grew cooler and darker. It was difficult to determine where one shadow left off and the next one began.

When at last he saw the stream before him Señor Ramirez broke into a run. The stream began somewhere high up in the hills that no one had seen before, that place where they said old voices called and new eyes watched over the world. Señor Ramirez leaned toward the stream as he neared it. He leaned so far forward that his body formed the same line carved between the sky and the sea by the western slopes. With a cry he tipped into the cold water, twisting as he fell.

It was not deep. The force of the current pulled at Señor Ramirez, tugging at his clothes, but he was not moved. He lay with the small stones which made the bed of the stream pressing into his back. The water ran clear and fast over all his body except his face. A large-winged bird of a variety he could not recognize flapped over him, and he felt the stirred air brush against his face just as the stream stirred the pebbles it covered. Tiny minnows darted among his clothes. Palm fronds fell and crashed through the underbrush. High above him, through a small crack in the roof of the jungle, Señor Ramirez saw the sky.

In the course of the following week the townspeople made their way down from the hills and back into their houses. The streets were filled once more with men, women, and children attending to the business of daily life. They made few references to any recent past except to say now and then, of the several older children who had not returned from the western slopes, "Well, at least in California they will learn English and become rich;" of Señor Ramirez's changed state they made no mention.

Everything in the village was nearly the same as before. Ingrita, the governor's daughter, the minor government offi-cial, the two disreputable citizens, and the unknown man were all gone. So had the four typists, their machines, and the notes and typed pages also disappeared. Only the old woman Chonita remarked on the absence of Ingrita and the gover-nor's daughter. "They were such sweet, lovely girls," she lamented to Señor Ramirez who, since the financial collapse and subsequent closure of his restaurant, had taken to sitting during the days and nights on a bench in the plaza.

He sat there, watching the children play their games and birds swoop through the flowers. The general citizenry did not disturb him; they delicately respected his apparent state of mourning. Only Chonita would sit with him, usually in silence. She brought him meals in a bucket covered with an embroidered linen cloth, and when it grew late she would lead him from the plaza to the room in her house previously occupied by Ingrita and the governor's daughter. Sometimes in the afternoons she would take him with her to the graveyard. The townspeople would politely turn their heads away at the sight of the man suddenly grown old leaning on the arm of Chonita and slowly being guided by her. Chonita would plant Señor Ramirez at a certain spot that he seemed to prefer over all others in the graveyard, then she would run off to play the games with her children.

All that remained of what had happened were large letters carved into the centre of the plaza's stone surface. Each letter was painted with a seemingly infinite number of fine lines, and each line was a different colour. Red, orange, pink, purple, blue, green, yellow, and all possible shades and mixtures of these tones. The colours were exactly those of the flowers which grew around the plaza.

The carved letters formed Spanish words of such enormous size that it was not possible to read them while standing in any one place. Rather it was necessary to walk along the lines of the letters and read them one by one. For a time, whenever they crossed the plaza the townspeople would walk slowly with bowed heads while they read the strange message. Then there came a time when the town decided to fence off the plaza and charge admission into it. The money would be used to build the long-dreamed-of new church. "We will do it for the sake of Señor Ramirez," the prominent citizens said. "It is what he would have wanted." As the fame of the message in the plaza spread far and wide, the venture was for a time an extraordinary success. Then it seemed that all the people from miles around had seen the plaza once and did not wish to pay to see it again. So the barbed wire fence was taken down and the plaza was opened up once more. The Swingtime Café was torn down and three walls of a new church were constructed on its site before the fund ran dry.

Several years later the townspeople decided that the letters were an unsightly stain on their square. A committee was formed to wash them away, and on hands and knees ladies scrubbed and sang for a month of Sundays; but no amount of soap or sand could dim the brightness of the colours. In time the citizens forgot that the letters spelled words, and then they forgot even the existence of the letters themselves.

The letters formed words and the words said: "The road leads to the stream and at the stream they wash their feet. That is why the road is dusty. That is why, says the little girl in the graveyard, but no one listens."

There came a time when the little children of the town discovered that several of the letters formed the pattern of a hopscotch game. They threw their markers and jumped amid the colours. When darkness came and all the grown-ups were sleeping safely in their beds, the children would tiptoe out onto the plaza to play hopscotch by the light of the moon. All the time they played, they laughed, but their parents did not waken. Still sometimes it seemed that the laughing voices could be heard all through the town, past the graveyard, and high upon the western slopes.

Never Tears for California

"Go away! Go away!" Chonita screamed, and the brats scampered away like mice. Chonita ran to the doorway of her restaurant and shouted down the street after them: "Go to the movies or go to the moon, just go away!"

There. They were gone. Chonita wiped her hands against her dress, getting them clean of those dirty kids with their filthy words and filthy lies. Those brats just knew how easiest to bother her, and that was to say the words "your aunt's restaurant." These words were a lie; the restaurant belonged to Chonita, it did, and that was the first thing and the most important thing. Some people said the movie place was more important than Chonita's restaurant. This was another lie. Proof: if you watched movies, you went crazy and cried over California; if you ate tacos, you grew healthy and fat. This was a plain fact, as plain as the stars in the sky, but only Chonita could see it. Of all the people in the town only she could see what was before her eyes, hear what was around her ears. The rest of the people were afflicted, and the disease that ailed them was the movies.

Every evening Chonita shook her head in disbelief as she watched crowds large as any fiesta-day parade pass by her restaurant to the movie house next door. Excepting Chonita, those too sick to leave their beds, and a few odd others, the whole town went to the movies every single night of the dry season. People of all ages and sizes flocked to the big bare room with dirt floor and no ceiling. Even the animals, who usually showed more sense than their masters, wandered into the movie house to catch a glimpse of the stars. Chonita had been to the movies only once, and she would never go again. Why? Because she had sense! Babies crying, children running around screaming, teenagers kissing, ladies gossiping, men smoking and drinking and swearing: it was all a bunch of craziness as far as Chonita was concerned, and the cause of it all was the fuzzy pictures flashing on one wall, the crackling English words messing up the air. "Oh, California!" cried the people, pointing to the pictures and swooning in their seats. Chonita knew that if there was such a place as California, it certainly was not a bit like the coloured lies dancing on the wall of the movie house. Of course not! Yet there was nothing she could say to make the people see the truth. The movies had cast a spell of California craziness upon the town.

Why else would the people leave their homes every night just to sit in the dark drafty movie house? But this they did, dragging along blankets from their beds and chairs from their kitchens. And the stink! People and animals went to the bathroom in the corners of the room when they weren't stuffing their mouths from big baskets of food. And that wasn't all. Some people couldn't read the Spanish titles, and they couldn't understand the English words, either, but they still went to the movies. This was not to mention the blind people and the deaf people who also sat there without understanding a single thing. Yes, it was a spell of craziness, and it made the people forget there was no roof above them. Even when a sudden shower fell and soaked them they sat there. They forgot there were any stars in the world besides Elizabeth Taylor, they didn't recall the real stars shining above, those eyes of God that watched all their foolishness. And Chonita wasn't about to waste her breath reminding them that water was wet and the world was round. There was no end to the craziness and no way of understanding it, so Chonita didn't bother to try. She had better things to do with her time.

Such as working in the restaurant. Foolish as they were, even the Doris-Day-dreaming people couldn't say Chonita didn't know the taco business inside out. After working in the restaurant every night of the week for three years she knew her work. She was cook, waitress, cashier, dishwasher, janitor, and manager all in one. No one could ever run the place half as well as Chonita, and everyone in town knew this was a fact, although some of the mean ones wouldn't admit it.

Like her sister, Rosa. Until her marriage to that Juan, Rosa had been in charge and Chonita only her helper. But Rosa hated tacos, she hated the look of them, the smell of them, the taste of them. She hated everything to do with tacos, and she didn't care about the restaurant one bit. Also, Rosa was lazy in the bones, sluggish with her dreams of Elizabeth Taylor. Those with clear eyes could see who really did the work. Who else?

Fifty times a night Rosa would run over to the movie house to see if the boy had got the girl, and sometimes she disappeared for as long as an hour, the reason being that these Hollywood hussies often played hard to get. This left guess who to make the tacos. Well, Chonita made them and served them to those teenaged boys with their blurry red eyes half blind from staring at Elizabeth Taylor. They couldn't have Elizabeth Taylor, so they took Chonita's tacos instead. Plus, to tell the truth, Chonita preferred it when Rosa was away staring at the kissing scenes, because Rosa was always sulky when making tacos, she was no joy then, crabby and craving, she felt she was missing something.

It was brains she was missing! When Rosa had been boss the restaurant was forever short of things. "No, we don't have any Cokes, tomorrow maybe," Rosa would say, as she helped herself to yet another sweet roll. Then, her mouth full, she would commence a discussion on the subject of Elizabeth Taylor's hair-do. "Try the place down on the corner, they might have Cokes," Rosa would say carelessly, her mind occupied with thoughts of Elizabeth Taylor, to whom she communicated through messages sealed inside old Coke bottles. Every week Rosa would pack a picnic lunch and make Juan row her far out to the place on the sea where currents would carry messages in bottles south to Puerto Vallarta, this being where Elizabeth Taylor lived when not in California, in a white house as large as a hundred white houses, but no longer with Richard Burton. "You'll be swept away, too," Chonita warned her sister. "But you won't end up drinking martinis on

Elizabeth Taylor's patio in Puerto Vallarta, no, you'll end up much colder and wetter and deader than that." Whereupon Rosa sulked and refused to say what she wrote in the messages to Elizabeth Taylor. As if Chonita cared!

On the day of Rosa's wedding to that Juan, Señora Sanchez, a modern woman and their aunt, made a formal announcement. Her voice heavy with a sense of family responsibility, Señora Sanchez said: "Now that Rosa is married, she has a family and a greater need. So she will run the movie house and Chonita can take charge of the restaurant." "Señora Sanchez paused and looked fondly at the bride, who was stroking the head of Juan that lay in the white lap of the wedding gown.

Rosa shot a look of triumph at Chonita, who quickly smiled and bent her head to kiss the bride in congratulation. "You only married that loafer Juan for the sake of the movie house and the sake of his strong arms that can row the boat so well," Chonita whispered into Rosa's ear as she nibbled upon it.

"Oh, my nieces," cried Señora Sanchez with emotion, while she pawed among the articles of feminine deception littered across her dressing table, in search of cigarettes. In a world-weary way she puffed smoke and said, "I am tired of working and tired of running the movie house. I have earned my pleasure and my leisure. You know, after my years in California, seeing the real thing daily, I have no need for the movies." Then, remembering responsibility, Señora Sanchez changed her tone and said, "Chonita has fourteen years now and she knows her business. We shall see how she does."

Well, they saw all right. Now that Chonita held the paddle the restaurant made more money than the movie house, profit clear as day. "Hmmm, yes," Señora Sanchez said every Thursday when she dropped by to collect the week's earnings. She looked on with a poor show of interest as Chonita pointed out the various tricks of an efficient money-making business. But before Chonita could finish explaining what was what, her aunt's eyes dropped and gazed tenderly at the notes she clasped in her hands. "This is very fine, my baby doll," she said, slowly smoothing the notes. "I can see already that one day you will be a woman as modern as I. One day you too will ride on the bus every Friday to shop and to eat fish dinners in the air-conditioned restaurants of the capital city.''

Chonita watched the money disappear inside her aunt's black dress. ''And of course you will go to California,'' continued Señora Sanchez, stroking the extra bulge near her bosom. ''You'll form night-owl habits there, I did. These banana-picking people fall asleep before the dogs do, and what kind of a life is that? I stayed up till dawn all the time in California, never slept in darkness for all the years I was there. Oh, I had myself a nice set-up in the States. That is, until my man got homesick for his mama and made me move back here with him to this old town. The least you can do is build me a movie house and a taco place, I told him, and while you're at it I wouldn't mind a modern white house. I knew I had the nose for business, but I didn't know what would happen next. Would you believe it? As soon as I had a show to run, my man wanted to lift his heels and head for the wild blue yonder. Listen, lover, I told him, you dragged me away from my gang of girlfriends in California, and you're a fool if you think you can yank my reins again. Go to the silvery moon for all I care, but don't expect to tempt me with your wooden carrots. So he went, and not a word from him since, but am I blue? The answer is: no. Men are like that. I've got my perfume and my jewellery and my shopping sprees in the capital, and I'm certainly not the kind of woman to feel discontent. I've had my share of the pie, and it tasted good. I still remember how it tasted.'' Señora Sanchez licked her lips and looked around with an expression of distraction. Suddenly she started up and said, ''Now excuse me, my little money-maker, but I must trot off. Tomorrow is my big day, the capital city awaits, and there are lists to be made, beauty sleep to be slept, and so on.''

After her aunt bustled away, Chonita sat quite still and looked around her restaurant. All the plans she had formed to improve the business were blurred by the scent of Señora Sanchez still hanging in the air; and though very old and familar, her aunt's words stuck in Chonita's head like the sap from papaya trees that blisters and whitens and clings to hands that touch it. Then Chonita stirred herself and began darting around the dim room. Her eyes shining, she placed a jar of plastic flowers on each table and hung pictures over the walls. But that was not enough. "I need something more," she thought.

One morning she woke in her bed and found the idea shining on her pillow with the sunlight that streamed through the window. If there were music in the restaurant it would be more crowded and make more money. Out of bed she jumped, over to her aunt's house she ran. "Tía, tía," she cried. "All I need is one thing."

Señora Sanchez was sitting before her mirror, the largest in town, with an air of weariness. She was wearing the black spotted dress and hat, plus the spots of red on either cheek, which comprised her city wardrobe. Though dawn had long been broken, all the electric lights were switched on. "I had a lovely time," said Señora Sanchez sadly. "A weekend filled with taxi rides and cocktails and established businessmen. Not a moment's sleep. Naturally, it was no Los Angeles, but it did. It did quite well." She spoke into the mirror, fumbling all the while with the bottles of perfume and cosmetics that covered the dressing table. "Love letters," she murmured, touching several sheets of paper. "Reading old love letters and writing new ones, and now the night is ended."

Chonita stirred impatiently behind her, and Señora Sanchez raised her eyes. For a long moment she stared with a peculiar expression at the reflection of her niece, which formed the background of her own image. "Yes, you do need something," she said. "And I have just the thing." Drawing a key from her bosom, she unlocked a drawer of the dressing table. "Take a jewel," she said, her voice quivering with generosity. "Take any one you want, but not this silver chain, and not this bracelet, either."

"I want something else. A record player," said Chonita.

"I have no record player," said Señora Sanchez. "Heavens, what would I do with such a gadget when I have real live music playing in my head?" She hummed lightly and quickly closed the velvet case.

"Rosa and Juan have a record player, and they don't need it," Chonita said firmly. "I need it for the restaurant."

Señora Sanchez began to apply another layer of make-up

over the one she wore already. Rosa and Juan had spent their wedding money not on furniture, but on a big record player. Instead of washing the dishes, they danced after dinner in their bare living room. "I'll give you a necklace, my favourite piece. It was a gift from a sentimental admirer, a widowed engineer of distinction and silvery hair," said Señora Sanchez, attempting shrewdness.

"A record player," repeated Chonita, watching the mascara brush tremble in her aunt's hand. She turned and glanced out the window. "Look," she said. "Look at all those pigs walking past. They look nice and fat, don't they? Think of all the juicy pork we'll someday have."

"Fun! Fun!" cried Señora Sanchez weakly. "Feathers and fun! These young girls of today don't know what it is to be modern and happy. The only song they can sing is of business and bills, and how can you dance to that? Well, it's the younger generation, tra la la."

Chonita bent down and sank her face into her aunt's neck.

The same day that Chonita obtained the record player, Rosa became her enemy, spreading stories — all bad, all lies — against her own sister to whoever cared to listen. Chonita didn't care, she just turned the music louder, and she couldn't hear the stories, and she couldn't hear the movie playing next door, either. Often Rosa came over and complained. "The music is too loud, Chonita. The audience can't hear the movie." This was another lie, and she said so right to Rosa's face. Other people might whisper behind backs, but they weren't named Chonita. And furthermore, there would be none of that slow, sad music. She played only the fastest kind of music, the bright kind that urged customers to spend more money quicker. She made her aunt buy the very latest American records in the capital and she played them loudly, so that people could hear them far down the street and know where to come for a good time. Who played faster or louder or more modern records than she?

No one! All the little kids swarmed around the restaurant, but Chonita permitted only the ones with money to enter. They just had to learn she wasn't a Rosa, allowing any old brat to help himself to free gum and candy. Yes, everything had to be paid for, and if they didn't have the money, why, the brats could just listen to the music from the sidewalk outside. And they could kindly save their childish dancing for the streets, too. Those brats thought that dancing was spinning around in circles, becoming dizzy, then falling over furniture and making a mess. That showed how much they knew. Grown-up dancing was the only kind Chonita permitted inside her place. If people wanted to dance like fools on the street, that was their business, but they could please stay away from her business.

Soon all the teenagers and young marrieds came to her restaurant, and they often sat over their tacos right through the movie. Every night the place was crowded, and sometimes there was a wait for tables. Even Rosa and Juan liked to drop over from the movie house, but she made them pay same as the rest. Rosa used to give the strong handsome boys free Cokes in the old days, but not her, not Chonita. They could say she was the most beautiful girl in town, yet she would budge not a single inch. "Look, boy," she always said. "Save your flattery for the other girls. They need it more than I do because they don't have restaurants to make them happy. If you want a girlfriend, you should treat one of them to a big bunch of tacos and Cokes. That's the way to go. Take my advice and you will be happier."

Well, they took her advice all right. The restaurant was a success. Still Chonita had another dream. As she ran about cooking and serving, she thought, "I have made my first dream come true. But one more remains." Her secret wish was this: tables crowded with Kodak cameras and sunglasses; Americans laughing and speaking in English, not Spanish; the smell of suntan lotion, not tacos. She saw it all so clearly.

This dream was more difficult, it made of the first dream a child's joke. One problem was the small number of tourists who visited the town. There was nothing much to attract foreigners — no ruins, no sandy beach, no stores or post offices. There was nothing in the town that counted except her restaurant. Another problem was that the few tourists who did visit were not the kind she wanted. They had little money, long hair (men and women both), and no cameras or sunglasses. They camped down at the rocky beach, and some people said they ate cactus and beans, and nothing more. Others said they lay naked in the sun. Chonita knew these were just stories, but still she knew it would not be easy.

Because her name was Chonita, she would not give up. When the real Americans came to her restaurant, some day soon, she would be ready for them. Whenever business was slow Chonita listened to the music hard and learned the American words. "Boogie woogie, dance dance, shake it all night, take me home," she sang as she stood beside the counter in her flower-patterned dress and high-heeled shoes, moving just enough to make the dress swirl against her knees. Now even the girls her age and older who still rode by bus to school in the next town knew less English than Chonita. They could never laugh at her again. She added hamburgers to the menu and made big signs in English. Continuous Music! English Gladly Spoken! Authentic Food! Soon hamburgers and speaking English were the craze with all the teenaged boys of the town. But still no tourists came to her restaurant.

As the months passed Chonita grew weary of waiting. The rainy season began, and then she knew no tourists would visit the town for five hot and wet months. She sat at the window and watched the rain fall upon the children playing baseball amid the puddles glowing darkly on the street. Yes, she was in charge; yes, the restaurant was a success; yes, she could play the same song over and over for as many times as she liked. Yes, yes, yes, she whispered to herself, but her heart answered only "no."

The rain wove a pattern upon the days, but it was one the people could never become easy with. The rain would fall steadily and as though without end for several hours, then it would cease for several hours, only to begin falling once more. Just when the people became used to the rain, it would suddenly stop; just when they forgot the rain, it would begin again, also suddenly. However, always the air was hot and wet, and steam rose from the streets like the smoke from some fire burning just beneath the ground. Because it lacked a ceiling, the movie house was often shut down, and on those evenings the people would wander the streets in a daze, like lost sheep. They cringed always in expectation of the first or last raindrop to hit them, and they walked straight through puddles, not seeing them though their eyes were turned to the ground. Above, stars still shone, but they could not see through the rainy mist, they could not see the town.

As the people sat quietly in the restaurant, slowly eating their tacos, Chonita looked at them and thought, yes, they have at last forgotten the movies and the false dreams of California. Then she noticed that the people were straining to hear the rain that drummed a song upon the tin roof even louder than the music. They were waiting for the moment when the song of the rain would end and Rosa would rush up the stairs of the church to the bell in the tower. She would ring the bell again and again, calling to the people, come quickly, we can show the movie, but we must show it right away, before the rain begins again, ring ring ring.

Those nights when the rain would not stop and the bell was not rung, Rosa would sit with her aunt beneath the old drooping tree in the centre of the plaza. With no movie to watch Rosa was irritable, and often she fidgeted on the bench beside her aunt. "You are happy," said Señora Sanchez, patting Rosa's hand. "You have your man and soon a baby, and that is enough for you. But your little sister, she is like me, and needs more. Swimming pools and freeways, oh, we women who need more are not happy," and the tears fell from her eyes like the rain dripping through the tree.

"That little cabrona," said Rosa, wrestling her hand from her aunt's tight clasp. "Elizabeth Taylor had babies, but she's never made a taco in her life."

"Oh, baby darling," sighed Señora Sanchez, seeing Chonita appear at the edge of the plaza. The aunt placed the bottle in her purse and ran out into the dark rain. Falling upon Chonita, Señora Sanchez wept. "My little Chonita will soon be a slave to the moon and to love, and then who will run the restaurant? Ah, but I will take you to the capital and buy you perfume and jewellery. You will marry the most handsome boy in town, maybe the son of Señora Lopez. All the girls are crazy to lie with him under the trees. I see them line up on Sunday nights and cry if they are not the chosen ones.

Yes, they cry if their brothers lock them safely in the houses, and they cry if they are chosen, too. The girls tell me he lies naked on the leaves and takes one after another, all night long. And when he is yours to take always, you will cry also, but never tears for California, no. You will cry for something else.'' Chonita smiled strangely and placed her head upon her aunt's bosom for one moment. Then she walked home to lie awake, as she did through other nights, while the scent of her aunt's perfume and her own sweet secret dreams blurred strangely together.

Then a crazy mood beset Chonita. At any old hour she would close up the restaurant. ''Out! Out!'' she screamed at the customers, whether they were finished their tacos or not. ''Get out of here right now!'' She herded the people out the door, then ran outside herself. She played baseball with the children in the street. The restaurant was forgotten as she ran the fastest, jumped the highest, hit the farthest, screamed the loudest. She kept track of the score from one night to the next, and soon figured her team to be more than three hundred points ahead of the opposition. Her hair was soaked by the rain, her dress wet also with sweat, and her high-heels muddy and scraped. People called her names up and down the street, but she would not listen. ''Why, oh why do you play with little children, big girl?'' they called. She would not listen when, tired but awake, she lay waiting through the hours while the English words and music came to her from somewhere, unbidden, and mixed across the night.

The rainy months passed slowly, and just as slowly Chonita's dream journeyed far from her heart. So it was that the night it finally happened she was caught by surprise.

It was a night that began like all the others, with a big rush at six before the movie began. These days she didn't care enough to see who was eating in her restaurant, for all the faces were the same. All the jokes and stories were spoken again and again until forever, and it made her sick to listen and sick to watch, so she didn't. She just did the work faster than ever to win a few minutes at the counter with her comic book.

Then there he was. There before her eyes, sitting alone over five tacos and a Squirt. But he had no camera or sunglasses, and she had detected no flaw in his Spanish when he ordered the tacos. That was how she nearly missed him. Chonita quickly brought to him the special coloured napkins usually saved for fiesta days, a knife and fork, and a glass of ice for his Squirt.

"Hello," he said. "What is your name? My name is Reeves."

Before she knew what words were in her mind, the answer was spoken. "Eugenia." Where that name came from she did not know.

"This is a nice place you have here. The music is pretty. I like to listen to music while I eat. It makes the meal more enjoyable."

Why did he not speak in English? She looked at him, and saw he was young and handsome and American, but she could see little more. She stared at the American boy, and the only particular thing she could see were his shirt-sleeves. They were long and, unlike the boys of the town, he did not roll them up on his elbows. They covered his wrists and arms.

He ate, paid, and left before she could remember a single word of English. He forgot some of his money beside his empty plate. She counted the little stack of silver pesos, five, then ran out into the street. No one was in sight. Back inside the boys were making jokes about the tourist. "Shut up, you hoodlums!" she screamed. "Haven't you ever seen a stranger before? Go home to your mamas and eat beans in the kitchens." She put on some faster and louder music and sat down to think.

The next afternoon she met her sister on the street. Ever since the signs of the baby had begun to show, Rosa had taken to standing on the corner all day long so that everyone could see her. "Are you on your way to work, Chonita? But what is this I see? The little businesswoman wears lipstick and eye shadow? What is next? Tomorrow you will smoke cigarettes? And you pretend the boys do not shake your heart!"

"Good afternoon, Eugenia." As he walked past, the American boy smiled at her with friendly eyes.

"Eugenia, Eugenia!" Rosa screamed with laughter. "This is the funniest joke yet." Rosa ran down the street, clutching her stomach, the faster to spread the news of Eugenia and her American boyfriend.

In less than one hour the restaurant was crowded with people of all ages. "Eugenia, Eugenia," they laughed. Señora Sanchez entered, anxious and breathless. "What are these stories I am hearing?" she cried.

"Chonita has a new name and it is Eugenia. She is going to marry a rich American and then they will live in Hollywood with all the movie stars."

"My Eugenia!" Her aunt hugged her tightly and cried tears of joy. "You will live in a big house and swim in the backyard. Now the dreams I had as a young girl will come true for you, just as I always knew they would. Go away!" she shouted to all the curious people. "Go back to your houses. Eugenia must be alone when her boyfriend comes for her."

So it was that the restaurant was empty when the American boy returned for dinner that night. Again he smiled at her and again he called her by name. He sat at the same table and ordered the same meal as before. "Good night, Eugenia," he said before he left. Five pesos lay in a neat pile on the table.

The next day Eugenia had many visitors. Everyone wished to know what had happened the night before. At first Eugenia would say nothing, but only looked shyly at her pretty fingers. Then she admitted, "We discussed tacos."

"Tacos!" wailed the circle of girls, falling upon one another. "You will make him a slave to your tacos, he will take you to California so that you can make tacos for him every night." Some girls wished her good luck, others were plainly jealous.

"Tacos, my foot," said Señora Sanchez, who stood outside the circle of girls, a thoughtful expression scarring her face. "No boy from California has ever been seduced by tacos. These local Juans and Joses, yes. But to charm this Californian, you need something more. I shall make a plan."

From that day on there were many facts and many stories, and they all concerned the American boy. One fact was that the boy took a room at Señora Lupita's house and did not blink an eye when she asked for fifty pesos a day. Another fact was that the American boy did not walk around the town with any of the tourists who camped down at the beach. He always walked the streets alone. A third fact was that the American boy did not go to the movies, but only paused for a moment in the doorway of the movie house and looked perhaps at the pictures flashing on the wall, perhaps at the audience beneath them. More facts were: he spoke Spanish better than any tourist ever; he came onto the plaza in the evening with hair so newly washed it was still damp; and he always ate at Eugenia's restaurant.

The stories spread like May fires around the town. Some said the boy was not young, but old, and not American, but French. An old man said he had seen the boy open an account in the bank in the neighbouring town with a three hundred thousand peso deposit. Juanita swore the boy had offered her one thousand pesos to visit his room on Sunday night. Señora Lupita claimed he slept in his room the whole day long and hung rainbow-coloured clothes like pictures over the walls. Señora Lopez's son whispered that he had walked down to the beach with the American boy one midnight, and there they had sniffed a strange white powder, not cocaina, that made the moon seem large and golden and close. These and many other stories were repeated time after time, and soon not a single person knew what was true and what was not. "There he goes," spoke the girls in the plaza, as the American boy walked by with no one hanging onto his rainbow sleeves.

Eugenia's dream possessed her more completely as each night the American boy came to eat alone in her restaurant. Now the people of the town no longer ate there, it was just Eugenia and the American boy. Always the same things happened in the same order, and the same words were spoken, too. Late at night Eugenia walked up and down the back streets of the town, and everyone knew who she was. The people came to their doorways to stand and watch her pass, but though they looked at her in a new special way, she did not see them.

This continued for fifteen nights. On the sixteenth night Señora Sanchez visited her niece bearing gifts and advice. "My Eugenia," she gravely said. "Here are jewels and perfumes my man bought for me in California. I have saved them for some special day, and in my heart I know that day has come at last. These trinkets are homesick, they long to journey back to California. They yearn to return to the place where they belong, and they will draw you back there with them."

Her aunt closed the curtains and locked the door, and all through the darkened afternoon she stayed with Eugenia. First she bathed her niece's whole body in clouded, drug-scented water. Then she washed Eugenia's hair and combed it for many minutes. She plucked her niece's eyebrows, painted her nails, and dressed her in a gown not worn for many years, an old gown the hem of which had once trailed upon the earth of California. Eugenia felt the warm hands upon her body and felt a strange slowing of her blood. The low voice of her aunt spoke words upon her that fell and covered Eugenia like thick tears. The perfume cast a spell upon her brain and all her limbs grew heavy. "Look," said her aunt, holding the glass before Eugenia, and her sleepy eyes opened and saw the face in the mirror. Eugenia recalled the seventy-five pesos, five for every night, that lay hidden beneath her pillow, and all at once they flashed silver before her eyes. "Now you are ready," said her aunt. She pushed Eugenia out the door.

Eugenia stood beside the counter of the restaurant, her body swaying to the music of its own accord. "God be with you, Eugenia!" cried the people as they passed by the open doorway. "Send me the autograph of a star and a picture postcard." All the people of the town wished her well before they went to the movie, and the last to speak the words of luck was Rosa. She approached her sister with mean eyes and a twisted mouth, but when she saw the dream within which Eugenia was standing, Rosa's face changed. Circling her arms around her sister's neck, Rosa rubbed her growing belly slowly back and forth against Eugenia. Then she too left, and Eugenia was alone.

She stood and waited, but the American boy did not come to carry her away. At ten o'clock the movie ended and the people walked past once more. "Where is your boyfriend?" they called through the window. "We thought you would be half way to California by now." But seeing Eugenia still silent in her spell, they walked quickly away, whispering like the leaves in the breeze, and Eugenia was alone once more.

At midnight Chonita shut off the record player, turned off the lights, locked the door, and walked home.

The next morning the whole town knew the story. Late the

night before two boys sleeping on the beach had been wakened by sounds of splashing. Beneath the eyes of the stars they saw the American boy and the son of Señora Lopez climb inside Juan's small boat. The two boys on the beach rubbed their sleepy eyes and saw the water dropping silver from the oars as the strong arms of Señora Lopez's son carried the boat far from shore. So far was the boat carried that soon the two boys on the beach could see only the wide black sea, and nothing upon it; so far away that even the bright eyes of the stars could no longer see the small boat moving slowly north to California.

The American boy had left all his clothes behind, and Señora Lupita made a small fortune selling them to the teenaged boys of the town. For a time it was the new fashion to wear the American boy's clothes. The streets were full of bright rainbow colours, but soon no one remembered from where they had come. As the dry season passed, with its warm clear evenings, the people no longer spoke of the season of rain.

Chonita's restaurant was once more filled with townspeople eating plates of tacos before the start of the movie. Even after Chonita returned the record player to Rosa and Juan and there was no longer any music, the restaurant remained crowded. It was not long before Chonita no longer noticed when a group of rude boys sat at the American boy's table, and it was not too much longer before she ceased walking down to the sea at night, looking for the vanished spot upon the water where she had cast the seventy-five pesos, one by one.

No, she did not walk down to the beach and look out at the sea. She and Rosa became inseparable companions fond of walking down the streets with linked arms while the older sister whispered words of Elizabeth Taylor into the younger sister's ear. Feeling the warm breath of Rosa upon her, Chonita would look down at her feet treading upon the dusty road, and she would remember how the silver pesos had arced silvery across the moon and splashed also silver into the water. When Señora Sanchez bought for Juan another boat, Chonita often accompanied her sister and brother-in-law on their expeditions out to sea. Juan rowed strongly, sweating in the sun, and Rosa sat tall and straight, one hand clasping the bottle that contained the message, the other hand shading her eyes as she stared far to the south, toward Puerto Vallarta. Chonita lay back in the boat, trailing one hand through the cold water, the same water that had grown darker and colder as the coins sank through it. The silver coins had flashed and shone, drifted down to the bottom of the sea, dazzled the fish. At last the coins had come to rest upon the ocean floor, where they would lie until they were silver no more.

People in the town marvelled at the way Chonita doted on her new niece. Frequently she would tend the baby for Rosa, holding the tiny girl in her arms while she talked with Señora Sanchez in the plaza. "Oh, my niece," Señora Sanchez said, tenderly and brimming over with pity. "You are heartbroken, California has lured your boyfriend away from you. But Señora Lopez has another son, and he is just as strong and handsome as the one that's gone away from us. He will be yours, he will, and you will cry in his arms every night, yes, you will cry, but never tears for California." And Chonita would laugh and kiss the wet cheeks of her aunt.

The laughing girl, they called her when she shouted jokes out the window of her restaurant to the people walking toward the movie house. Chonita laughed with bright eyes when, some time later, a big hotel that catered to Americans too old for work was built on the dirty shore. If ever the old Americans entered Chonita's restaurant, she would laugh at them, saying "I don't speak English," even when they ordered their meals in Spanish.

All the little children were allowed to play inside the restaurant once more. Chonita laughed with them and played with them, and she gave them free gum and candy. "California, California," the children would say to their mothers, who sat gazing at the coloured pictures flashing on the wall. "California," the children would say, and then they would run out of the movie house and over to Chonita's restaurant. There Chonita and the children played games all evening long, raising their voices above the sound of the movie playing next door. When Chonita closed the restaurant and walked home, the children ran down the streets after her, calling "Tía Chonita! Tía Chonita! Please don't go away!" and the words fell upon her ears like something sinking deeper and deeper.

Love in the Devil's Arms

While the bell was still ringing the end of Sunday prayer and song a dozen girls skipped past their dozing elders and ran from the church to the house of Gabriela Fernandez. There they began to prepare for the evening dance. Again and again water was heated for baths, and from the old tin tub clouds fo steam rose to curl lovingly around the girls' bodies. The iron singed and smoked, and the room grew hot. Girls floated half naked through the foggy rooms, helping one another to fix dresses and hair and make-up.

Gabriela went to the open doorway and for a moment stood just inside it. She waved away the clinging steam and tilted her face toward the evening falling cool, the moon rising clear. Bats swooped around street lamps, flitting in and out of light like memories of a dream. Down at the end of the block five little girls danced on thin brown stick-legs around the maypole of a street lamp. As she listened to the rhymes they sang Gabriela's starry eyes clouded, and she did not see a group of women approach slowly down the street. Then one of her girlfriends cried, "Gabriela, come and tie a ribbon in my hair," and she turned back inside the house.

The group of neighbourhood women gathered on the front steps of the Fernandez place. They lounged lazily, arms folded across chests, skirts pulled up like sails to catch a cooling breeze. The woman spit shells of pumpkin seeds upon the road, fished cigarettes from down fronts of dresses, and talked of this and that.

Señora Martinez, a nervous woman, walked rapidly toward

the ladies. "Look!" she wailed at once. "The moon is only half."

"What of it?" drawled one of the lounging ladies. "It happens every month, it's natural. They call it waxing and waning, and it just goes on and on, like everything else."

"A half moon is not complete. It lacks its other half to make it full," cried Señora Martinez. "Think, please! Tonight is Sunday, is it not? This means, of course, a dance. All our young girls will be going mad with love, doing anything and everything to complete themselves. Dance! It is no dance, it is folly, danger, temptation set to music!"

The gathering of ladies sighed with one breath. Although used to the thin, anxious woman, they were unable to take pleasure in her company. "See here," they said. "We lock up our daughters six nights a week to keep them out of trouble. We chain them to the kitchens, we fasten all the doors and windows. But they must be allowed a taste of pleasure one night a week. Otherwise, they will go crazy with longing, pierce their hearts with knives, and so on."

"One taste of poison can mean death," exclaimed Señora Martinez, as the scent of flowery perfume drifted from the house and into the street. Señora Martinez heard the rustle of new dresses, the whispered names of handsome boys, the excited giggles of anticipation. She caught sight of young girls slipping through shadows in the rooms beyond the doorway, white slips gleaming against brown skin, towels wrapped turban style around hair newly washed and still wet.

"Besides," yawned and stretched the ladies. "We are looking forward to the dance ourselves. A little dancing, a little drinking: you should go yourself."

"Ha!" choked Señora Martinez bitterly.

"By the way," mentioned Señora Fernandez, "how is your daughter these days? It's too bad what happened to Juanita up in Mazatlan, but don't you feel ashamed. These things can happen to any girl."

"That baby! It wasn't because of any boys she had that baby!" cried Señora Martinez excitedly. "It was that city who put the baby inside my Juanita. Mazatlan! A pigsty fit only for Americans. We should sell it to them, and good riddance to bad rubbish."

"I never quite did understand how the baby died," remarked one woman casually.

"Juanita didn't kill it, she dropped it by mistake. You know my girl has always been clumsy, and how could she know its head would crack open like it did?" Señora Martinez's heart heaved against the visible bars of bones encaging it.

Gabriela came out from the house. "Mama, can I wear your blue high-heeled shoes?" she asked in a clear, high voice. "Yes, my love," answered her mother with emotion. "But not my green ones. I plan to wear those myself tonight." Suddenly Señora Fernandez turned sorrowful. "Not that anyone will notice my shoes or anything else," she sobbed. "My man will be drinking and gossiping with those other worthless men. Yes!" she cried to the women around her. "My husband and your husbands! Oh, this game of love!" Whereupon the women took comfort in the sharing of tears and brandy, and Señora Martinez ran away unseen.

She found her daughter standing before a mirror and shoving a paper gardenia into her tresses. "That dress," moaned Señora Martinez weakly. "Where can you be going in that red dress? To the Sunday dance or to hell?"

"You must be joking," laughed Juanita, smoothing the tight silk sheath across her shapely hips. She bent over and adjusted her black fish-net stockings. "The dances in this one-mule town are for babies and fools, and thank God I'm neither. No, I'm off to the discothèque in the next town. It's always thick with rich American men too stupid to know how to hang on to their money. I guess I'll do all right for myself."

Juanita caught sight of two young girls running lightly with joined hands down the road. She looked greedily at their white dresses and fresh skin. "Virgins! Señoritas!" she called tauntingly out the window, and then applied another coating of lipstick around her mouth.

After Juanita swayed out the door, her mother fell weeping silently upon her bed. Suddenly, she started. The sound of the band striking up another Sunday dance floated clearly across the town, and with it came other noises: quick footsteps, slamming doors, barking dogs, and young girls laughing and calling and laughing.

Señora Martinez looked through the window and saw the half moon, now a deeper yellow, poised amid the darting, dancing stars.

The young girls of the town sat at unsteady card tables on one side of the large enclosed courtyard, and on the other side men and boys stood drinking and smoking. In the central space several couples danced before the band, stumbling occasionally on the uneven cement surface. Dotted around the Casino were mothers and wives, some with eyes fixed vigilantly upon their daughters, others relaxed and enjoying a festive mood.

Gabriela's girlfriends whispered and giggled and chewed chiclets beneath the ceiling of sky. They craned their necks to spy on the handsome boys, they glided their eyes quickly over the ugly ones. Twisting the rings on their fingers and counting the beads on their necklaces, they sat with backs straight and stiff.

"It's better not to dance at all than to accept the invitation of one of those drunken, smelly thugs," remarked one girl crisply.

"Oh, but I want to dance," said Gabriela, looking at her friends with wide brown eyes. "I am wearing my best dress and my mother's high-heeled shoes, and the music sounds just right."

"It's still early yet," said another girl without hope. At that moment the girls turned their heads and watched five of the most handsome boys in town leave the Casino together.

"Well, that's that," snapped one girl. "We might as well kiss those boys goodbye. They'll be down at the beach playing games in the sand all night," and the girls drooped like flowers folding at dusk.

Gabriela shivered as some breeze brushed against her heart. "Dance with me," she begged the girl beside her. "Just one dance."

Her companions gazed moodily down at the tin surface of the table, and they did not look up when Gabriela sprang from her chair. Dress sweeping and folding about her knees, long hair flying, she twirled around again and then again.

When she fell the other girls laughed. "You need a boy's strong arms to hold you up," they crowed. "See what happens when you dance alone."

Gabriela lay on the rough cold floor, her face turned up to the night. For a moment she was still, her eyes closed. Her body began to move as slowly as a sleepy snake, and then to shudder, to twitch, to shake. Her limbs jerked with increasing speed and force, as though trying to break free from her torso. With eyes now frightened the girls watched Gabriela's hands reach to the sky, fists clenched tightly at one moment, opened and grabbing for the stars at the next. A film of sweat sprang upon her skin, glistening in the moonlight; and like the fish pulled up from the deep dark sea, she thrashed and gasped.

The band fell silent, and the townspeople stared at the girl with an interest that quickly turned to horror. Her eyes rolled back in their sockets. Fearing the girl would injure herself, several men attempted to hold her still; but with a strength beyond herself Gabriela threw their hands away. Her neck arched and her throat curved in offering to the night.

The girl's motions slowed, then stopped. She lay limply, a peaceful drowsy look washing over her face. She yawned and stretched, and then her eyes cleared, looking with puzzlement at the crowd encircling her.

The band started up again and couples recommenced to mambo. Gabriela raised herself from the ground. From the Casino and through the empty streets she strolled. Everyone was at the dance, nearly all the houses were dark. Only one window held light. A thin woman with burning eyes sat alone there, waiting for her daughter to come back from the arms of strangers, turning her hands in her lap as though trying to untie a very complicated knot. Passing by, her clothes and body dishevelled with love, her face lit with a triumphant and knowing expression, Gabriela looked directly into the red eyes of Señora Martinez, who was swept by flames of shame.

For the rest of the evening and far into the night the townspeople spoke of what had happened. At first everyone had their own idea of the meaning behind the incident, but gradually all came to agree that it was the inevitable outcome of preserving a girl too long from love. "It is only to be expected," said older matrons. "A healthy girl of sixteen without husband or babies! In the old days we were firmly established in marriage at thirteen, and there was none of this rolling around on cement dance floors."

"I will lose no time in finding my Gabriela a good, clean boy," vowed Señora Fernandez, whom the other women made to feel somehow responsible for the evening's spectacle. "I have a little saved, enough to buy some linen and a sewing machine and a big double bed, all things a girl needs to catch a boy. A busy married life will be just the answer for my baby."

Other mothers of young unmarried girls agreed with Señora Fernandez's sensible words. They felt that Gabriela had been struck down by a whim of fate, and that this blow could just as easily have befallen their own daughters. To be on the safe side, the women resolved to marry off their girls as quickly as they could.

The following days were a time of great planning. As there were only so many eligible boys to go around, mothers schemed and plotted to snatch one for their own daughters. Women who for many years had been closer than sisters now become suspicious of one another. Eyes spied out from behind curtained windows, secret meetings were arranged at the dead of night, deals were made behind closed doors. Mothers of handsome single boys gave themselves airs, and they marched around town with the satisfied expressions of possessors of rich treasures. Mothers of pretty and healthy girls were fairly certain of obtaining one of these finer boys. However, mothers of girls less fortunately blessed by nature lay sleepless at night, worried lest they might be forced to take into their families boys who were ugly or mean, drunken or lazy; or worse, boys with some defect: a stutter, a clouded eye, a lame or missing limb. It was feared that certain girls would be required to marry boys from neighbouring villages or, if truly desperate, from the capital city.

The air was thick with the fevers of romance. The priest prepared for a rash of weddings. Mothers of unwed girls retrieved money from beneath mattresses and bought fancy household goods, which they displayed temptingly in front of their houses. Single girls were freed from household chores and were paraded day and night though the streets and plaza, dressed always in their finest clothes. Many young boys came to have a hunted look, and they would glance nervously over their shoulders, as though fearful of a clutching hand. As the days passed it was gradually noticed that a number of young boys had vanished, fled up into the hills to hide until this mood of marriage had passed and they might return safely single to the town.

Those boys who remained behind took pleasure in the company of Juanita. Usually this girl had nothing but contempt for her fellow townspeople and lived only for the business of love that flourished in the larger town nearby; but now she seemed to take greater interest in her place of birth, and seemed also to feel the planned weddings posed a direct threat to her. In revenge she offered single boys the rich pleasures of affection outside the binding chains of matrimony. While unattached girls dragged themselves around the treadmill of the streets, boys ran past them to the beach, to where the arms of Juanita stretched wide and waiting through the dark.

"Look," said Señora Fernandez to her daughter on the following Sunday night.

In the mirror Gabriela saw a face she could not recognize. It was a mask of paint and powder. Bracelets and necklaces and rings hung upon her like heavy chains, and perfume swam around her as thickly as water she could not breathe.

"Look," repeated Señora Fernandez. "You are very beautiful and sure to snare a dozen boys at the dance tonight." Despite her words, the mother had a secret fear that the episode of the previous week would frighten suitors from her daughter. Now seeing Gabriela sitting so queerly silent, Señora Fernandez's fears grew stronger. "Go! Go! What are you waiting for? Those sly girls will be vamping and vixing around the Casino already. Now remember, don't sit with those girls and don't talk with them, either. They'll be full of tricks and games, and not worthy of a speck of trust."

That night in the Casino there were five eligible girls for every eligible boy. The band was nervous, and played even more uncertainly than usual. The girls stood each alone, their paint so thick and necklines so low as would before have caused a scandal. Those boys forced to attend the dance were losing no time in drinking too much beer too quickly, and they moved only to stumble into a dark corner where Juanita was entertaining. Mothers watched these proceedings with the sharp darting eyes of fishermen searching a wide sea for swirls of fin or tail.

When Gabriela fell upon the ground again, to be thrown around in the clutches of a spell more fierce than that of the previous week, a commotion occurred. Many women cried foul play, intimating that the fit was false, a scheme hatched by Señora Fernandez to focus all eyes upon her daughter. The single boys took advantage of the ensuing ado to slip unnoticed from the courtyard.

"I see what this is," cried Señora Martinez, pushing her way through the crowd around Gabriela. "It's a disgrace, a shame, a scandal, this girl making love in the devil's arms. And in public!" Señora Martinez turned to the women. "See what you get!" she screamed exultantly. "You have invited the devil to our town with your talk of lusty love. I hope very much that you are happy now," and the excited woman looked around with wild eyes, swaying and teetering as though about to join Gabriela on the ground.

Immediately the townspeople saw that for once Señora Martinez was right. They stepped several paces back from the moaning, thrusting girl, whose lovemaking with the demon was growing more passionate and explicit; and before it could draw to its terrible climax, they turned together and fled the Casino.

The girl awoke in the emptied, silent courtyard, her heart rising and falling to the beat of the sea. The cement on which she lay was hard and cold. She felt hands stroke the damp hair off her brow, wipe the sweat from her skin. Juanita's face hovered like a moon above her, but upside down, inverted, and finally lowering closer and closer.

Juanita's heels clicked away. The sound echoed in the courtyard, then faded. Gabriela lay still, looking up at the wide black sky, now empty of its moon, and stars fell like tears from the eyes of God.

This second incident only served to increase the marriage mania that swept through the town. Mothers now felt it was a race against time: sooner or later the fickle devil would grow weary of the arms of Gabriela, and he would turn to any girl not protected by the sanctity of marriage. Astounding lengths were resorted to in the name of holy matrimony. Some mothers let it be known that their daughters might be visited in the middle of the night by the right kind of boy, to give him a taste of what could be his forever. Other women, feeling need for more drastic measures, climbed the western slopes in search of Indian brujas who could cast spells. Bitter and sweet smoke rose from pots of potions and hung in narcotic clouds above the town, and chanted prayers floated down streams and fell hissing into the sea: oh, cast a boy upon the shore of every girl.

The house of Señora Fernandez stood closed and silent, its doors and windows fastened. The townspeople avoided passing close to its doomed front. Gabriela was not to be seen, and her mother left the house only to fetch food, hurrying through the streets with head bowed in shame. A group of women, led by Señora Martinez, had visited Señora Fernandez and demanded she keep her daughter away from their blessed girls and off their sacred streets.

Gabriela's eyes grew familiar with the darkness of shadowed rooms. When by chance a blade of bright sunlight cut through some crack in the walls or windows, Gabriela would stare in fear, and a pain would flash through her head. The girl did not sleep, but paced slowly around the house with dragging footsteps, peering into the darkest corners with hopeful eyes. She shivered and her teeth chattered, and her skin was colder than ice to her mother's touch. In silent fear and awe Señora Fernandez watched her daughter wait constantly and restlessly for the caress of the devil's firey breath, and she could not help but notice that as time passed the demon came more often to his lover.

Outside the church bell chimed its wedding spell with increasing frequency, and for a period of several weeks the air was broken continually by the song. The dirt streets were painted pink and blue by a carpet of confetti and the blossoms of bridal bouquets. The priest's eyes grew red from lack of sleep and his voice came to trip over words of the wedding ceremony. No one chose to notice that as time went by he began to skip certain parts of the ritual in order to hasten proceedings. Soon the town was half deserted as all the newly married couples left for extended honeymoons in Acapulco and Puerto Vallarta. These were furnished by mothers of brides, women grateful their babies had been saved from the devil's arms and anchored safely in the calm harbour of marriage.

The wedding bells shattered Gabriela's dreams, and with their every stroke she screamed out loud, running to the bolted door. She would fling herself against it, bruising and bloodying her body until she fell onto the ground and into the arms of the devil. So great was the injury she did herself that Señora Fernandez finally felt she had no choice but to chain the girl to the bedpost. Gabriela crouched on the stone floor, imprisoned in irons, and she rocked herself back and forth. Near to her the spitting candle flickered and flared, wavering strangely in the smoky breath of the devil. Above the bed the silver cross shone red, the colour of flame and fire, the colour of Juanita's eyes peering through a gap between the shutters, fixed by a look that might have been love or pity or longing, or something else instead.

When the newlyweds returned from their honeymoons, weary with lovemaking, the town went back to its old ways. Boys who had been hiding up in the hills came down. Now that all their girls were secured within the strong brown arms of boys, the women of the town offered no objection when Señora Fernandez unchained her daughter and unlocked the door.

Gabriela walked the streets and plaza both day and night, neither avoiding nor seeking out her friends of old. She did not seem completely aware of her surroundings, and often tripped over a stone on the road or walked into a wall. These accidents did not jar the yearning expression that was fixed on her face. Gabriela acquired the habit of continually licking her lips in the way people do when looking forward to a tasty meal. Now when she fell upon the dusty road, laughing and sobbing with pleasure, the townspeople took little notice, only stepping over or around her writhing body. Sometimes small, dirty boys poked sticks in the space around her with the hope of spearing the devil in her arms. When accidentally they stabbed Gabriela, her acts of love were not interrupted. In their beds and groaning beside their smooth boys, young brides would hear Gabriela crying in the street outside. What is it? asked their boys, still twisting brown on the white sheets. What is it? they asked the suddenly frozen girls. In reply the young brides laughed somewhere deep inside themselves, then coiled around their boys once more, groaning louder.

The town was filled with sounds of love day and night, and Señora Martinez sat very still behind her window, twisting her hands in her lap. With glowing eyes she watched her daughter follow Gabriela through the streets. Having abandoned suddenly and without explanation the commerce of love in the next town, Juanita spent her days trailing after Gabriela, always at a distance of several feet. Her appearance, previously so carefully maintained, altered drastically, and Juanita wore a soft and sloppy look upon her face. She seemed to wait for the devil to visit his lover with as much impatience as Gabriela herself, and when he finally appeared she watched the act of love with a naked fascination disturbing to behold. This was despite the fact that the sight apparently brought Jaunita only a feeling of pain that mounted in intensity with every passing day.

One afternoon when Gabriela swooned with love upon the road Juanita fell upon her with a hysterical cry and a monstrous fury. She slapped Gabriela's face five times, hard. At once the two girls became calm. Gabriela sat up.

"There, now," said Juanita roughly. "Let's end this

foolishness. Come with me.'' And for the next two weeks the two girls were always together, sharing a bench in the plaza while one taught and the other learned. Through this time Juanita returned to her careful way of dress and her hard, scornful expression, and Gabriela was free of the devil's love.

"Now the first thing and the most important thing is English," instructed Juanita. "Say like this: hello handsome, what is happening, have fun with me." Juanita repeated the English words slowly several times, and Gabriela tried to echo their sounds. "Hi there, big boy," said Juanita in the foreign tongue. "Want to dance, take me home, my baby is dead," and she laughed and laughed and laughed.

Juanita showed Gabriela how to smoke cigarettes and how to flutter her eyelashes. She taught Gabriela the ways of Americans and the aspects of financial love, and when she felt her pupil ready she dressed the girl in a bright, flimsy garment and tall, wobbly shoes. As she adorned Gabriela, Juanita said in a hard and sure voice, "Now you will never have to worry about that craziness of yours again. You will forget all about it, you will forget everything. I promise you."

So Gabriela accompanied Juanita to the discothèque and the arms of American men in the neighbouring town. The two girls left their village each afternoon and returned with the sun the next morning, their make-up smeared across tired faces, their shiny dresses soiled and wrinkled, their feet aching in tight, high-heeled shoes. They returned to the house of Juanita and her mother, where Gabriela had come to live. Señora Martinez had cool baths and iced fruit drinks awaiting them. When the exhausted girls dropped heavy heads onto pillows, to sleep through the heat of the day, Señora Martinez sat on the edge of their bed, fanning them with a movie magazine. The woman's lips pressed tightly together in a thin smile, and a bright, satisfied light shone in her eyes. She watched the sleeping girls, then paced her own dim room, with arms wrapped tightly around herself in a passionate embrace.

Sometimes Gabriela wakened in the middle of the afternoon when the sun was at its height of strength. Her skin would feel damp and sticky, and the bed full of burning coals. She would slip into one of her old and faded flower-patterned skirts, pull on a white blouse, and walk through the town. Invisible to the eyes of her former friends and neighbours, she searched for some cooling breeze, a patch of shade. From all sides around her came cries of babies conceived one year before.

The early moon, appearing nebulous as a puff of smoke, rose from the east and hovered there, waiting for the sun to sink. A warm breeze stirred the parched leaves above Gabriela's head, catching her eyes. Now and then a hot breath blew in her ear, intimately, caressingly, and the girl turned her head quickly to see only a fire over which a woman was stirring beans. "Hello, big boy, want to dance," Gabriela whispered to herself in English. "I love you, your arms look so big and strong," she repeated over and over again, but still a note of something lost struck inside her head, like a bell chiming through the hot, unrepenting air.

The National Circus of Argentina

Emilia dumped the slop into the trough, then stood gazing into the distance. The pigs butted against her knees, almost knocking her onto the ground. They made loud sounds of hunger.

Her sister called from the house. "Emilia, hurry up! I asked you to feed the pigs, not tell them your life story."

"I'm coming," Emilia answered, and she slowly began to cross the slippery sty.

Suddenly, a voice blared in her ear. "Men, women, and children. All good people. This is your one and only chance to see the National Circus of Argentina in all its glory. Direct from the land of gold and silver, this renowned circus has fascinated kings, queens, and movie stars. See daring feats and savage African beasts! Ride the ferris wheel into the sky! Come to the music and dancing and laughter! Come to happiness! Come to the National Circus of Argentina!"

Emilia stood entranced. A battered truck tore down the main street of the village, throwing great clouds of dust into the air. The driver tossed an empty bottle onto the side of the road, where it smashed. From a loudspeaker fixed on the hood of the truck the voice droned: "Men, women, and children. All good people . . ."

"Sister Selene!" cried Emilia, running into the house. "Listen! A circus!"

"I've got ears, haven't I?" retorted Selene acidly. "There ought to be a law against these tricksters proclaiming their lies in broad daylight. They aren't content to whisper their false, silky promises in the dark, these Don Juans and Joses." She gazed bitterly out the window, but could see only a reflection of the shabby room in which she stood. Wheeling around, Selene moodily surveyed her boudoir. It was a jumble of knick-knacks, old momentos, faded photographs, cheap presents lavished by past suitors. In the centre of this her bed, the biggest in the village, stood like a throne.

Selene's glance fell on her sister's shining eyes. "Are you intending to turn into a cow?" she shrieked. "It isn't enough that you're a fool, I suppose. Get to work!"

"I want to go," said Emilia, gathering the breakfast tray off Selene's bed. "I want to see the National Circus of Argentina. I want happiness."

"Happiness! Argentina! A dirty land full of dirty cowboys. They ride the mares until their hooves fall off and their mouths stream blood. You know, of course, who that coward driving the truck was? The very same shyster who's been sneaking around all the villages and doodling the simple girls. If he's from Argentina, I'm from Paris, France. I dance the cancan in a nightclub, I sleep on silk sheets, I eat snails." Selene's voice trailed off and her eyes grew moony. They quickly narrowed. "This imitation Argentinian hasn't doodled you, has he?"

"I've never been to Argentina in all my life," mumbled Emilia, blushing. "Not even when I was a little girl."

Selene placed her hands on her ample hips. "Pesos!" she screamed. "They'll charge the moon and the stars to see their tinny tricks. How do you expect to pay? With the tears falling from your eyes?"

"I had a dream," thought Emilia, wiping her wet cheeks. "I dreamed I was swimming at the bottom of the sea, and fish were slipping and sliding around me. They whispered secrets in my ears and kissed my eyes and looked in wonder at my streaming hair. I reached out to touch them and they turned to silver and gold. All around me the sea was shining as brightly as a million jewels. But no more secrets were whispered in my ears and no more kisses brushed my eyes, and I cried. Then I drowned in my tears."

"Snap out of it, sister," said Selene. Her eyes became

suspicious. ''You haven't been stealing, have you? Must I turn my sister the thief over to the Chief of Police? They have rats in jail, you know. Big ones.''

''I didn't steal anything.'' Emilia began to sweep the floor, causing dust to fly thickly around her, a cocoon which Selene's sharp eyes could not pierce. Emilia swept and thought of her silver coins. They were wrapped in a rag and hidden in a hollow of the old mango tree behind the house. She leaned on the broom, and her eyes grew as large and round and bright as the silver coins of which she was dreaming.

Early every evening Selene fell asleep after her copious meal and brandy. When her snores filled the house Emilia slipped outside and wandered the streets. Villagers tossed stale crusts to the poor, thin girl. She nibbled at the bread, and when she reached the shore it was gone.

Emilia walked naked and alone beside the sea, trembling beneath the eyes of the stars, the hands of the wind. The moon drew pictures upon the waves, and Emilia's heart ached to see them. They were so beautiful. She tried to run from the pain that lay beneath her glistening skin. But the faster she ran the more wildly and loudly beat her heart, until it broke with a deafening sound. Emilia felt something fall from her, and she was all lightness. As a strong current pulled pieces of driftwood and a broken heart far out to sea, Emilia believed she could run forever. Unburdened of her heavy, hurting heart, one day she would fly.

The cold sea boomed in her ear and flooded the empty space inside her. Above the sound of the waves Emilia heard a voice calling. She stopped running and turned her face toward the water. Her lost heart was crying somewhere at the edge of the moonlight, past the point where the endless ocean vanished into darkness.

Suddenly the night turned cold. When she pulled the faded dress over her head, its cloth stuck to her skin with a glue of sweat. Emilia walked back toward the shining lights of the village strung along the wide curve of the bay, her face turned down to the waves foaming beneath her feet. But no matter how she strained to see she could not find her missing heart. In pity the sea threw pendants of ruby and amethyst upon the shore, and the stars cried diamond tears.

Emilia gathered up the jewels without wondering. She did not think of someone crying for something loved and lost. Nearing the bright, blind eyes of her village, her arms full of treasure that brought her no happiness, she felt only the gaping wound inside her chest.

"Anyone who walked along the shore at night would find these things," Emilia told herself. Yet she stole like a thief down a dark back street and knocked softly on a door marked by no name or number.

Old Rafien peered out, then pulled her inside. "No one else would give you what I give you for these cheap baubles," he muttered, his eyes as bright as the jewels he stared at. "They would cheat a girl like you. But I'm an honest man, a businessman. I don't ask how or where a girl like you finds trinkets such as these." Rafien's tongue licked his toothless gums. "Yes, yes," he mumbled, seeming to forget he was not alone. He swept away the shining treasures. Then a brighter light burned in his eyes. "Now, you know where your money is, eh? See how my pockets are bursting with coins tonight? Just reach inside and take them, and they're yours."

Emilia stretched out her hand and felt inside the old man's pocket. But the coins were never there, and the pocket was never sewn shut, and it was always something else she found. Rafien grabbed her wrist and held her hand there. And while they stood like that Emilia looked past the old man's closed eyes, through the grimy window, and at the round, blank face of the moon.

He released her suddenly, pushing her away. "Here's your payment, my sweet business partner." He laughed and threw several coins out the door. Emilia scrambled in the dirt for them, then ran through the sleeping streets to her sister's house.

The mango tree that stood alone in the back yard had old and hollow and barren branches. Emilia reached for a rag in a small niche high in the tree, and she added the coins to the ones already there. Entering Selene's snoring house, she wrapped herself in some scraps of cloth and lay on a corner of the floor. She forgot at once about the silver coins. Her hands pressed against her ears, she waited for dreams of fish to swim through the empty space inside her, and to fill it.

The next day Emilia worked with the thought of the silver coins shining before her eyes. In the hot afternoon she walked through the village on an errand for Selene and she saw a girl wearing a pretty, bright dress. Looking at her own faded shift, Emilia thought, "With my coins I could buy a dress just as pretty as that." Passing an open window, she saw two girls lying and laughing on a bed, spraying perfume from a green glass bottle into the air above them. The scent floated out into the street, and in its spell Emilia stood still. "I could buy a green glass bottle of perfume, too," she mused. The thought took her by surprise, for never had she dreamed of removing the silver coins from their hiding place. She knew that if she stretched up her hand to take the money from the hollow of the old mango tree she would not feel the coins, but something else. "It's something other than pretty perfume and dresses that I want," Emilia thought.

That night as she was walking home from Old Rafien's the stars rained through the sky, and upon hitting the ground they exploded into words: "Come to the music and dancing and laughter! Come to happiness! Come to the National Circus of Argentina!" Feeling the words of promise fill the empty space inside her, Emilia reached up into the niche of the mango tree. The rag of coins fell easily into her hand. Emilia entered the house and roughly shook her snoring sister. "Pedro? Alfredo?" muttered Selene sleepily.

"Look," said Emilia, and the silver coins fell upon Selene's bed. They glinted in the candlelight. Selene sat up, rustling the movie magazines scattered over the covers. Emilia grabbed her sister's throat and held it tightly "We're going to the National Circus of Argentina. Tomorrow." The moon smiled through the window.

The next evening the two sisters rode in the back of a neighbour's truck toward the larger town some twenty miles away. The wind tore around them. In one corner of the truck Selene clung weakly to its side with one hand, while with the other she desperately tried to keep her freshly curled hair in place. "Faster!" cried Emilia, as the air beat against her face. "Faster!" she cried, as the truck sped along the coastal road.

Selene glared at her sister. Since the moment her beauty sleep had been destroyed, Selene had felt full of hate and some fear of Emilia. The slut! Hoarding money from her own family's needs! Earning pesos in God only knew what shameful or sneaky way! As far as Selene was concerned, Emilia had taken leave of the little sense she had once possessed. She would not listen to reason and she would not do a stitch of work. Selene vowed to teach the little tramp what came of trying to play the princess, plus have a little fun herself.

They entered the next town, which though larger than their village was still a small, country place. Emilia scrambled from the truck and danced on the road. "Hurry, Selene," she implored. "I can hear the music of the circus, and it sounds so close!"

Selene descended from the truck with some difficulty. She attempted to rearrange her damaged curls and wipe a portion of the dust from her satin dress. "First things first," she commanded. "Give me that filthy money right now, unless you desire to lose it. These two-bit circuses are full of pickpockets who become rich thanks to fools like you know who."

Her eyes fixed down the street in the direction from which sounds of laughter and music carried clearly, Emilia dropped the rag full of silver into her sister's hand. "Now you go on ahead," stated Selene, "and get rid of your dreams. I'll just step inside this café for a glass of something cool. Plus, I need to redo my face. I'll join you directly."

Emilia ran down the street. At the edge of a thronging crowd she halted. The National Circus of Argentina lay before her eyes, and it was a sight so perfect that Emilia could not believe it true.

Looming over the square was a large tent on which was painted various pictures of savage beasts, funny clowns, cute monkeys, pretty ladies flying on trapezes, and much, much more. All around the square were small booths lit up by bright lights. Before them boys were shooting pistols and throwing rings at targets, aiming to win prizes for their girls. Taco stands and candy carts and refreshment booths were set up here and there.

Emilia looked at the circus anxiously, her eyes darting in every direction at once. They came to rest on a large wheel that towered over the crowd, the square, the town. It turned around and around, and the coloured lights fastened to it turned also. Emilia craned her neck, looking up at the highest point of the spinning wheel. People seated in little chairs around it screamed with joy, and they reached out to grab the stars. "That must be the ferris wheel," thought Emilia, and the vision floated on her wet eyes.

She entered the crowd. People bumped and pushed against her, rushing to take everything the circus had to offer as quickly as they could. Emilia wandered without direction, pulled this way and that by the magic of the circus. A woman with wild hair and eyes sat just inside the fortune-telling booth, and she beckoned for Emilia to enter the darkness. A dark man grabbed her wrist and held it tightly. "Step inside," he chanted. "See the fattest woman ever born. Her waist is wider than the world, her thighs are larger than a dozen Americas, her chest is taller than the highest Alps."

Emilia pulled away and ran in fright until she became lost in the crowd. Suddenly she found herself directly beneath the ferris wheel and inside the turning circle of its song. Now and then the wheel stopped, and people climbed off or on. Emilia stepped forward.

"Where's your ticket?" asked a man, holding her shoulder.

"Ticket?"

"You need a ticket to ride the ferris wheel. You buy it from that lady over there. It costs one hundred pesos."

Emilia looked at her empty hands. The wheel began to turn again, carrying its passengers high into the sky. Their cries of joy seemed to come from so far away. "They can see everything," Emilia thought. "They can see across the mountains, they can look across the sea. They can touch God." She noticed that when the revolving wheel carried the people back down to earth their faces looked wiser and the laughter died on their lips. What they had seen in the sky had changed them. "The world doesn't seem the same when they return to the ground," thought Emilia.

She turned and drifted through the maze of people. From all around came the music of a hundred different songs, but no single one could be heard clearly. A thousand different faces pushed past her, yet she did not recognize any of them. Emilia tried to make her way to the edge of the crowd, so she might walk up the road to where she had left Selene. But she could not find her way, and the mass of people pushed against her, streaming in the opposite direction. The strong current pulled Emilia deeper and deeper down. The water turned black, there were no fish swimming around her, and no silver coins flashed before her eyes.

The waves of the crowd threw Emilia out onto its edge. She picked herself up from the ground, trembling. Her feet carried her down the dark road that lay before her and she discovered herself by the sea. Waves beat silver against the shore. Emilia slipped her dress over her head and ran beside the sea. She tried to run as quickly as she had run all the nights before, so swiftly the sea and moon and stars would marvel at her speed and shower her with their treasures. On jewelled wings she would fly higher than the ferris wheel.

The beach was strange to her feet, and rocky. Several times she tripped and fell. Although she rose and raced onward, she could not feel the moon and stars gazing with love upon her, and the wind did not brush against her. She felt only the pain where stones had scraped her skin, and the larger hurt that was her heart.

Water splashed around her feet. Emilia saw she had reached a river that cut across the shore on its way to the sea. It smelled of waste. The light was such that Emilia could not see across it. She did not know how deep or wide it was, or what she might find on its further shore.

Stumbling now more often on the stones, Emilia retraced her steps. Her dress was crumpled in a ball in her hand. Her eyes searched the ground, but no treasure lay waiting to be gathered. At last she fell and did not rise.

He stood over her like a shadow falling across the moon. "Rafien," she said. "I have found no treasure, but please give me your silver coins. Let me reach inside your pocket. I need to ride the ferris wheel. Tomorrow night I will find more treasure than I've ever found before, and I'll give it all to you."

The shadow sank down over Emilia and covered her. But her face was still exposed. As she was pressed again and then again against the ragged rock, she saw one large, mocking eye of the moon. She heard the jeering laughter of the distant crowd, the music of the circus, and she saw the wheel turning.

Selene held tightly onto the arm of her new beau. Together they weaved through the crowd. The high heel of one of her shoes had somehow broken, and Selene was forced to hobble along. "Where can she be?" she asked irritably. "She's apt to wander off the edge of the world if you don't keep an eye on her. Do you see her, lover boy? She's a thin, scrawny thing with crazed eyes. Of course, we're not really sisters, we're hardly of the same species. But I'm a large-hearted woman, I take any stranger into my soul. I can't help it, that's how I am. Now give me another drink from that bottle."

They found Emilia sitting on a bench beneath a blooming gardenia bush, somewhat removed from the bustle of the circus. "Emilia," said Selene, suppressing anger. "Where have you been? This is Alfredo, a gentleman aquaintance of mine. Say hello."

"Hello."

"Why are you sitting here like this? I thought you would be running wild around your precious National Circus of Argentina. I must say, it is a shabby affair. But what can you expect? Not now, Alfredo." Selene giggled girlishly. "Just wait and we can have ourselves some fun later." Selene looked with contempt around her, then spat. Her unfocused eyes returned to Emilia.

"Don't just sit there!" she shouted with sudden fury. "What kind of trick is this, after you've nearly talked me into the grave with your circus this and circus that. Ride the ferris wheel! Find happiness! And hurry up about it. Alfredo, give the fool a few pesos."

Seeing Emilia motionless on the bench, eyes turned to the ground, Selene grabbed her sister's shoulders and pulled her to her feet. "What have you done now? Where are your shoes, and how did you tear your dress like that? What is all this blood? I swear," Selene fumed to the teetering Alfredo, "this is the fine thanks I get for giving a simpleton its way."

"I fell off the ferris wheel," Emilia said flatly.

"People don't fall off ferris wheels, and if they do they die! At the very least they break some bones!" screeched Selene. A number of spectators looked with curiosity at this scene. Selene's eyes shrank small with hate. "You're just out to ruin my good time. I sit in that hovel for months on end with only an idiot for company. Is this what I deserve?" Selene demanded of the onlookers. "Is it? No! Come, Alfredo. Show me that funny thing you were talking about. Man and woman both in one? Can it really doodle itself?"

Alfredo and Selene swayed off together. "And don't wait for me, either," Selene called over her shoulder. "Alfredo has promised to take me over the mountains on his motorcycle. How I live for fast rides! We'll race to the capital city for cocktails and fish dinners in air-conditioned restaurants. We may be gone for days and days."

Emilia remained on the stone bench. Though the crowd had begun to thin out, the motion and music of the circus continued. She heard the ferris wheel creak as it turned around. It jerkily started and stopped. You rode around ten times, then they made you get off. You had to buy another ticket if you wanted to ride again.

Selene poked her sister in the back as they walked arm and arm out the church. "Smile," she hissed. "Do you know how much that dress cost me?"

On the church steps they waited for the groom, who had remained inside to have a drink with the priest. A large crowd milled around; nearly everyone in the village had come to see this curious wedding. Emilia stood stiffly in the heavy bridal gown. The flowers she clutched gave off a scent that made her eyes want to close, her legs fold, her arms wrap themselves around herself.

"But it was worth it," whispered Selene. "Old Rafien will feed you and clothe you, and I'll have the house to myself, free to entertain my male friends. Old Rafien's place has three rooms, running water, and electricity. He has an ironing board, an ice-box, and an electric blender. Count your lucky stars."

Selene lit a cigarette and showily puffed smoke. "Now throw those smelly flowers, I certainly don't want them. Have no use for them. Weddings were invented for fools like you. Look, here comes the handsome young prince of a groom."

Rafien shuffled toward them and took Emilia's arm, holding it tightly. The bridal couple passed through the crowd, which stared stonily at them.

Emilia's long white dress trailed in the dust, sweeping the street like a broom. Rafien led her to his house, and they entered the door without a name or number. "Now, my golden goose," the old man said, "you can start to lay your golden eggs. But first lie here."

He pushed her onto the wide bed, and Emilia thought she would fall through it. She would sink through the waves, and the light would change from blue to green to gold to black. But the bed rocked, she floated on the waves; and though the old man pushed her down, she could not drown.

When the room grew dark the old man got off her. "That's enough of that," he said. "There's time for more of that later. Years and years. Now go and gather treasure for your loved one. Go."

He pushed her out the door. Emilia walked slowly to the shore. Once more she pulled the dress over her head and ran naked beside the sea. Her pulse hammered, blood pounded through her veins, her heart beat cruelly. She ran more swiftly than she had ever run before, so rapidly she would surely soar into the air and on a high trapeze swing from star to star. Through the sky she flew, somersaulting in space, fearless even with no net below. She spun around like a whirling planet, and the crowd gasped and cheered and held its breath with fear. The sad clowns and lion tamers and bareback riders also turned their eyes up to the first star of the National Circus of Argentina. Then she missed the bar, her hands grasped only air, and she fell and fell.

Emilia lay upon the sand. She turned her face to the sky, but great clouds covered the heavens, closing the eyes of the moon and stars. She looked at the sea, but no jewels were carried upon the foaming waves. There was no sound from her heart. She felt it inside her, silent and heavy as a stone. It didn't hurt a bit. Emilia knew it had been there all along, it had never dropped. It was lodged firmly inside her, and there it would always be. It would never fall upon the shore and release her.

Music made faint by distance grazed against her ear. Emilia looked out across the sea. Lights of a wheel turned around and around, red and purple, blue and green. They moved between the heavens and the sea. The National Circus of Argentina was floating out in the centre of the dark, wide water.

Emilia waded through the shallows. The sand was firm beneath her feet and the water cool around her legs. She waded farther, then began to swim. Though her heart was a massive weight inside her, for a moment she felt light. She could swim a great distance without becoming tired. Ahead the circus beckoned.

Her heavy heart sank like an anchor seeking rest. As she drifted down Emilia saw the coloured lights of the circus also sinking. Beneath the water the circus lights looked so funny that Emilia almost laughed: they grew soft and large as coloured moons. Attracted by the bright lights, fish swarmed around the girl, slipping and sliding around her. They whispered secrets in her ears and kissed her eyes and looked in wonder at her streaming hair. They were changed by the sea's love into silver coins and golden treasure as bright as coloured circus lights. For a thousand and one nights the waves threw themselves upon the shore, pendants of ruby and amethyst for another girl to gather.

There Must Be More to Life Than Kissing Boys

She hated it, that's all. Estrella just hated the rain, and she wished it would go away. "I can't stand it, the way it falls on you and covers you like a million slobbery kisses of a million stupid boys," she said, striding quickly between the four walls.

"Stop," her mother said, but not to the rain that pounded on the roof, demanding entry. "Stop. It makes me dizzy to watch you rush around like this. Where are you going? And what on earth are you doing with that measuring stick?"

Since the rains had begun one month before, the room seemed to shrink a little more each day. Estrella was sure it had grown smaller, but upon taking measurements she found the damp, dark space to be the same size as always. "I can't believe it," she said, frowning at the ruler.

"God is sad," murmured her mother, who sat very still in a little chair, her eyes as clouded as the sky. "He is crying for all of us."

"Beans!" cried Estrella. "Rain is made from the earth's moisture being absorbed into the sky and formed into clouds, which rise into thin air then drop their water. We learned all about it at school."

"There's no need to get scientific," replied her mother primly. "Don't play prima donna with me. You become wet in the rain the same as the rest of us, my proud little lady. School! You haven't learned a single thing yet."

"I've learned I'd rather drown in the rain than stay in here with you!'' shouted Estrella, and outside she ran with neither umbrella nor hat.

She visited her girlfriends, but they were no comfort. As soon as the season of rain had begun, Estrella's friends had changed. Their brains had turned soggy. Now they sat for hours in silence, looking out windows, listening to the sound of the rain upon the roofs. But they wouldn't listen when Estrella talked about Florence Nightingale or Madame Curie, and they showed no interest when she spoke of the time she would be old enough to leave the tiny town. She would move to the capital city, and there she would live the life of a sharp, modern, independent young woman. Estrella talked quickly and loudly about her plans, but her friends only stirred themselves from time to time and sighed that the rain was so romantic.

It was as romantic as a slap in the face, as far as Estrella was concerned. It caused all the dirty smells in the streets to be raised to nose level. And the mud! Please don't mention the mud! To avoid the mud Estrella was forced to stay inside that dark little house with her mother. All she wanted was to keep neat and clean like any normal civilized person, but how could she with the rain? She'd rather kiss a hundred boys than play out in that rain.

Her friends did that, which only showed. Now and then they rose from their stupors to run around and scream in the rain, feet and legs bare as bare could be. Their games had no rules and made no sense, those girls just squealed like pigs in the mud. They liked to paint their skin and hair with mud, and the filthier they got the louder they shrieked, making Indian and animal noises, announcing their crazy joy. Then they danced and splashed in the puddles, those girls, their dresses soaking up water like sponges, clinging to those girls, allowing the boys to see everything. Those girls might as well have been naked for all it was worth. No thank you! Keep your rain! thought Estrella, as she walked through the darkening afternoon to the coop of a house where her mother would cluck anxiously all though the night.

When Estrella woke the next morning there was no rain in the sky, but that was only a trick. It would begin to rain again that afternoon, surely as sin, and meanwhile the streets were all soaked and shining from the night full of rain, and the air was already so hot and damp. There was not a breath of freshness, you couldn't breathe, you might as well be lying in a tub of water as in your bed. Estrella's skin felt sticky, like it was coated with spit from a boy's mouth, or with glue. She'd have to be extra careful not to brush accidentally against some boy or she'd find herself stuck to him for life. Ugghh!

Away she ran to buy the day's tortillas for her mother. Before the tortilleria was a large crowd of girls holding white cloths stitched with red and green. Usually these girls scratched and clawed to be the first to buy tortillas, and there were often injuries. But on this day instead of fighting in line the girls were standing around, whispering and giggling like half-wits.

Estrella stepped up to buy her tortillas. The machine clamoured and clanked. A ball of dough as large and round as the world was fed into a gadget, where it was flattened and cut into a million tortillas. These followed one another down a moving belt, passing over a flame that burned and branded them. They all came out the same.

Estrella stood there, surprised at how easily and quickly she had made the purchase. Always the first girl to buy tortillas would lord over the others, bragging of her victory, and now Estrella held the full heavy warmth of her cloth above her head. "Look!" she cried. But the girls paid her no attention, not the slightest bit, cheating her with their meanness.

A boy happened by. All the girls shrieked as though they'd seen a ghost or a goldmine. "A boy! A boy!" they shrilly screamed, and they started dancing around more crazily than dying chickens. "I bet he's a good kisser. Look at his mouth. It looks just right for kissing."

The boy quickened his step, glancing back at the girls with surprise. Estrella left the tortilleria at that moment, by coincidence walking in the same direction as the boy, and her foolish friends called after her: "Catch him! Catch him and kiss him, Estrella!"

That day school was even more chaotic than usual. The teacher tried to explain about geography, but the only places of interest to the girls were those where boys were sitting.

Around and around the boys ran the girls, flouncing their dresses and shaking their hair. Knowing the meaning of the word impossible, the teacher did not attempt to shout over the girls' screams. He spoke as though to himself of capital cities and countries.

"Donkeys!" hissed Estrella to her friends, "Shut up! I want to learn geography. I want to know where Paris is."

"Paris is where they kiss in the streets," was all these girls could say. The day was ruined, thanks to those giggling geese. As Estrella walked home from school, her important plans seemed to turn soggy and useless in the rain, which was falling with unusual force.

Because of the heavy showers, the boys and girls had the plaza to themselves that evening; adults and small children preferred to stay dry inside the houses. Estrella herself didn't go to the plaza to look at the boys, or anything like that. She was only curious to see what madness her friends would think of next. Under the shelter of a thickly leaved tree Estrella sat on a perfectly dry bench. She watched her girlfriends walk arm in arm around the square, promenading in the rain. At first they ignored the boys who rustled like dark leaves in the bushes, who huddled there to keep the ends of their cigarettes fiery and hot. Estrella could smell the stink of the perfume the girls were drenched with, she could see the thick globs of make-up sliding down their faces. Driven wild by the stinging rain, soon these girls pointed at various boys and smacked their lips. "Kiss me! Kiss me!" they called to the boys, and then they ran away.

This kissing business was not new. Two years before, when Estrella and her friends had been eleven, the boys seized hold of the idea that kissing was fun. They were stupid enough to want to copy their parents. For one whole season of sun the boys had roamed in packs, hunting for any stray girl who might be captured and kissed. At that time the girls agreed unanimously that there was nothing worse in the whole wide world than having to touch lips with mean and dirty boys. They would cry in frustration when forced to undergo this torture, and to prevent it from occurring the girls had contrived to walk in twos or threes whenever possible, knowing that safety lay in numbers.

Some time later, when they tired of chasing reluctant girls, the boys had begun to go down to the beach at night. They slipped down the dark roads in pairs, returning very much later when all the town had gone to sleep and no eyes could see them. During daytime then the boys were always sleepy and dopey. You had to ask those boys a question twice before they'd hear you, and even then their answers made no sense.

A time came when the girls had looked up from their hopscotch games and stared after the pairs of boys. "Where are you going, lovebirds?" they had shouted tauntingly. When the boys' backs disappeared down the road leading to the sea, the girls would begin to quarrel for no reason. The hopscotch game would end amid crying and chaos. Girls who had been best friends for years became worst enemies in an instant, and they fled home to lie alone in their beds. There they had cried until the rainy season had come to wash the chalk outlines of the hopscotch games away, leaving the surface of the plaza blank.

And now this! Estrella couldn't stand watching these dumb girls, who shivered in the rain and stared after boys slipping past them to the shore. "You're getting all wet," Estrella called to the girls. "Come and sit with me on this dry bench."

"The rain makes us more beautiful," they cried out from the darkness. Which only showed! If straggly hair were glamorous, these girls were movie stars. Estrella watched the bravest girl in town hesitate for long moments at the edge of the plaza, then finally venture down the dark road toward the boys on the beach. One by one the other girls followed.

"Estrella means star," thought the only girl who remained in the plaza, looking down the now deserted road. "A bright point of light that stands alone in the dark, shining by itself, needing no one. Estrella," she thought, and the word sounded inside her like a promise.

She stared hopefully at the sky, waiting for a moment when the clouds would shift and all the stars would be revealed to her, shining in the darkness like lights of a beckoning city. When this did not occur, she squeezed her eyes as tightly shut as she could. Upon opening them a minute later, little dots of coloured light seemed to dance just before her, though clouds still concealed the faraway heavens. Then the coloured points of light vanished, like fireflies at the end of the rains.

Several hours later the girls straggled up the road. Wet sand was smeared on their dresses and hair. They looked more dead than alive. "See," triumphed Estrella, when the girls stumbled up to her. "Now try to tell me the wonders of kissing boys."

However, these fools would not admit to the terrible time they had suffered down at the beach. No, they stood there with swollen lips and glittering eyes, and they wouldn't say a word. "You've caught the chills and fevers," observed Estrella. "See what comes of kissing boys."

"Boys," repeated her girlfriends dreamily. "Their lips are so soft and their mouths are so warm. They taste like milk and honey."

Well, it was perfectly plain what had happened. These girls had caught germs from all their kissing, and every one of them was sick. "You're sick in the head," Estrella told them plainly.

"Just try it, Estrella," they answered, looking at her strangely, as though she were the stupid one who knew nothing. "Try it once and you'll see. And instead of Paris and pesos, you'll dream of kissing boys."

After that night there was no reasoning with those girls. They had been brainwashed. They could think and speak of only one thing. When Estrella tried to discuss with them sensible subjects like Florence Nightingale or Madame Curie, as in days before, the girls would always find a way to change the topic. "Florence Nightingale," they would say with envy. "She was the only woman among thousands of men, she could kiss a different man every hour and never run out of new lips. She healed the wounded soldiers by kissing them." That was the sorry state into which Estrella's friends had fallen.

The girls held endless discussions about boys and kissing them. "When my eyes are open, I can see his face so near to mine, but it's all blurry. I can't tell if I'm kissing Manuel or Miguel," a Maria would say. "But when I close my eyes I can see with my lips. I can see clearly what he looks like: his dark eyes, his strong legs and arms, his wide shoulders, and everything else, too." And all the girls around Maria would squeeze their eyes tightly shut, and they stood there just like that.

"You might as well be blind. God didn't give you eyes just to close them," Estrella said. "They are for seeing."

The girls laughed. "You don't know everything, though you think you're so smart."

"Well, I would maybe kiss boys," Estrella admitted once, "but for the fact that in this town there are no boys I like. They're all so stupid, their jokes are so bad, they don't even know how to talk."

The other girls just laughed harder. "A boy can be stupid and still be a good kisser. You know Vicente and how he is the dumbest boy in town? Well, he's also the best kisser. Who cares what a boy can say if he can kiss like Marlon Brando? Everything a boy needs to say he can tell you with his mouth and without words."

Crazy! You can't kiss boys twenty-four hours a day! There must be more to life than kissing boys! There must be! There had to be, and Estrella knew it. For old time's sake she stuck with her friends for a while, thinking that this kissing fad would pass like a fever, hoping that maybe she could talk some brains back into their heads.

Things only got worse. The girls made lists of all the boys their age in town. They placed the best kissers at the top of the lists and the worst ones at the bottom. Sometimes a girl would race up from the beach, her lips especially swollen and bruised. "Rene!" she would gasp. "He has learned some new kissing tricks. We must move his name higher up on the lists." To hear these girls, you would think kissing was the latest modern science. They experimented, took notes, wrote up data, compared the minutest details. Sometimes they would go off beneath the dripping trees to practise on each other. "It's easier to advance our skills when we kiss each other," claimed the girls. "You can't think clearly when you're kissing boys."

Of course you couldn't! At first it seemed to Estrella that the boys were pleased about this kissing craze. They did not seem able to believe their good luck. Their eyes became more goofy than usual, if that was possible, and they walked around licking their sore lips and smiling at some memory. Soon, however, they began to slip past the girls. "Give me a holiday from kissing," a boy would beg as he ran over the streaming streets pursued by a dozen determined girls. "Have pity on my tender lips and aching jaw."

The boys took to approaching Estrella where she sat alone in the plaza with her plans. They would sigh as they sank down beside her on the bench. "Just let me talk," a boy would plead. "Your friends won't let me speak. As soon as I open my mouth, they pull me toward them and start kissing again."

"Look, boy," Estrella would tell them. "If this is just a trick to recruit me as a new kisser, then forget it. It won't work. And those girls aren't my friends."

August arrived, and the rain fell with greater intensity. The streets turned into rushing rivers, and the school was closed because the walk to the classroom was too difficult for too many students to make. But girls still wandered the wet streets with thirsty, searching looks. They would stand still in the square and laugh as the rain washed them clean. They would turn their faces up to the sky, open their mouths wide, and drink the rain. The girls sometimes cried out in sudden pain as sharp arrows of rain pierced their hearts, and their blood ran red down the street, swirling like pictures in the puddles.

Estrella sat inside the dark room with her mother, who took greater and sadder pleasure in the torrential downfalls. "The world is flooding," said Estrella's mother. "We will have to climb aboard the ark, two by two, or we will be washed away. All of us, two by two," she repeated meaningfully.

Estrella became sarcastic. "I think it's just wonderful. It's surely a blessing when a mother urges her own daughter to partake in madness. You'd be positively delighted if I took leave of my entire mind."

"Listen to me for once. Try. If you aren't careful, you'll be left behind. Your girlfriends will grab up all the best boys and you'll be forced to take leftovers. I'm warning you because that very thing happened to me. I had to settle for your father. Oh, he's not bad, it could be worse, but why settle for second best?"

This kind of talk did not deserve an answer. Through the window Estrella saw girls walking steadily down the street, headed for the beach, their heads bowed beneath heavy sheets of falling rain; and though no pane covered the window, it seemed she watched them through a thick layer of clouded glass. After the girls passed by, the town appeared to be a place abandoned to the rain. Across the way, three cows stood chewing weeds in Ramirez's field; they did not take shelter beneath the old amapa tree there by the fence, but only gazed with wide eyes at the wet, empty landscape around them, like the last survivors of the world.

For days on end Estrella sat in that room and watched the world outside the window, until she was just about to lose her mind, rush crazy into the street, kiss the first boy she saw. At night she would lean out the window and look up at the sky, but God closed the curtains of heaven and she could see no stars.

She could feel her mother's worried eyes always on her. Sometimes her mother would sneak up behind Estrella and thrust a mirror before her face. "See how pretty you are. Don't be afraid. The boys will like you." Estrella's mother spoke quickly to the reflection in the glass. "It's not so bad. You get used to it. You have your babies and your home, and for those things you can bear a lot."

Estrella turned away. She could bear it only when she concentrated upon her plans. In two years she was going to climb on the bus and ride away to the capital city, and she was never coming back. She would live in a place where people thought about more than kissing boys. If she couldn't be a nurse like Florence Nightingale or a scientist like Madame Curie, then she'd be happy enough working in a clean, air-conditioned office. She would write a million words a minute on one of those typing machines. At night she would go home to where she lived in one of those tall apartment buildings she had read about. She would live high up in the stars. She could take off all her clothes, walk naked around the rooms, and no one would see her. She'd wash and iron the clothes she needed for the next day in the office, and she'd eat a meal. But not too much, she didn't want to get fat. She would have friends who could talk about anything in the world, who read newspapers and books, who weren't married and were happy to be alone.

But it seemed so far away. Though the capital city was only forty miles distant, it seemed much farther away than that. It lay just over the mountains, and every day of the week an old blue bus carried people to it in only one and a half hours. Estrella had been to the city, three times, and though she hadn't seen much, she had seen enough to know that it was there she wanted to live. But two more years! How many more days of rain remained?

When the rain let up to some degree and school began again, Estrella noticed that a number of girls no longer came to the classroom. Their seats were empty. If she asked other girls whether the missing ones were sick or just bored with school, they wouldn't answer her. If she approached her former friends, they stopped talking and just stood in silence, looking down at their feet until she was gone. Then they began to speak again. But these girls no longer screamed and shrieked as before, they no longer ran in circles of excitement around the boys' seats in the classroom. No, the girls sat still, with brooding expressions on their faces, and they always turned their eyes quickly away from the boys, as if in fear. Maybe they're no longer so fond of kissing, Estrella thought. Maybe they've changed.

Now the classroom was more quiet than it had ever been before, and every word the teacher spoke rang clearly between the four walls. But though she wanted to hear and tried to hear, Estrella could not comprehend the teacher's words. They slipped past her head before she could catch them. She could only wonder about the missing girls, and she puzzled still harder when one by one more of them stopped attending school.

The boys left the classroom also, to begin work on the hills or in the sea. One day the teacher looked around at all the empty desks and sadly told the few remaining students: "Congratulations. You have graduated. Now you are ready to begin your lives."

I want to learn more! Estrella cried inside. I haven't learned a single thing yet. I still don't know where Paris is.

"Well," said her mother in a sharp, pleased voice. "Thank goodness that foolishness if finished. You'll begin to learn now."

Estrella started to work in the tortilleria. She stood amid machines that rattled every thought from her head. Endless tortillas passed before her eyes every day: they were all round and they were all wrinkled and they all gave off the same hot, heavy smell. Estrella stacked, weighed, and sold tortillas to little girls who fought in line with their clothes stitched red and green. "I won!" the first girl to buy tortillas would cry.

Estrella would often see older girls she had once known walking past with slow steps, bundled up against the rain. These former friends did not turn their faces toward Estrella, and she did not call out to them. Only silently did she cry: remember Florence Nightingale, and Madame Curie, too! She saw boys walk by also, on their way to the hills or the sea, where hard work awaited them; and there was a puzzled look on their faces, as though something had happened which they could not understand.

"Yes," her mother said when Estrella returned home in the afternoons. "This is not so bad. Maybe some day a boy will see how much money you make in the tortilleria, perhaps the silver sight will tempt him into marrying you." Estrella's mother held out an open hand and quickly said, "Food is so expensive these days, there are thieves in the government."

Estrella dropped most of the pesos into her mother's palm, then put the remaining few into a box she kept beneath her bed. On a piece of paper she calculated how long it would take her to save enough money to move to the capital city, attend school there, and learn to write on a typing machine. Five years. She would be so old. She would be eighteen and fat, her body thickened and her hair dulled by too many tortillas.

Estrella took out her old school books and opened them. There were the stories about Florence Nightingale and Madame Curie. She looked at the words, but somewhere on the journey between the page and her mind they turned into round tortillas, each one the same and meaning nothing, filling her head with a bland mass and making it so heavy she could not hold it up.

Estrella went to bed and laid her head upon the pillow. September passed slowly, and the rain fell less forcefully and steadily with each succeeding night. Winds came out from the west, tearing leaves from the trees and tossing green globes of avocados upon the earth. Estrella lay awake and listened to the dripping trees outside her window, and it seemed the blood was slowly leaking from a hole in her heart. Often when she could not sleep and the darkness would not end she would leave her hot bed and steal outside.

The town lay dreaming in the rain, and Estrella roamed past the darkened houses. For brief moments the night would clear, and through a great dark distance, farther than any city, solitary points of light would shine. Then the heavens blurred, the stars vanished.

Just above the earth, just by Estrella's eyes, coloured bits of brightness glowed, like pieces of red and purple stars, like drops of green and yellow rain. After washing colours from the stars, the rain fell and fell all the way to earth, and fireflies were born. They flickered and floated in the dark the way they always did at the end of the rains. Kisses soft and wet and warm rained upon Estrella, and she was afraid.

The Spanish Princess

"And then," continued Rosario, "princes from the most powerful lands came to Spain to beg for the hand of the beautiful Spanish Princess. They were all handsome and they all brought presents. They knelt before me and kissed my pretty foot and pleaded for me to accept their gifts. 'Ho, hum,' I said. 'I already have a million silver slippers and a billion ruby rings, for my pirates bring me all the earthly treasure I desire. If you princes want me to smile one little smile in your favour, you must bring me something more.' I looked through the castle window and saw the Spanish moon floating in the Spanish sky. 'That's what I want!' I cried, pointing. 'The first prince to bring me the moon may kiss my lips and carry me in his golden carriage to his far-off land . . .' "

"Please shut up your baby mouth!" shouted Rosario's oldest sister, who was named Linda and who was mean.

"Yes," snapped Lupe, Rosario's other mean old sister. "Are you trying to drive us out of our minds with your silly Spain? Take this coin and go away. Buy candy. Stuff your mouth with sugar and be silent for a while."

Rosario took the coin, but she didn't go away. She stared hard at her two sisters, turning them into ladies-in-waiting who were frightened of their royal mistress. When the Spanish Princess became angry with people, she ordered them taken away by the castle guards. Sometimes she had heads chopped off. The executioner would hold up the severed heads of the ladies-in-waiting by their hair and the crowds would cheer. The beautiful dresses of the ladies-in-waiting would become ugly with blood.

In white slips Linda and Lupe sat side by side before the big mirror. Fresh from baths, their brown skin glowed like dark blossoms in the night, and the scent of magnolia rose from it like heavy steam. Their faces were smooth, their bodies curved, and their hair was thick and full of curls. Linda and Lupe leaned with love into their reflections, and sitting behind them on her bed Rosario could see both their backs and faces. She closed her eyes against this double vision.

Those two girls stuck together like glue, and you would think the constant sight of their twin selves would be enough to turn their stomachs, but no. They clung for hours to the big mirror in the bedroom. On the corners of the streets they would take little mirrors from their purses and stand entranced before the glass. They stared at themselves as though at all the world. At night, when after forever they finally finished dressing, Linda and Lupe went out to gaze greedily into the round mirrors of boys' eyes. Too stupid to know they were only windows through which Linda and Lupe could see themselves, all the boys trembled with love.

Rosario tucked her knees against her heart, then wrapped her arms around them. She was secret and tight. In her hand she felt her sister's coin. It was silver and perfectly round, like the moon when it was big. Rosario held the moon tightly so it would not slip from her grasp and float up like a red circus balloon that vanishes into wide blue sky.

"And then," Rosario said, more loudly than before. "After three years a Swedish Prince with golden curls and blue eyes came to the Spanish Princess, who was sitting on her throne, and he said: 'Beautiful Spanish Princess, I have flown up into the sky in a big red balloon and I have brought the moon back for you.' The Swedish Prince opened a blue velvet box, and inside there was a silver crescent. 'Sweet Swedish Prince,' I said. 'I'm afraid this is not quite good enough. It is not a quarter of a moon I desire, but a full, round one that I can throw like a ball to my friend Marie Antoinette. Then I catch the ball when she throws it back to me. That's our favourite game. Go away and bring me all the moon, and then . . .'"

"Mama!" screamed Linda and Lupe with one voice. "Rosario is driving us bananas again, and meanwhile the boys are becoming restless."

Señora Gonzalez ran into the room with the little steps of a baby who is just learning to walk. "Where did I get such beautiful daughters?" she cried, the very question she posed a hundred times every day. She threw her arms lavishly around Linda and Lupe. "If I hadn't seen you come out from me with my own eyes, I would believe you angels."

Linda and Lupe scowled, shoving their mother away. "You're messing us," complained Lupe. "Just take that baby brat away somewhere. Give her to the gypsies, give her to the sea. Just get rid of her this exact instant or we'll both lose our heads. We'll say yes instead of no when the boys whisper in our ears."

Señora Gonzalez saddened, then turned to Rosario. "My last child!" she quivered. "You are so much younger than your sisters because I was so madly in love with them I desired no more gifts from God. It wasn't until years after their birth that Señora Carranza, who knows such things, said God had allotted three girls to me. At once I heard you inside me, screaming to be let out. Then you started kicking and pushing and shoving your way into the world."

Señora Gonzalez dashed drops from her eyes. "My Linda and Lupe are two delicate flowers, and my heart is forever frightened that they will fall and bruise their petals. But you, my strong, sturdy señorita, you will kick and push and shove your way through the world, and I need never worry that you will come to harm."

"You're as bad as that baby brat," said Linda in the hard, even tone that meant she was immediately about to lose her temper for three days and three nights, during which time the household would know no peace. "Look! My hand slipped because of your prattle, and now my lipstick is smudged."

"Forgive me, my sweet angels!" emoted Señora Gonzalez. Unable to restrain herself, she patted the curls of Linda and Lupe.

Rosario bounded from the bed. "Mama, it's time for tea," she said, leading her mother from the room. "You always feel happy when you have your tea, don't you?" Rosario felt her mother's hand holding tightly onto hers. In the kitchen Rosario washed green leaves, then put them in a pot of water. She held a match to the gas ring, and a blue circle leaped at her hand. The water heated, then boiled, and the scent of cinnamon spread through the house.

Rosario sat on the little stool she had sat on since always. Her head rested in her mother's lap. She felt a hand stroke her hair, smoothing away a problem. "You know," said Señora Gonzalez in a shy voice. "It's wrong of me, but sometimes I think Linda and Lupe don't like me. They look at me as though I were a stranger. And it is strange — they don't in the tiniest way resemble me or that sad fool who was father of you three."

Señora Gonzalez fell silent; words always deserted her after she spoke of the man who had gone away. Her hands brushed Rosario's head more slowly. Rosario felt herself grow sleepy. Her mother was sending her to Spain.

Sharp, hard taps of heels on concrete roused Rosario. Flounced dresses rustled and magnolia stirred through cinnamon. The front door banged shut behind Linda and Lupe, and it would not open again until very late. Far into the night the two older girls would return to the house, yawning and murmuring as they pulled off their dresses, unaware that Rosario was not in her bed. No one heard Rosario steal from the house because she did not creak open the door. There was a window in the bedroom, and it led to the world.

"We're exactly the same," said Señora Gonzalez, pushing away the silence with her voice. "I look at you and see myself at eight. I need no photographs turning yellow in an album. And you, you need not waste pesos at the fortune teller's booth when the circus comes to town. Look at me. Your future breathes before you."

Rosario closed her eyes and saw her mother standing before the stove, peering puzzled into pots, a big spoon in one hand. Señora Gonzalez was short and squat, and in the afternoons she pushed the pedal of the old sewing machine with a hopeful and excited foot. She made suits of skirts and blouses, carefully copying big coloured pictures of American fashion magazines. When she tried on the suits her shining eyes died. I don't understand why this doesn't fit, she would wonder, pulling at the cloth this way and that, tugging with trembling fingers at the suit she had made for someone taller and thinner than herself. She drooped with disappointment inside the ill-fitting skirts and jackets. They quickly wrinkled, there was always a button missing, a stain, a tear, a loose thread. Rosario's mother had blue rivers running down her lumpy legs, and dried-up creeks criss-crossed her face. The streams in her hair shone silver.

Rosario sat very still. Her mother's hands came to rest on Rosario's head, and her breathing grew even, in and out. Rosario slipped from her stool and entered the room she shared with her sisters.

One side of it was dwarfed by a messy double bed, which was surrounded by a carpet of cast off clothes. There were dresses not chosen for that night, dresses soiled from nights gone by, dresses of girls who had fallen fainting with love, bruised petals which would soon turn brown and dry, then fly away with the wind.

The other side of the room was neat as a nun's cell. The narrow bed was made up smooth and flat. Things were in their place. Faces of movie stars and world leaders looked through the wall, and sometimes they spoke to Rosario. They asked her advice on important matters. Above the faces spread a map of the world, painted by God with a big brush, and each country was a different colour. America was green, China was yellow, England was pink, France was orange, and Spain was golden.

Rosario sat on one of the two empty chairs before the dressing table. It was littered with: bottles of perfume and jars of cream; tubes of lipstick and boxes of powder; strings of beads and brooches and bracelets and rings. Rosario looked into the mirror. She gazed very far, over the mighty mountains, beyond the seven seas, all the way across the world and back to where she sat next to a chair that was empty of someone who belonged by her side.

Her hands moved of themselves, opening jars and bottles. In the air they repeated patterns Linda and Lupe had made through a thousand and one nights. The world spread over Rosario's dull, dark skin. Green America, yellow China, pink England, and golden, golden Spain.

The world was not quite right. It was flat where it should have been curved, pointed where it should have been smooth. It was a place where catastrophes occurred: two dark lakes flooded their banks and streamed over the earth, sweeping away houses and trees and girls who cried as they drowned.

Rosario blurred the world until it was one nothing colour on the tissue. Then she turned off the light and climbed into bed.

She slept alone there. Neither Linda nor Lupe would sleep with Rosario. They said she kicked. They didn't know she was moving her legs to travel to the places she went at night. Sometimes she found herself so far away.

She played with Marie Antoinette in the Palace of Versailles, which was so enormous a game of hide-and-seek could go on forever there. But she and Marie Antoinette always found each other, and then they danced out into the palace gardens. Beside a fountain that always flowed they played with a silver kitten who spoke French. The two royal girls twirled in the moonlight until the Spanish Princess saw the sky begin to turn red as Spanish soil. Her mother the Queen would cry for fifty years if she found her daughter's bed empty at morning, and the Spanish Princess knew she had to leave. "Goodbye! Au revoir!" she called. "I will come to play with you again, Marie Antoinette!" And the Spanish Princess ran quickly across the world to her bed in the castle tower.

Rosario opened her eyes, and there was the ceiling with the cracks in it. There was the wrinkled old house and the funny mother who cried: wake up, sleepy head, you'll be late for school again, my dreamy doll. Hello, hello, goodbye, sang birds outside the window, diving off to swim in the blue sky. Rosario felt tired from playing games with Marie Antoinette and from galloping across the globe. "But a princess cannot lie in bed all day," she told herself. "She has her royal duties."

In the kitchen her mother poured beans into the frying pan. The hot fat jumped, frightening Señora Gonzalez. "Mama," asked Rosario. "Do you remember where you go at night?"

"Well," said Señora Gonzalez, squishing the beans with a spoon. "I do have this one dream. I am with a big bunch of people, celebrating something in a sophisticated restaurant.

The place is so elegant I can hardly believe my eyes. One delicious dish after another is brought to the table by a handsome waiter dressed in immaculate white. Everyone eats with great enjoyment. The dishes become fancier and fancier until I hardly know what I'm putting in my mouth. Then the food begins to taste very funny, as though made from the most unappealing and even disgusting ingredients. I see that everyone else is still eating with appetite, and I'm afraid to say anything because the restaurant is so rich. Then I wake up, and so it is with joy I fry beans in my kitchen, just as I am doing now.''

The sun spilled through the window. It leaked into Rosario's eyes as she walked slowly to school, making her squint and making the world look strange. The schoolyard was full of gangs of rough, playing children, whom Rosario sometimes tried to imitate. She would run in little circles that took her nowhere, like they did; she would shout and cry meaningless sounds, like they did. But inevitably she tripped and fell, or ran into a wall. On a very few occasions she would stand with the other girls in a ring and play the catching game. However, when the ball was thrown to her, Rosario held her hands in the wrong place. She held them hopefully up to the sun, and the ball fell to the ground or hit her in the face.

On this morning Rosario sat quietly at some distance from the children with her empty hands clasped together. She remembered: how cool and dim were the castle rooms; how bravely the knights jousted on the shining streets, fighting for her favours; how gracefully she danced the first dance at every ball; how still she sat in the tower window, piercing cloth with needle, painting Spain with coloured thread. In the distance, very far away, the Spanish Princess heard the happy voices of playing children.

A bell rang. The children pushed and shoved into the classroom. They sang songs and threw things and chased each other around and around, knocking over desks and chairs. Boys bullied and girls cried, and the teacher clapped his hands helplessly and said, ''Children, children.''

The Spanish Princess was busy working at her desk. The life of a princess was not all fun and games, and every morning she spent several hours writing laws and proclamations to guide her people. They needed her to look after them. All my subjects will spend every Thursday telling jokes, she wrote. Pink ink flowed from her pen, which was made from a grey feather. When the Spanish Princess grew weary of writing she would pause to brush the feather against her skin. It tickled the tiredness away.

Rosario heard the teacher's voice: "Yes, the cruel Spaniards came to our country to steal our gold and silver. They made the people of our land work as slaves in the mines, and even the littlest children had to swing the heavy shovels. If they didn't work hard enough, they were whipped. Many of our people died. The savage Spaniards robbed the riches from our earth, then left it dusty and poor and empty . . ."

"Precious jewel," her mother said when Rosario appeared in the doorway before the day of school was done. "Your sisters have the beauty and you have the brains. You must stay in the classroom until you have learned everything. Then you'll be able to explain to me all the things in this world which I do not understand."

"The teacher tells lies." Rosario threw her books into the pail of scraps. "Just feed his fibs to the pigs, that's all." The Spanish Princess would never allow such terrible things to be done in her name. She would never accept stolen diamonds stained ruby red by the blood of murdered children. Her pirates were good and kind, and the treasure they gave her they found floating lost upon the sea.

At that moment Linda and Lupe entered the kitchen. They were cross-eyed and crabby like every day, and they wouldn't say a word. "My Sleeping Beauties!" gushed Señora Gonzalez, rushing to offer them the delicacies she had spent the morning making. The two older girls picked fussily at their food, then returned to the bedroom to begin preparations for the night ahead.

Through the afternoon Rosario helped her mother with the housework. She moved quickly and she did not stop to rest, for there was a fear inside her that was trying to catch her. She shone her sisters' shoes, washed their fancy dresses, and tidied the messy side of the bedroom. Señora Gonzalez glowed at her youngest daughter's sudden interest in household affairs. "You will make a fine home for some man, and maybe you will be lucky like me and have two beautiful daughters," she said.

As darkness fell the sweat on Rosario's skin turned cool, and prickly as needles. She slapped her face clean with cold water, then on her bed she sat watching her sisters toil to fix themselves for the boys. Several times Linda and Lupe turned from the mirror to ask Rosario why she wasn't telling her lies about her stupid Spain. But Rosario did not answer. She studied the ways her sisters painted their faces until they looked like other girls and not themselves. They painted the two girls who lived inside the mirror, too.

The front door banged shut. The scent of cinnamon stole through the house. In the kitchen Rosario's mother made sounds of invitation with dishes and her throat. Rosario listened for the movie stars and world leaders to speak to her from the wall. She waited for the coloured-paper world to fall and cover her like the beautiful brilliant robes of a Spanish Princess. She heard her heart knocking like a fist on a door: let me in, let me out.

"Sometimes," Rosario said when no other voice would speak to her. "The Spanish Princess grew weary of her castle. She became restless sitting still upon her throne, and the bejewelled crown felt heavy on her head. Sometimes she heard her people laughing and singing, and she stood in the tower window and gazed down upon them. Far below they danced in circles around fires that burned orange on the black paper plain. Dark shapes moved in the dark Spanish night. Beyond the plain the Mediterranean breathed, and the Spanish Princess longed to know that water was wet and sea was salt."

Rosario heard the sounds of the town crowding in the streets. Radios blared hot music, passionate voices smouldered in the movie house, smoky noise drifted up into the sky, then vanished. Children screamed and cried, and one sudden voice callled.

"And then," Rosario said "one night the Spanish Princess climbed down the ladder of a sycamore tree that grew beside her tower window. She landed lightly on the Spanish soil.

It felt unfamiliar to her feet. Disguised in the dress of a lady-in-waiting, she walked through the streets of the town that crouched around the castle.''

Everything looked very different than it had from the tower window. In wonder the Spanish Princess walked past spitting taco stands and children playing baseball before the church and old men leaning on sticks at the corner. The Spanish Princess followed the road to where it led. None of her people recognized her in disguise, for they had only seen her far above them in her window.

Although the people had no riches, they seemed happy. They had not the cares of a kingdom and thus could play all night long. ''I must rule my people well if they are so contented,'' the Spanish Princess thought proudly, walking through the gay and thronging streets. Yet at the next moment she felt sad that no one sat on a throne to look after her while she played. ''If I were not a princess, I could walk down this street every evening. I could sit on a bench in this plaza,'' she thought, entering the town's square. She saw boys and girls floating like flowers there, whispering and rustling sounds she could not understand. The Spanish Princess passed down the dusty road that led to the sea, and barking dogs announced her coming. ''My Mediterranean,'' she whispered to the big round moon above.

Waves broke upon the beach in silver pieces. A breeze breathed the dark, rich secrets it had stolen from Africa across the water. Some distance from shore lights of Spanish galleons swam like stars. On board the rum ran in rivers and the Spanish pirates revelled roughly, golden rings in their ears and bright bandanas around their heads. For one moment the Spanish Princess yearned for her pirates to sail her away from the heavy load of her land.

The moon touched the sand with a silver smile, and on this shining street the Spanish Princess walked, taking care not to trip over rocks that huddled dark and moody at her feet. On the side away from the sea bushes grew. Rounding a point, the Spanish Princess heard giggles and whispers coming from the shadowed shrubs. She smiled to herself and thought, ''Of course, my people enjoy sitting beside the sea on fine, fresh nights like this. They are fond of simple pleasures." Suddenly the Spanish Princess felt a desire to speak with her subjects. She thought that it might be interesting to know what they had to say about various matters, and that with this knowledge she might guide them more wisely. She approached the voices.

In a hollow carved from the dark bushes two white pieces of cloth hung like sails from branches. Two dark shapes twisted beside two dark shapes. The Spanish Princess stood unseen and watching. Then she started, and turned her face up to the mirror of the sky. She gazed deeply into the glass, but no reflection appeared upon it.

"I think it is time to return to my castle," the Spanish Princess thought carefully. "It must be quite late, and princesses especially require much sleep. They become so tired from carrying the burden of their land that sometimes they feel like sleeping and sleeping and sleeping."

The house was empty, and the looking glass, too. Rosario could hear her mother, calling her name at the far edge of town. Her mother cried in fear, like a child suffering a bad dream from which she cannot wake. Rosario! Rosario! Where can you be?

"Where can you be?" Rosario asked the Spanish Princess. "Where is the window from which you gaze?"

The Spanish Princess murmured from far away: "My people, you will not see your Princess for some time, because she has fallen ill. She cannot wave to you from her window each day at dawn as she used to. But do not be sad, my subjects, for I love you all as much as ever, and soon I will be better."

The voice faded, the glass filled. Rosario picked up one of Lupe's high shoes, and with the heel she hit the mirror. She beat the girl with the flat, broad face who stared so stupidly at her. She smashed the girl until she cracked and broke and fell in slivers upon the floor.

Rosario floated, and days drifted by with seaweed and driftwood and bobbing bottles containing dreams of girls on land. She swam in a magnolia sea, her hair streaming around her, her dress sailing like a shroud. She was taken by the tides;

they pulled her far from shore, then back to land again, in and out. In the black sky above a mother moon gleamed darkly and cried sweet tears that slaked the thirst of a drifting daughter.

Her heart was a stone that pulled her down and deeper down, and she sank forever. She fought to the surface, gasping for breath, to hear the clink of a perfume bottle, a brush pulling through hair, a hand patting powder on skin. Cinnamon smelled. A mother pushed the pedal of a sewing machine and sang a little song. I am a child with no name, the mother sang. Where is my father?

Where is my Father the King, and why did He leave me here alone to rule this wide, dark land of gypsies and pirates and roses that fall at night? Where is the Prince who can wake the Sleeping Princess with a kiss and carry her away?

"She's awake, she's come back." The girl found herself floating on the bed. Her head lay on the pillow, her mother's hand lay on her head. The girl tried to remember, to cast her mind over the big black sea to the places she had been. But she could not recall the Palace of Versailles, and the face of Marie Antoinette was faded like the world upon the wall. Its colours had dimmed.

And when the Spanish Princess finally rose from her bed in the castle tower she found her kingdom pale and poor, robbed of its riches in her absence. She looked from the window upon a world that was strange to her eyes. "I am the beautiful Spanish Princess," she reminded herself. "This is my kingdom and those are my people I see below, and it all belongs to me."

And then the Spanish Princess remembered the time she had walked through her world for one evening, and what she had seen then. She knew she belonged in her castle, on her throne, but she had a desire she could not silence to go out into the world once again. She wanted not only to walk through and to watch the world, but to live in it.

So one night she climbed again down the ladder of the sycamore tree that joined her window to the world. Once more she leaped lightly upon the ground. This time she was dressed in the disguise of a poor peasant girl, and no one recognized her as their Princess.

She ran laughing through the village where the poor people were making merry after a long, hard day of work. They forgot they were tired as they danced and sank in the barn, and the Spanish Princess forgot she was a princess as she twirled around and around like a world. The sawdust was soft on her bare feet, the hay smelled sweet, and the wine was warm.

The fiddler played away the night, and when the stars began to fade in the Spanish sky the Princess knew it was time to steal back up the sycamore tree and into her bed in the tower. But God was angry that she had played like a peasant girl when she was a princess born, and during the night the sycamore tree had shrivelled into a thorny bush. The Spanish Princess could not climb to her room high above, and, seeing her bare feet and poor clothes, the castle guards would not let her through the gate. They did not believe she was a princess.

For the rest of her days she wandered across the world crying: I am the Spanish Princess! I am the Spanish Princess! Her clothes became more ragged and her face became a mask of grime. Her feet grew tough and scarred by the sticks and stones she trampled upon. Over a world that had lost its colours she searched for someone who would recognize her as being the Princess she was. "Perhaps one day," she thought, "a Prince who was once in love with me will swoop down upon his silver steed. His love will show him the Princess beneath this dirty skin, and he will carry me away. He will take me to the moon."

Beneath a moon poised high in the sky she stumbled. She was always drawn back to her Spanish Kingdom, and throughout that land she became known far and wide. Villagers gave her rags to wear when her old ones tattered into only air, and they fed her scraps meant for the pigs. Some poor people gave because they felt that any girl might a Princess be; perhaps when restored to her rightful throne this Princess might remember who had helped her in her hell, and she would reward them largely. Others helped the girl because they believed she was of God, and her search for a castle was a pilgrimage. She is looking for the King who sits on His throne above, they thought, and when she finds Him she will speak in our favour. Some people aided the girl for no clear reasons: anything is possible in Spain, they shrugged.

Sometimes old women would think the poor girl a missing daughter, and they would take her into their homes and long for her to stay with them forever. They wove cloth from cinnamon to dress her. "It is another lost daughter for whom they search," the poor girl would think when she left the old women to wander more.

Always she was pulled toward the castle that once had been her home. She crossed the wide, flat plain toward it. The castle could be seen from very far away, and its towers pierced the blue cloth sky like needles. The poor girl's heart beat very fast as the castle loomed larger and taller and nearer before her. When at last she touched the cold grey stone walls of her true and former home, it towered over her, blocking out the Spanish sky, casting a shadow into which the girl fell fainting. She slept beside the castle wall, and when she woke it was to gaze with longing at a tangled, thorny bush that grew close by. Each day its thorns grew sharper.

Sometimes she walked the streets of the village that spread itself around the castle. She saw the poor people playing when the fair came to town. Red balloons sailed into the wide blue sky and vanished there. In fine gowns her former ladies-in-waiting swept by the poor girl, and she saw that their faces had grown sharper and their eyes more cruel. The poor girl wandered to the sea and swept its breadth, looking for a pirate ship to come for her on shore. She prayed to be taken away and made a Pirate Queen.

At night the tower window was a square of yellow light. It was empty, and no Spanish Princess leaned from it to look down upon her land. The poor girl closed her eyes and saw: crimson curtains, jewelled tapestries, and candle flames rising from silver sticks. Incense from the East breathed around the rooms. For a moment the poor girl could not smell the scent of magnolia that clung to her always like a shadow that would not let her free.

I will rise like the moon and spill in light through the window high above, the poor girl thought. Red balloons vanish into blue sky on circus days, and trumpets ring round, silver notes that float through the air like coins of pirate treasure. Who stole the riches from my land and left it empty?

A girl appeared in the castle window. She leaned from it and gazed down upon her land. The crown that caught the moonlight in its diamonds did not tumble from her head. Her hair was dark and long, and it fell from the window to dangle in empty air. The Spanish Princess looked with longing at her people playing far away, still playing though the circus had left town. She had not the ladder of a sycamore tree by which to climb down to her world, and the tears of the Spanish Princess fell upon the tangled, thorny bush below. Flowers as big and round as coloured moons bloomed there. The poor girl plucked them before their petals could fall and bruise. She threw the round, full moons high into the air, and the Spanish Princess leaned farther from her window to catch them.

All moons melted in the hot, close night, and the Spanish sky was dark and empty of light. It was smooth as glass. The girl gazed into the mirror.

The Scent of Young Girls Dying

After Chonita's husband died, the old woman devoted her days to tending the flowers which grew in such profusion around her white house. As she and Hector had lived in California for a number of years, returning to their home only just before the latter's painful death, the flower garden was gone quite wild. "The poor woman is trying to keep busy and forget her grief," said the ladies of the town. Soon the scent of Chonita's roses became remarkably more pronounced and drifted entirely through the town, being strongest in the hours just after and before dusk. "How pretty," said the town women, standing in their doorways with folded arms.

After the burial of Hector, Chonita was not heard to mention his name again. She showed no signs of sorrow and shrugged off any sympathy offered her. For a time she was not observed visiting the place where her late husband lay.

This was not unusual. The graveyard was neglected. It lay on the edge of town behind a sagging barbed-wire fence and beside a road on which many people walked every day. However, except on infrequent occasions of burials, the townspeople seemed to forget about the graveyard. It was a lonely place and the plastic flowers faded in the sun. Grass grew thickly around the graves, obscuring them, and cement crosses cracked, then tumbled onto the ground. Occasionally one or two of the more civic-minded citizens, seeing it was becoming an eyesore, took an afternoon to slash at the brush. Their machetes glinted in the sun. Sometimes at night the townspeople were woken by wild dogs that came down from the hills to fight over graves.

Chonita seemed as unwilling to visit her fellow townspeople and former friends as she was the graveyard. Her years of absence in California had made her a stranger to her place of birth; it was decided she had acquired airs as well as money. The town ladies took offence and felt slighted by her seclusion.

Chonita's house was surrounded by a tall red iron fence, and no one was invited inside the yard. When the gate was briefly opened, people passing caught sight of masses of roses and witches' broom and japonestas. All day long they heard water splashing against leaves, running through flower beds, flowing into the earth. "Wasteful," commented the women of the town, who viewed ornamental gardening as an odd and somewhat unwholesome practice. "Chonita is trying to change God's seasons, she pretends she has the fountain of youth in her own back yard," the ladies said. Very quickly their nerves became strained by the sound of water bubbling like a hidden spring behind the fence, by the scent of roses wafting unavoidably into their houses.

One day the ladies realized with strange suddenness that the old woman had been visiting the graveyard daily for a number of weeks. Although the visits were made with complete frankness, the town ladies felt any action that had escaped their notice even momentarily was suspect; they took pride in their keen powers of observation, and were irritated by any failure of them.

Every morning the iron gate banged shut and Chonita walked through the streets. "Maria! Isabela! Veronica!" she called, and the twelve happiest and most beautiful little girls in town abandoned their mothers' mirrors and their jumping ropes and jacks to run to the old woman. Singing and laughing and clinging, the little girls frolicked around Chonita, forming a merry procession that passed to the graveyard. There the little girls skipped among headstones and crosses, and chased each other around and around. They looked like floating flowers, coming to light upon the long grass, then sinking into it in a circle around the old woman.

"Look around you," Chonita exclaimed. "Your grandmothers and aunts and sisters lie suffocating in the ground. I knew these women and girls; they died silently, though in great pain. Now they cry. Listen!'' and the grass sighed and sobbed in the wind. "They want us to dig them out, pull the dirt off them, and allow them to breathe the open air again. They want to sit up and stretch themselves, they long to comb out their matted hair.''

The little girls sat quietly, their faces made grave by the mournful sound of Chonita's voice. After a while they began to fidget. Then they scampered off to play again. The little girls hid behind gravestones, then jumped out at their friends, shouting "boo," causing the air to ring with screams of joy and fear. The old woman took a green glass bottle from her purse and held it to her mouth. She spoke soothingly to the women lying beneath her. These sad and buried women called out to the little girls who danced above them. "Play!" they cried. "Laugh and play! But remember us who listen beneath you.''

Most mornings the town ladies gathered before Doña Lupita's store. They sewed and sat in little chairs on the sidewalk. Now and then the mothers of the girls who accompanied Chonita to the graveyard lifted their heads at the sounds of laughter floating down into the town. Initially these mothers were quite pleased their girls had been chosen by Chonita as her companions; they vaguely believed that somehow a part of the old woman's wealth would rub off on their babies. These hopes rapidly soured. The ladies took exception to the fact that while Chonita would hardly speak a civil word to them, she felt free to waltz off with their daughters whenever she pleased. Because they were somewhat in awe of the rich, proud woman, the town ladies were reluctant to confront her directly. They preferred to share their complaints among themselves.

"She should mind her flowers and leave our girls alone," stated a certain Señora Juarez.

"She'll kidnap our babies to the graveyard, yes, but would she deign to bring a single of her million rosebuds to the Queen of Spain's grave?" questioned Señora Fernandez.

"Oh, that strange, sweet smell," moaned Señora Aquino. "It makes my head hurt so.''

"Her precious, freakish flowers," snorted Señora Ortiz. "She grows them just to torment us with their stench, I swear."

"It's unhealthy," Señora Martinez cried with emotion. "Our daughters will fall into old graves and break their necks. Our beautiful little girls will grow to be sick and sad, and they will wander pale and weeping in the moonlight. They will languish in their beds, and the scent of young girls dying will hang over our town like a dream."

Chonita sat beside a fallen angel and grieved, "Oh, what's become of you?" The angel had crashed down from heaven and lay face pressed into the earth. The old lady dug it out from the dying leaves and crumbled off caked dirt. She polished the white figure with her skirt, them kissed its smooth, blank eyes. The fat, smiling angel rested in her hand, arms floating in frozen flight.

Ravens swayed in the wild, old amapa tree with its arms that drooped down to the ground, its fingertips that brushed the waving grass. In the round house of the tree's shade Chonita sat stiffly, her legs stretched out straight before her, running shoes on her feet, a faded orange peasant dress crumpled about her knees.

Waves of emotion carved the old woman's face. She looked now at the angel, now at the golden-crowns nodding yellow heads nearby. "Oh, how could such a thing have happened?" she cried out suddenly, seeing broken Virgins in distress all around her. Mutilated, crippled, missing an arm, half a leg, their lower portions, they lay stretched helpless in the long grass.

Chonita trembled, listening to the breathing earth. "My daughters," she called, and a dozen heads bobbed over the tall grass toward her. Some were adorned with plastic wreaths.

"Her husband's death unhinged her," said the town ladies. "She drove him into the ground, but still she's not happy. No, she must sit beside his grave, ranting and raving. No peaceful sleep for that poor man."

"But my little Maria says she doesn't even look at Hector's grave," commented Señora Alamena.

"No, she's too busy keeping an eye on the dead and buried women. She's afraid their ghosts will flirt with Hector."

"California changed her," remarked Señora Ortiz. "Since she's returned she thinks she's Susan Hayward, smoking and drinking and wearing slacks."

"Of course, Susan was a redhead," added Señora Lopez, and all the other ladies nodded heads in interest.

Señora Martinez couldn't stand it. "Susan's dead!" she screamed. "Cancer took her. But our little girls are alive! Listen," she hissed. "I hear my Fransesca whispering to her older and younger sisters, spreading the old woman's tales of tainted love. How will our babies find boys, homes, children?

"Chonita is placing a curse upon our girls. She is jealous that God never gave her a daughter of her own. Our young girls toss and turn in their sleep, tormented by dreams of tragic love. They call out to be saved. Their hearts are withering before they've ever bloomed."

"Look, I've fallen!" laughed Chonita, lying helpless in the grass. The little girls flocked around her, heaving and pulling, their faces straining and ribbons falling from their hair. Chonita laughed breathlessly, and with the girls skipping around her passed through weeds and grass and graves.

The old woman halted and tears flowed from her eyes. "Violetta Valquez. As white as a ghost and as pretty as a picture. Her long black hair was as heavy as the cross of Jesus. She died at seventeen. A fishing boy disappeared at sea, and she paced the shore for a hundred nights, her hair blowing in the wind, her nightdress soaked by the spray of crashing waves. Then blood spilled from her broken heart, pouring out her throat like red wine upon the white pillow."

The little girls looked at one another in puzzlement, their eyes clouding with questions. When they started to cry they were frightened, because they did not know why they felt so sad. They screamed and wailed. "That's all right," said

Chonita, bending over and patting first the graves, then the backs of the sobbing girls.

"Petra Delgado," she lamented, pointing to the ground, though no gravestone stood there. Wild flowers trailed across a slight hollow. "She married a white-toothed charmer, and that killed her, though it took her twenty years to find death. I would hear her screaming for death to come, but he wouldn't. He was as cold-hearted as the rest of them. They hear you crying for them night after night as they steal down the dark back streets. But they will not come for you."

Chonita stood lost in thought, while around her the little girls screamed with high, piercing voices. Their eyes were closed and their faces tilted up to the sky. All at once they fell silent, then turned away as one. They ran through the long grass. Flashing red and yellow in the sun, they played hide and seek, and tag.

The little graveyard girls would not play with the other girls of the town. They walked in a cluster down the street. Huddled together, they threw glances at the men and boys around them. "Señor Marquez," the girls whispered loudly, pointing to an old man asleep on a bench. "He killed his wife. He drank and filled himself with poison. When his wife kissed him, all the poison flowed into her. She died for him, while he walks around healthy and strong and looking at other women."

Their mothers heard these words and were filled with passions. Old scandals and secrets long buried were unearthed by this talk, and scenes occurred. "You Devil!" screamed the woman. "We were like sisters until you came along. Murderer!"

The next day, their passions abated, the woman ran inside their houses at the sight of the accused man. "Look at this mess you've got me in!" they scolded daughters. "I must now hide from my own neighbours. What is next?" they asked their little girls, who gazed raptly into mirrors.

It was a relief when the twelve girls grew old enough to

attend school. Their mothers listened with satisfaction as chanted answers to unheard questions rang through the town. The girls would learn to read and write. They would learn that l-o-v-e spells baby and one plus one makes three.

The twelve little girls quickly worked charms upon their teacher, a tall young man both romantic and single. They brought him armfuls of flowers from Chonita's garden every morning. They sat closely around him, combing his hair, filing his nails, brushing his cheek with their warm breath. The perfume of the flowers and girls stole around the teacher. In a daze he watched them dance out the doorway of the school before classes had hardly begun, laughing shrilly as they ran hand in hand to the graveyard.

They always found the old woman there, although more and more she left her sorrowful strolls and sat still beneath the amapa tree. "Clean off Señora Alonza, she is getting so dusty," Chonita implored. "And see how that big thistle is feeding off that slip of a girl over there? Oh, I'm becoming too old to care for the dead."

On the other side of the graveyard the girls wandered among cracked stones and crooked crosses, not seeing the words inscribed to speed young girls to heaven. Their skirts brushing the grass and grasshoppers flying up in clouds around them, they discussed romance and love. Sometimes their words carried to the old woman, snatches of song mixing in with her dreams. If he is tall and handsome, she heard. When he kisses you. His lips are soft. And his mouth tastes of honey, the young girls said, blades of grass twirling in their mouths and hands. Love hurts, they said, pacing, faces turned down to the ground, in prayer.

Isabela lifted her head quickly, like a deer, and saw the sea lying in the distance. They go out in boats. And they don't come back. Though you wait for them, she said in a clear, calm voice, brushing her hair from her face.

With crushing feet the girls tramped trails. They made tunnels in the long grass, secret passages that closed behind them. Woken by their words, Chonita looked across the graveyard for the girls. Only tilted crosses rose from the sea of grass, and the graveyard appeared deserted.

At a meeting of the town junta one Sunday it was decided something must be done. "We are concerned," stated a group of women, and an eloquent speech was made on the topic of the sacred dead. The junta agreed that the girls must be kept from the graveyard, although it was not clear how this could be achieved: the town was famous for its headstrong girls and women. "Signs," proposed Señor Lopez. "Playing In The Graveyard Is Prohibited. That should do the trick." Chonita's name was called out by someone at the back of the crowded Casino. "Which one of us will ask her to stay out of the graveyard?" another voice demanded. At this question the junta fell silent. "Mourning the dead is not a sin," muttered a third voice, before the junta quickly moved on to a new and unrelated topic.

At around this time the girls began going to the graveyard less frequently, although it was widely known that Señor Lopez's signs were not the reason. "Oh, yes, we tore down those stupid signs," laughed the young girls carelessly. They mostly came alone now, Veronica or Isabela or one of the others, walking quickly up to the amapa tree beneath which the old woman sat amid the falling poppies of February.

Upon hearing her name spoken, Chonita turned her head slowly and squinted up at the girl. "You have grown taller and more beautiful," she said musingly. "Yesterday you only wanted to run all the time. Breathlessly you ran with the other girls around and around the plaza. Now all at once you feel tired, too weary to lift your feet. You want to lie in bed all day and cry, though you feel no sadness. You sit in the doorway all night long, fanning yourself with a magazine and waiting to be caught."

The young girl looked quickly and guiltily away from the old lady's bright eyes, and she would not venture alone to the graveyard again.

As with every passing season their daughters grew further from Chonita and closer to womanhood, the town ladies lost most of their awe of the old woman. They felt they had defeated her in a battle for their babies. Now when Chonita made the daily journey from her white house to the graveyard she was often accosted by the town ladies.

"Doña Chonita," they said. "You are not going all the way to the graveyard? It is far."

"California is far and Argentina is far," said Chonita. "But the graveyard is close."

"I must have told my Guadalupe to visit you a million times," simpered Señora Gonzalez. "But you know how selfish and thoughtless these young girls are. Lupe is exactly the same as I was at her age, wild and boy-crazy as anything. I suppose you miss the girls."

"Old age, it happens," said the ladies, patting their curls. "You must find it difficult to take proper care of your flowers now. Your roses don't seem to stink so much these days. They haven't died, have they?"

Chonita gave a small smile to the ladies, then walked slowly on. Passing down the main street, she saw figures sitting motionless on straight-backed chairs, just inside open door-ways. The rooms were dark, and the still old women stared directly before themselves with blind, black eyes. Chonita remembered girls running through fields, hats with red ribbons falling from their heads. Wait for me, she had called to the older girls who ran in front of her. Next year I will be older and able to run as fast as you. Wait for me, she cried silently to the ghosts of girls dancing before her, beckoning her toward the graveyard.

Sometimes, turning a corner, Chonita found the sidewalk blocked by several of the girls who once had come singing and clinging to her. Now growing tall and curved, they wore uniforms and clutched books to their chests, like shields. They walked in twos or threes, long and shiny hair swinging to the same secret beat. "Chonita," they said, their smiles sliding slyly past her.

The graveyard fell into a state of greater ruin and the paths worn by the girls became lost in waves of grass. Often the old woman fell asleep beneath the amapa tree in the afternoon heat. She lay there like a splash of red or purple paint. Yellow poppies fell upon her. When she awoke, suddenly, she sat up and in a voice of command called, "My daughters!" After a moment she called again. But no figures emerged from behind the headstones, and the graveyard was still.

One December the girls began to come calling at Chonita's gate in early evening. They passed through tangled flowers and shrubs, which crept closely around the white house, enfolding it. Inside they looked quickly at the glass and bottle on the table, the record turning on the record player. "You have so many things," they said in the blue light of Chonita's bedroom. Small dust-covered flasks and jars and bottles lay scattered over the dressing table.

"They're all I brought with me from California, and now I can't think why I wanted them. Isn't that funny?" Chonita asked, looking up at the girls from where she sat on the edge of the bed. "Take them," she said, after a moment's silence, and the young girls picked over tubes of lipstick and pots of paint.

"And all these beautiful flowers growing wild. They just grow and die. Oh, Chonita, just one gardenia for my hair!" the girls implored. The old woman snipped the blossoms with scissors.

The girls ran away with their treasures. Chonita looked after them, the scent of gardenias bleeding in the dusk.

Like sleek, wild cats the twelve girls prowled around the plaza at night. Their eyes glittered cruelly and their fingernails were long and sharp and pointed. Silver paint hooded their eyes, gold powder clung to their cheeks, red lipstick slashed their mouths. Gardenias grew from the roots of their hair. The girls wore strange dresses which they fashioned themselves while gathered together in the afternoons. Sparkling and glistening, phosphorescent in the dark, the gowns trailed carelessly across the ground. Plunging backs and necks exposed smooth, glowing skin. "And at their age!" cried older women, shocked.

"What can we do with them?" shrugged their mothers. "They blow cigarette smoke in our faces and laugh. They take after us. They're smart and know what they want, and how to get it, too."

The twelve girls swept like brush fire around the plaza, their mocking laughter and cigarette smoke burning the air. A heady, powerful scent surrounded them, and it caused the plaza to empty quickly. Choking and coughing, most of the townspeople stumbled away, in search of clearer, cooler air.

As evening drew on the laughter of the twelve circling girls grew more wild and wicked. Their heavy perfume thickened. Still huddled where they had been all night, the boys of the town cast frightened glances at the smoking girls.

Chonita dreamed she was floating on a sea of scent to a place and time far away and unfamiliar. I don't like it here, she cried in her dream. Carry me back to where I was before. But the scent died in the air, leaving her stranded.

She woke in complete darkness. Sounds of abandoned laughter drifted down upon her. For a moment the old woman lay still, waiting for the familiar scent of her flowers to carry her back to the certainty that she was in her bed, her house, and not some other, distant place. But with the laughter came a strange, unknown scent both deeper and darker that that produced by her flowers.

The old woman sat up and turned to the bedroom window. It was covered over by leaves and blossoms of climbing rosebushes. Chonita pushed her face into the flowers and breathed deeply.

Other women, also woken by the reckless laughter, looked from bedroom windows and saw Chonita's candle dancing in the dark. What is that old woman looking for? they wondered. Their eyes passed to their daughters' empty beds, then turned in the direction of the graveyard, and to the lights weaving there.

As the solitary woman grew more alone, the gate to her yard was opened less often. However, the people of the town saw Chonita's rosebushes grow above the fence, then trail over it. Glad to be diverted from a rising anxiety over their girls, the town ladies for a time showed renewed interest in the old woman. "At last we see her famous flowers, but that's not enough," said the mothers of the twelve girls. "Visit Chonita and tell us: is her house clean? Are the bottles empty?"

"Oh, leave us alone!" snapped the twelve girls. They sat long hours before mirrors, examining their beauty with troubled eyes. They were nervous and irritable, and spent the days in bed.

Aching heads made their mothers moan. "Perhaps," they suggested timidly, "you might wear a little less perfume. We can't even smell Chonita's roses any more. Your perfume is pretty, but it's too strong, darlings."

"I wear no scent," cried each of the girls. "There goes Chonita now," they sobbed. They ran from windows and fell crying into chairs.

The road to the graveyard was becoming long. Once arrived there Chonita was too tired to walk among the stones and raise the fallen Virgins. Angels lay buried in the grass. Chonita sat in silence with the dead, her eyes wandering slowly from grave to grave.

When she took a few steps around the graveyard Chonita found bright, lost buttons, torn scraps of pink silk, broken bottles, wilted gardenia blosssoms. She came upon places where the grass was flattened, as though graves large enough for two had been dug in it.

Now and then she stayed beneath the poppy tree after dark. Upon returning to town, she found the main street brightly lit by streetlamps and music and calling children. It seemed she had been gone long and far away, and the townspeople looked at her as they would at an unexpected and unwanted visitor.

When Maria died in childbirth at fifteen, the ladies of the

town shook their heads. "A woman's life is not easy," they said to one another. "Such is our lot." In the church the priest spoke over the coffin, and he told the people that this seed they would now sow into the earth. While little girls played around the coffin, the priest said that this was the time to let tears fall, so the ground would be watered. From this seed would rise a new plant, and the flowers would shine in the sun.

After the priest's words, people crowded around the open coffin, and it was agreed that Maria had never looked more beautiful than at this moment. The coffin was closed, and on the back of Señor Lopez's old blue pick-up truck it was carried to the graveyard. The townspeople followed, streaming down the road, bending over to let themselves between strands of the barbed-wire fence, flowing into the graveyard, milling over the weeds and grass. There they wept and sang and prayed beneath dripping torches all through one night. Men smoked and drank, empty bottles smashed against the gravestones, and ravens fluttered from the amapa tree in fear.

Isabela wandered out to sea one moonless night. Her filmy white dress floated around her in the dark water, covering her like a shroud as she sank.

Yolanda roamed the cliffs above the bay, scanning the horizon for a white sail. Her foot slipped, her body fell and fell. She drifted slowly down through the blue sky, her red dress filling with air and billowing about her like a parachute. Then she lay dead upon the ragged rocks below, and blood dyed her dress a richer red.

The town was filled with tragedy as the twelve most beautiful girls died one by one. "Stay safe inside the house," mothers of the surviving girls implored. "Soon you will grow older, and the dangers will pass you by." However, the surviving girls would not understand their mothers' words of caution. They did not appear to grieve for their dead friends, or even notice they were gone. Their finery grew finer, their smiles more inviting, their eyes more sparkling. As they swept heedlessly around the plaza at night the air had an increasingly unbearable scent. The square was no longer the favourite place of relaxation for the townspeople, and even bats and owls deserted it.

Many people became frightened of the girls with their doomed laughter and poisoned kisses. Mothers warned sons. Yet the boys of the town were compellingly drawn to the condemned girls, and at night the plaza was crowded also with boys from neighbouring villages, and even from the capital city across the mountains. The dying young girls became famous throughout the state.

The noises from the graveyard in the hours after midnight turned more wild and raucous, and in the town below people shuddered in their beds.

Quickly, slowly, with or without pain, the young girls died in any number of ways. They clutched their hearts and cried out, swooning into the arms of gardenia bushes in the plaza. They gasped and screamed for weeks in bed, thrashing within the embrace of strange chills and fevers. They coughed, and in one moment the bloom left their faces as blood poured like thick purple wine upon the pillows. Several simply drifted off to sleep and never woke.

The town became immersed in the subject of young girls dying. Talk centred around diseases and accidents and details of funerals. Mothers of girls still living accepted the inevitable and planned ahead for their daughters' deaths. Each woman attempted to outdo the others in terms of lavish mourning parties, sumptuous funeral feasts, and fashionable gowns of grief. Black became the most popular colour in town, and a mood of festivity prevailed.

A steady hammering sound descended from the graveyard during daytime. Hearing it, the townspeople felt the pride of progress. At last their town was growing! Mothers of girls dead or dying sunk all available cash into the creation of splendid monuments to their babies' memories; most spent more than they could actually afford. "When you think of it, it's not so much," they reasoned. "Imagine how much it would have cost to feed and clothe and keep happy my poor darling for fifty years." The townspeople agreed with this logic one hundred per cent.

Chonita abandoned the graveyard to the carpenters and masons and mourning mothers, and remained almost always inside her red iron fence. In its excitement over the dying girls, the town had forgotten the old woman; and she was neither notified directly of the deaths, nor invited to share the graveside grief. On the rare occasions when she ventured out into the streets, Chonita walked unnoticed as a ghost.

The light inside her house was green and gloomy even on the brightest days. Leaves and blossoms pushed through the windows. As the rosebushes grew more thickly around her house, Chonita was drugged into drowsiness by their sweet, sickly smell. The uncontrolled growth was making it difficult to enter or leave the house.

Chonita listened to the screams of death and blows of hammers filtering through the plants which surrounded her. She started to spend several hours each day pruning the rosebushes, and she halted the flow of water to their roots. It was quickly evident, however, that these actions did not stunt, but actually encouraged, growth in her plants. Sometimes, after several drinks, Chonita would stagger outside with an axe. She swung at the thick, twisted trunks of the rosebushes. But the wood was like iron, the old woman had grown too weak, and she dropped crying upon the ground littered with fallen petals, her face pressed into the dark, rich dirt.

At night Chonita lay gasping for air. Wild roses trailed across her bedroom. The old woman had waking nightmares about vines growing like ropes around her and binding her forever. As she tossed in bed, she often pierced herself upon thorns, staining the white sheets red. The thick scent filled her the way water must fill drowning lungs.

Nightly the cries from the graveyard sounded more loudly. Dragging herself from her bed of green leaves and red rose petals, Chonita pushed aside the thick growth that blocked the window. The graveyard lay gaudily lit in the distance. Music mixed with laughter and drunken shouts and cheers spilled down into the town. Another girl was being buried.

Chonita heard a furtive shuffling, a snipping sound. Then footsteps fled. Going to the gate and opening it, she saw strangers running down the road, blossoms overflowing from their arms, falling in the moonlight, leaving a trail upon the road. Those flowers which had trailed over and hung outside her fence had been picked.

When she walked through the town the next day, Chonita could scarcely recognize it. Strangers in city clothes and carrying cameras, milled about everywhere. Men stood at corners, with baskets of flowers at their feet. "Fifty pesos!" they shouted. "The scent of young girls dying!" they called. "The most beautiful fragrance in the world! Buy the blossoms that adorned the hair of the glamorous Violetta Valquez! In memory of the lovely Isabela Inocence!"

Women of the town knocked into Chonita, then hurried on. They ran up and down the crowded road, and scampered in little circles. They wept out loud and wrung their hands. Falling upon strangers, they soaked shoulders with their tears. Then they lifted their faces, they became animated. "There are still three left, you know, but we have no hope. They say the governor himself will attend the funeral of the twelfth. Oh, it will be a great, grand affair. We have no hope, we have no hope!" they cried, skipping down the street.

When eleven of the doomed girls had died and only one remained, she was watched expectantly. As this last girl, Veronica, walked through the streets, people stared at her, called out to her, took her picture. At every moment it was assumed she would fall dead upon the dirt. Sometimes she was shaken from sleep in the middle of the night when her anxious mother believed she had ceased breathing. There was an air of impatience in the town, which quickly turned to disappointment as time went by and Veronica would not die. Certain citizens felt the girl was thwarting their hopes deliberately and out of meanness; on one occasion, a group of masked figures gathered in the dead of night before her father's house, chanting that she had an obligation and a duty to die.

Veronica grew to be as healthy as a horse. She turned into a dull and listless girl, prone to plumpness. Since all her girlfriends had died, she spent most of her time with her mother, pounding dough for tortillas in the kitchen, beating clothes clean in the sink; and she did not seem unhappy with this new domestic life. For a while curious strangers occasionally came to see "the last of the twelve," as she was called; but invariably they went away disappointed. Veronica had abandoned her finery and exotic ways, and little trace remained of the panther of a girl who had run wild in a pack of twelve. The flower vendors and city people melted into thin air, and for the most part the townspeople reverted back to their old habits of daily life. There was no more talk of a visit by the governor, and as months passed it was generally forgotten that Veronica had at one time been "one of the twelve."

She renewed her friendship with Chonita. Every afternoon she entered the iron gate, emerging some hours later with a flushed look. "We sit, we talk, we look at the flowers," was the girl's only answer to the questions of the town ladies. "I would like to marry now," Veronica announced one day, and in time her mother found her a nice, steady boy.

The graveyard was changed. It was now the favourite gathering place of the town ladies. They sat with their sewing and talked there through the afternoons, often in neglect of household duties. The town junta elected several men to caretake the graveyard, and it became a neat and pretty place. Weeds were cut, grass trimmed, and fallen Virgins restored to a more fitting state.

The ladies always sat near one or another of the eleven

magnificent graves which dwarfed the site, and as they spoke their voices drifted down into the town. The eleven mothers of girls who had died young formed a kind of clique among the town ladies. ''When my Rosario died,'' was the frequent beginning of conversations. ''She was never more beautiful than at the last moment,'' it was averred. ''The cigarette fell, and in one second her dress became a ball of fire! It was the most fantastic sight!'' The ladies would shake their heads with sad pleasure, stitching and sewing, while ravens swayed in the amapa tree above. Now and then the town ladies lifted their eyes from their handiwork. Breathing the clean, fresh air deeply, they looked at the graveyard. It was always so pretty when the sun began to set!

The house of flowers, they came to call Chonita's place. Roses and gardenias and japonestas grew more wildly in her yard, until they completely obscured the white dwelling. The old woman sat in her back yard, looking at the flowers and listening to water drip through the leaves. Veronica's babies tumbled over her. Dripping with sweat in the hot afternoon, the plump young matron wielded the machete. ''They grow so quickly,'' marvelled the old woman, bouncing babies on her knees. ''If you could just trim those bushes over there,'' she would murmur, pointing. After Veronica and the babies left, Chonita burned the clippings in a fire beside her tall papaya tree. She stared raptly into the flames.

Sometimes she was startled by a woman's voice calling at her gate. ''Doña Chonita, Doña Chonita, have you some roses for poor Guadalupe's grave?''

The old woman's face was inscrutable as she left the fire and cut an armful of blossoms. Her scissors were sharp, and they glinted in the sun. The mother of the young dead girl held the flowers to her face, then looked as though she had been tricked. ''These blossoms have no scent! They used to make me dizzy a mile away! What happened?''

The Boat in the Stars

"One man cannot fish alone," Señora Aquino heard hidden voices say behind the masses of leaves and blossoms that surrounded her. "Two hands are not enough for fishing," she heard the unseen men say, and again she knew it was her son, Victor, of whom they spoke. Señora Aquino turned her head in the direction of the speakers, but she could see only the dark whispering leaves, trembling against each other. The stone bench on which she sat was cold and hard and, like all the benches in the plaza, it was imprinted with the name of some townsperson long lying in the graveyard or still wandering lost, unseen, ghostly. Señora Aquino sat stiffly forward, so that the letters carved into the stone bench would not press against her back. But still she felt her mother's name branded upon her.

Women sitting and standing close around Señora Aquino also spoke of her son. Their voices rustled in her ears, above her head, across her neck, along her shoulders. "Your son has come home," said the women, flinging their hands with each word they spoke. "Victor has come back from the sea. He has been gone for many days and now he is safe on land again," said the women, pressing against Señora Aquino. "Now once more you can sleep at night."

"My sons would never leave me," boasted one woman.

"My sons would die before they would ever leave my house," said another.

"Even when they marry my sons cannot leave me. They bring their wives into beds they slept on as small boys," a third proud woman said.

The women on the benches fluttered and fidgeted, their hands spinning webs of thread or reaching out to touch one another. Señora Aquino, however, sat motionless in their midst, her hands resting stilly upon her lap and her eyes now gazing straight before her.

All around the sitting women narrow cement sidewalks wound this way and that, bending through shadows of trees and shrubs until disappearing behind them. Playing children darted along these paths, also vanishing, and they left behind cries that called to the women on the benches. Walking slowly in twos or threes or larger groups were youths all dressed in their finest clothes. They sought the eyes of the one they desired with shy glances or brazen stares, and called to one another, softly as sleepy birds. It was evening, and first stars appeared in the sky above the plaza.

The women surrounding Señora Aquino shifted restlessly, their eyes darting about in search of children belonging to them. They were anxious that the younger ones had not fallen in the course of their tumbling games, and just as anxious that the older ones had not slipped down to the beach in the company of another older child. The sounds of their husbands' voices washed against the ears of the women like the stream that fell down the hills and through the thick, dark jungle. Señora Aquino gazed intently at the lamps spaced along the twisting paths, the shining globes of light that led away from her. The calls and cries of the crowded plaza formed a net that caught her up, gathered her inside it, and drew her to the surface of the still pool in which she had been drowning.

"It is not natural that he has good luck all the time," said one of the men obscured behind the bushes. "One week a man finds many fish, the next week he finds few. There is good luck and bad luck, the sea is calm and rough. But Victor sails on different waters than we do."

"He does not bring his fish to our shore, he will not sell them here," said another man. "He sells his fish to strangers in other towns."

"It is not good to be alone at sea," a third man said. "When you wish to sing, your voice cannot be heard alone above the wind."

A breeze rose up from the Pacific and drew across the town. Señora Aquino shivered and pulled her shawl more tightly around her shoulders.

"Look, there he is!" hissed the women to Señora Aquino. They fell silent, as did the men behind the bushes, the screaming children, the calling youths. There was a moment when only the owls perched at the tops of the dark trees could be heard, hooting suddenly, as though startled from sleep. Victor appeared, floating down the paths, swooping along the cement sidewalks, and all the townspeople stopped to watch him. His figure was straight and tall, his face carved clean and strong, and his feet did not touch the ground.

Around and around the plaza Victor flew, passing now beneath the shining lamplight, now amid the shadows of trees, moving always so quicky that no one could see him clearly. the huddled men glanced at the racing boy, then shoved fists deeper into pockets and looked down at the ground on which their feet stood firmly, naked and brown, crusted and scarred. The little children, squatting in their games upon the sidewalks, looked up at the tall figure advancing so rapidly upon them. Though it appeared that surely he would knock into them and send their bodies crashing and breaking, the children felt no fear. Always at the last moment Victor dodged around them. "Disgraceful," each woman whispered, neither to herself nor to another. "Disgraceful," they whispered, just as they had done two years before when Victor had walked with an unknown American boy through the streets. "Disgraceful," they had said when the American boy suddenly left the town after giving Victor a pair of roller skates and making of him a stranger who went far out to sea alone, returning to land only to race around the plaza, coming and going, never standing still.

The people listened to the sound of Victor's skates rolling over the paths. When this sound died away there was a moment's silence before the people continued talking. But now their conversations sounded strange and disconnected, like broken threads, and each word spoken was an unanswered question that wavered waiting in the air. Then a noise that sounded like a rushing of water would draw near, washing and cleaning what it touched. Victor would reappear, gliding on his roller skates, coming full circle around the plaza once more.

"He is almost a stranger to us now," said one woman to another.

"But you have other children, both older and younger," said another, addressing Señora Aquino in a voice of comfort. Victor's mother pushed her head forward against the breeze that sang down from the trees, but she did not answer.

Then, suddenly, Señora Aquino turned to the women next to her and cried in a voice of surprised pain. "He is my son!" Her heart flew away from her and toward Victor, and she was just about to run after it when a hand pressed down on her shoulder, holding her on the bench. Señora Aquino felt a familiar warm touch, a gentle and firm touch, and she twisted her head to look into her mother's eyes. But no one stood behind her, and only the shining eyes of God looked down upon her.

The women looked at Señora Aquino's swimming eyes with pity and curiosity. "But surely you knew he was back in our town," murmured one woman. "Everyone knows he returned this morning with the light from the east. Didn't he come to see you?"

Before Señora Aquino could answer, another woman burst out loudly, "Well, I remember when my Pedro returned home from the city and his troubles there. Oh, the feast we had that day! We killed a pig and ate it all up. It is true that the pig was sick and dying anyway, but we killed it, ate it, and it tasted good. Did you prepare a feast to welcome home your son, Señora Aquino?"

"I was making cactus soup," said Victor's mother, staring raptly at the salia bush before her.

"Cactus soup, cactus soup," clucked the women, turning from Señora Aquino in embarrassment.

He had appeared in her doorway just when the morning light was beginning to whiten and blaze upon the town. Inside Señora Aquino's house it was still dark and cool, and the fire she was building still burned low. The older children were off at school or were helping their father mend the fishing nets.

Señora Aquino was sitting on a stool beside the sink. She had finished scraping the spines off the cactus and now she peeled it. The hard green skins fell into a white basin resting on her lap. Near to her the youngest children were playing beside the fire, watching the flames leap and the sparks fly upward. The smoke drew water from Señora Aquino's eyes.

His head nearly touching the ceiling, Victor stood still in the doorway, blocking the light. His mother wiped her eyes and looked at him. Though eighteen years of age he seemed still to be growing, and each time he returned from the sea he appeared much taller. His height did not seem to come from either Señora Aquino or her husband, and it made her house seem strange and small to her. The new clothes her son wore on each occasion of his reappearance were the clothes of a stranger. She had never scrubbed them in the sink behind the house, she had never used all her strength to pound them clean. She had never seen them draped over the bushes in the yard and drying in the afternoon sun.

Señora Aquino turned her face down to the basin upon her lap and watched the meat of the cactus, fragrant and sweet, reveal itself beneath the hard green skin. Every stroke of the knife was halted when the dull blade hit against her thumb.

There was a silence in the room. The small children stopped their fighting and sat quietly beside the fire, staring up at the tall stranger. Señora Aquino heard her son enter the room, pause beside the table at its centre, then leave again. When the sound of his footsteps was gone from her, she raised her head.

Her youngest children were staring at the heap of silver coins and shining diamonds that Victor had drawn from his bulging pockets and placed upon the table. The children looked at their mother with questions in their eyes. "He is your brother," she told them, slowly. "You remember him. He used to sit beside the fire when he was a small boy. He was just like you." When her children continued to stare at her, Señora Aquino clumsily gave them some of the silver coins and told them to run to the corner and buy themselves Coca Colas. After the children scampered away, she placed the jewels with all the others hidden at the back of a drawer in which she kept those things belonging only to her. Then she turned to the fire and saw that it was nearly hot enough to cook the soup. A scent of salt and sea, of Victor, lingered in the room. Señora Aquino picked up the knife and finished peeling the cactus, and when she cut her thumb one jewel of blood rose to the surface of her skin. In the dim light of the house the blood looked not red, but black, and the cut was made more painful by the stinging, salty scent of Victor.

"Cactus soup, cactus soup," repeated the women in the plaza. They watched Señora Aquino, silent and dreaming beside them. She seemed to have forgotten her son; her eyes did not follow his swooping figure. Now and then an irritated expression crossed her face, and she waved her hand in the air beside her head, as though brushing away some cobweb that hung around her. The women were afraid to try to comfort Señora Aquino, and they looked at each other, shrugging their shoulders. Each one knew that Victor would not stay in his mother's house when he returned to the town. During the days he worked down at the shore, strengthening his boat in readiness for another journey out to sea. In the afternoons he slept on a large flat rock beside the river, and he did not see the people who crept close beside him to stare and to listen to his breathing. When evening came he was seen skating around the plaza, but no one knew where he went when the hour grew late and the plaza became a solitary place.

The boy with black eyes who raced around the plaza did not seem to see the children he dodged, the girls who stared at him, the boys who looked away from him, the men who scowled at him. He did not seem to see any of the people, and this included his mother. Yet for a time each person in the plaza was certain that it would be him, only him, whom Victor suddenly stopped beside, and only in his ears would Victor speak of what he saw and where he went on his journeys out to sea. Each person waited for this moment, and the sound of Victor's skates rolling around and around the plaza created a circle inside of which the people were imprisoned.

As the night blossoms began to unfold and reach toward midnight, a young boy suddenly scaled the side of the church that faced onto the plaza. One by one the people turned their eyes away from Victor and toward the boy climbing daringly upward by means of large spikes driven into the side of the church. "Look!" they cried, pointing to the boy, and they watched him ascend until he vanished into the darkness above. Then the plaza was filled with the sound of the church bell ringing over and over. The small boy hit the bell again and again; and wildly and unsteadily it pealed, not calling the people to church or celebration, ringing in no rhythm. All at once the bell fell silent. The boy became tired, and he leaned against the wall of the tower, breathing hard, and there was the plaza beneath him. It looked far away and filled with figures made strange by distance. Dotted around it, like dark breathing flowers, were the forms of children curled into balls, lying wherever they happened to fall asleep.

When the church bell stopped ringing the townspeople stirred themselves, and it seemed the pealing bell had woken them from sleep. As the final stroke of the bell drifted from the plaza in ever-widening circles, one voice called out. "I hope he falls," said the voice, clearly and loudly, and the people turned back to Victor's fleeting form, yet now with expressions of indifference or contempt upon their faces. People began to leave the plaza and the sound of Victor's skates, for the hour was growing late.

Around the huddled men cigarette packages were passed until empty. When the burning butts were crushed beneath heels, the men split off into groups of four or five, each one of which would work together in a boat. Away from shore the boats would be pushed by the youngest man in the crew, who waded through the shallows with his trousers rolled up on his legs, water licking his skin. A lamp burned in the bow of each boat, looking out upon the black water beneath which the fish ran in dark crowded masses, waiting to be pulled up into the starry night.

As the plaza slowly emptied, the girls without boys walked more quickly around it, and they laughed more loudly. "Victor will not look at us because he loves the mermaids who call him out to sea," laughed those girls without boys. The girls twined their bodies together as they walked, and their laughter

rang shrilly in the air, echoing around the plaza, then returning to mock their ears. In secret shame the girls without boys
left the plaza one by one and made their way to their mothers'
houses, to the empty rooms where only candles burned
beneath the crosses.

The women still sat together on the benches. Slowly they
ran out of words, and their interest in the dreaming woman
beside them also died. The women became as still as Señora
Aquino, and in their darkening minds each saw one point of
light, one lamp bobbing in the boat that held her husband.
The women were reluctant to gather up their children and
return to houses and beds where no men lay waiting and warm
for them. The plaza grew more still and more quiet, and the
moon rose in the sky.

Floating within their drowsy trances, the women did not
see the older boys and girls steal down to the beach in pairs.
Two together, one boy and one girl lay on sand that was cool,
pressed against a body that was warm. "Tell me about him,"
a girl would ask with lips that trembled against a boy's skin.
"When you were younger and he was younger, he was your
friend and you were his," said one girl to one boy. "While
I was skipping with the other girls in the plaza, you would
go off with him into the dark. You would climb along trails
that wound through banana trees and up into the hills. What
did he do and what did he say?"

In answer the boy pressed his face into the girl's neck. She
felt his hair beneath her hands, and his searching lips. Arching
her neck, she looked up to see stars drifting across the sky.

When the boy opened his eyes later, to find the girl lying
quietly beside him, he saw the beach stretching down to the
dark sea. The sand was printed in a pattern of small hollows
where water had lapped and washed over it at high tide. The
boy saw those hollows that looked like craters on the faraway
moon, but he could not see the traces of long ago, those marks
upon the sand that showed where he had fought with Victor
late on nights like this one. They had stood facing each other,
Victor and one boy, their faces shining clear, then blurring.
They fought until both were in the sand, and one of them had
won.

And in the plaza Victor turned around and around, past the sleeping children and dreaming women, dodging and weaving patterns that vanished as they were formed. Only now when there were no crowds to watch him did he perform leaps and spectacular turns, throwing himself up into the sky and catching hold of it with strong spead arms, then gathering the night and everything in it to his chest. Twirling round and round like the planets Victor danced alone. When the hour grew close to midnight the women roused themselves from their stupor and gathered up their sleeping children. After these smallest ones were put into bed, the women stood in the doorways of the houses, calling and calling to the older children who lay down upon the sandy shore.

Señora Aquino, still sitting on the bench, heard the bell-like voices calling names of children, many names. Come home, come home, it is late, come home, cried the women in the doorways. Señora Aquino listened, but she could not hear her own name being called. Once her mother had also stood in a doorway, once her own name had been called. And however far away she was, the girl who become Señora Aquino would hear her mother's voice calling to no one but her. Across miles of air she would hear her name called again and again, falling through the night like a star.

The voices of the calling mothers died away, leaving only the sound of Victor's skates rumbling over the plaza. He danced around his mother, not looking at her. In the sound of this dance Señora Aquino could hear the voices of the heavens, angry and threatening. She turned her face up to the sky in search of cloud or rain, but the night was clear. So transparent was the sky that Señora Aquino could see far through it, beyond this single night, and past other nights to come. She felt a sudden fear. "Victor," called Señora Aquino. "Victor," she called, but softly, so that only she could hear the sound of her voice.

The world turned round and round, and the planets spun. Wet and dry, wet and dry, the seasons passed into years and the town became older. Victor went out to sea, was gone for several weeks or a month, then returned to the town, bringing diamonds for his mother, not saying where he had been. Then he left again. The townspeople became as familiar with Victor's comings and goings as they did with the rising and falling tides, the clear and clouded skies, and when they spoke of him it was as something that moved around them, apart from them, untouched by them.

Her children grew used to waking from dreams or nightmares or sickness to find Señora Aquino standing by the window, looking out at the dark empty street of midnight and the rising star-filled sky above. She was looking for Victor. Sometimes the children woke to see her sitting at the kitchen table, dwarfed behind a huge stack of stones that glittered. They watched their mother look with puzzlement at the shining diamonds, but they did not see her touch them. Then the children shut their eyes against the blinding light and fell back into sleep. The next morning the kitchen table would be bare, and the children would recall only the distant memory of a dream.

Señora Aquino's children grew older, and one by one the eldest ones married. Victor neither married nor grew older. But his mother aged more quickly than was natural; before her time she looked like the women whose men have died and children left them. She looks just like her mother, said those people in the town who remembered the terrible illness and agonizing death of Señora Aquino's mother. Some said that Señora Aquino had the same sickness. Soon, they said, the pain would begin, and like her mother Señora Aquino would suffer for three endless months. The pain would be so bad that she would scream day and night in a voice that was not human, and her heart would turn black. She would spit black blood and curse God for giving her the pain, and she would form a monstrous hate for all the people of the town because they did not suffer also. The pain would not end at her death, but become only more awful, and like her mother Señora Aquino would wander as a ghost through the town, trying to find revenge for her suffering by inflicting evil upon the people, trying to ease her pain by doing good.

As this story grew older and stronger, the people began to

have a kind of fear for Señora Aquino. Anxious that she would not haunt them after her death, many people crept to her house at night, and in the morning Señora Aquino would open her door to find presents that bore the names of the bestowers. However, she never thanked the people for their gifts. When she walked through the streets of the town passersby would pause and say her name respectfully, even if they were unacquainted with her or her family. Señora Aquino would not answer them, but walked slowly to the bench in the plaza that was kept always empty for her. Even the smallest children knew not to sit on Señora Aquino's bench, and none of the women who had been friends with her in years gone by would sit with the aged woman. The people of the town allowed Señora Aquino to sit alone and remember her life in peace. When Victor danced around the plaza and flew past his mother without seeing her the people said, "He does not recognize his mother, she has grown so old." Or they said, "He still comes to her house when he returns to land, seeking her favour with gifts from faraway lands. But she does not remember who he is and leaves his gifts untouched."

The stories about the old woman sitting alone in the plaza were told again and again. Small children grew to know these stories in the same way they grew to know the streets and houses and hills around them. Often people would stand quite close to where Señora Aquino sat dressed in black, and they would repeat her story in clear voices that carried to her ears. But she did not turn her face toward those who spoke of her. She looked as always up into the sky.

Just as the stories about Señora Aquino became old and familiar, so did the story about her son also spread. No one could remember who had told the story first or when that had been. The story about Victor was told by everybody and belonged to the whole town, though each person believed it to be his own. "Victor told me once," every person would begin, and then they would tell the tale of how Victor travelled far out from land in his boat, farther out to sea than anyone had ever been before. He journeyed to the great cities that lay to the north and south, to the ports of California and Peru. He journeyed still farther away to the islands lost in the middle of the great Pacific, the islands that had no names and were known by no one but Victor. Sometimes, the people said, he crossed the sea all the way to the horizon. He sailed beyond the end of the ocean and up into the sky.

The stars were islands, floating, and their beaches were made not of sand but of diamonds that glittered even in the night, more brightly in the darkness. When the tide of night was high, waves washed upon the moon and made it new; when the tide was low, the moon was old. Sometimes waves flooded over the moon and it could not be seen at all. Victor sailed over the sunken moon, he drifted from star to star, and he was the only one who walked upon the diamond beaches. Alone in the stars he sailed, all alone except for God.

No one in the town asked Victor about the times he spent in the boat in the stars. But sometimes when he had not been seen for many days the townspeople would look at the face of Señora Aquino turned up to heaven, and they would turn their eyes up to the stars, also. They would search to see Victor's boat sailing through the night.

The sea is calm, the sea is rough; luck is good and bad. The people of the town were long familiar with the ways of the fish and the sea, the moods that changed from favour to disfavour. Sometimes there would be no fish for a month, and the people would lie awake with an empty gnawing feeling in their bellies. Sometimes there would be more fish than the men could catch and more than they could sell, and then each person's belly would be bursting full to the point of pain.

But a time came when there were no fish, and this time would not end. Night after night the men cast their nets into the sea, and they fished all through the days, too. But except for the clinging, dripping plants that stank of salt the nets were always pulled up empty. With every week that passed unblessed by good luck the empty nets seemed to become heavier, until it required all the strength of every man to drag them to the surface of the sea. Yet still their labour was not rewarded, and gradually the men spent more of their hours at sea sitting idle and drifting with the currents. They cast their eyes up to the blank, faraway heavens. The men who drove in trucks from the city to buy fish from the villagers ceased coming when day after day there were no fish to buy. Finally, the men of the town no longer went in the boats out to sea.

The school closed, and the children were sent up into the hills each morning to look for bananas and papayas and oranges. Young boys crept through the jungle, speared sticks in hands, in search of armadillos. Women slaughtered their pigs and goats and chickens one by one, until there was nothing more to kill and no more meat to eat. All the people searched for food from dawn to dusk, but there was never enough. Even the land had forsaken them.

In the evenings the plaza was empty. The people of the town closed themselves inside their houses. Small children lay upon mattresses, moaning and whimpering with hunger. The older children no longer slipped down to the beach in pairs, but lay silent and alone in bed, an aching that was not hunger creeping through their blood. Women lay weakly beside their men, and in low voices they would speak of ways of finding food to feed the hungry children. They whispered of the bad hungry times, and when they might end. God has forgotten us, they despaired. He is angry with us and will not listen to our cries. Oh, what did we do wrong? They tried to remember all the small sins they had committed through the years, but they could recall none too large not to be forgiven. They listened for an answer to their prayers to come through the darkness, but the only sounds they could hear were the moans of their children and the cries of ghosts who wandered the empty streets of the town, weeping with loneliness.

Yes, the town was empty in the evenings, and Victor did not roller-skate around the plaza. During all this time of evil he did not return to the town, and this was the longest he had ever stayed away. Gradually the people came to believe that the bad times would not end until Victor's boat touched their shore again. Through the long and sleepless nights the people would rise from their beds and go to their windows. Turning their faces to the sky, they looked for Victor's boat in the stars.

Now when Señora Aquino looked out her window in the

dark hours of early morning she saw faces in the windows of every other house, and these faces burned like lamps. Twisted with longing, they looked strange and not like the known faces of her neighbours. They looked like reflections of her own face, and seeing them did not make Señora Aquino feel less alone. She looked away from them and searched to see Victor's boat, its bow piled high with diamonds gathered from beaches of stars, sailing and shimmering toward her.

One night Señora Aquino lay beside her husband, listening to the restless turning and ragged breathing of the children beside her. Her husband's eyes were open wide and gazing at the ceiling. Señora Aquino did not go to her window this night, but waited in her bed through the hours. Floating through the town were the whines of starving dogs, the chants of sorrowing women, the fevered prayers of the hungry. The town twitched and shivered with sorrow and hunger and despair, and it seemed that never would it sleep again.

But as the night moved toward its deep heart and centre the sad cries and calls became softer, lower. They grew weak, then died away. One nightmare scream sliced the sky, then ended. One by one the children of Señora Aquino fell asleep, and then her husband slept, too. Father and children breathed together, sharing the same rhythm of their blood.

Señora Aquino rose from her mattress and by the light of the moon that flooded through the open window she stepped over the still forms of her children. She moved to the drawer where she kept the things belonging only to her, and reaching to its back she pulled out all the jewels given to her by her son. Señora Aquino sat at the kitchen table, silently turning the cold jewels over in her hands, feeling their hard surfaces, weighing them, warming them. At times she turned her eyes away from the jewels, and looked around the dim room and at the dark shapes of her sleeping family. Then she stared again at the diamonds, peering into their light as though something was revealed inside it. The bronzed crucifix nailed to the wall above her head burned with the light of the jewels, a cold fiery light that seared Señora Aquino's vision, blinding her even when she closed her eyes.

Even when she closed her eyes she had been blinded by

the screams of the woman who lay on the bed. She had sat there for days and nights, enclosed within the screams of the woman on the bed who was her mother, unable to run like her father and brothers and sisters as far from the screams as was possible, but never far enough. The woman on the bed could or would not talk, she only screamed at the god who had given her the pain. The girl beside the bed felt the pain flowing from the woman like tears of blood, tears of black jewels that would not stop flowing, tears for a death that would not come. With every scream that would not end the girl beside the bed felt the tears of black blood dripping upon her, burning her skin, then entering her. So she sat, until at last the room was silent, as silent as the waiting, listening town. And the girl opened her eyes to see tears still falling from the bronzed figure nailed upon the cross, upon the wall.

Señora Aquino sat upon the chair for a time, her shoulders sagging and tears dripping from her eyes like burning wax from a candle's flame. Then she gathered the jewels in her arms and slipped out from the house.

The town looked barren and strange, and the emptiness of its streets was made more clear by the streaming moonlight. The dusty road was shining. Dogs that had been barking all through the night now were silent, and the owls did not cry. Señora Aquino walked slowly, brushing past the ghosts who wandered lost and aimless. She entered the plaza and sat on a stone bench at its centre. The jewels resting on her lap, she turned her head this way and that, not nervously, but steadily, as though ensuring that no one or thing should slip by her unseen. She sat waiting for several hours, and while she waited the tide crept upon the shore.

Suddenly Señora Aquino's heart bolted inside her. She sat straight and tense and trembling. Her face quivered against the breeze and she felt all its secrets washing over her, caressing her. She rose from the bench and walked down the paths that wound and twined through the plaza. As she walked she dropped the jewels, one by one, and they glittered behind her, illuminating the steps she had taken. Down the main road she moved, the jewels falling like stars into the dust. Their points of light formed constellations and patterns of gods. When her hands were empty Señora Aquino returned to her house and slipped onto the mattress beside her sleeping husband.

When she woke next the sun was reaching toward her through the open window, and by its light she saw that her husband and children had gone from the house. She listened to the cries of excitement and surprise that rang around and around the town. Above these cries the churchbell pealed loudly, clearly, steadily. Señora Aquino saw people running by her doorway, diamonds clutched within their hands and their eyes fixed upon the ground in search of more. "Victor has dropped them from the stars, they have fallen from the sky," the people chattered. They quickly planned how they could travel to the big store in the capital city, where the diamonds could be sold for money. There would be a feast in the town that night, there would be more food than anyone could eat, and singing and dancing in the plaza, too.

Señora Aquino passed unnoticed through the crowds and walked down the road to the beach. For several minutes she stared out at the waves that glittered and danced in the bright morning sunlight. A cool breeze touched her face. She began to pick her way slowly across the rocky part of the shore, her eyes turned to the ground.

Upon reaching Victor's boat she halted. It was smashed upon the shore, its body torn and splintered. Señora Aquino looked at the small boat without surprise, though she knew there had been no storm to drive it against the shore during the night just passed. The boat was beached upon the rocks, abandoned by the ebbing tide. But now already the sea was flowing and reaching toward it.

Señora Aquino returned up the road and into the town. It was deserted. All the people had departed with the jewels to the capital city. Señora Aquino walked past her house and into the plaza. She sank down on a bench and felt the letters of her mother's name press against her back.

She waited as the sun rose in the sky and became more hot. The trees and bushes around her, which seemed so protecting and luxurious in the evenings, now appeared weak and frail, and they offered little shelter from the sun. Flowers that bloomed and scented the night air now were drained and dry.

Señora Aquino waited through the afternoon. The sun reached its apex in the sky and slowly began to sink down to meet the climbing, rising sea.

In its final moments of power the sun burned with vengeance upon the town and glazed it white. Señora Aquino closed her eyes. Her mother's hand would feel cool, and the shadow of her figure would fall over Señora Aquino like soft wings of a bird, offering peaceful and endless sleep. Señora Aquino could almost feel the presence of her mother appear under the force of her own longing. But she only became more dazed and weary, and no ghost appeared.

A hot breeze, heavy and stinking, passed over Señora Aquino, and the leaves around her shook feverishly. Señora Aquino felt dizzy and drowning beneath it, but the breeze washed against her eyes, compelling them to fight against it and open. She saw the breeze stir through the plaza and down the street as it moved toward the graveyard at the edge of town.

When the breeze had passed by her the air was suddenly cool. The tide crept higher upon the shore, cooling the burning rocks, nearing the broken beached boat, then reaching it. Small waves nudged its skeleton, slowly freeing it from the rocks. All at once the remains of the boat were floating. Señora Aquino felt them drifting far out to sea, beyond the reach of her vision, past the horizon, and up into the sky. The first star of early evening appeared, and Señora Aquino turned her head toward it. Something inside her loosened, then floated to its rightful place. Señora Aquino sat on the bench, her arms clasped tightly around her sides, and slowly she rocked herself back and forth, her own mother, her own child.

Poppies Always Fall

A man threw his only son up into the air, then caught him just before he fell onto the ground. The baby screamed in fear. He made a noise that was a mixture of the words "wire" and "war." When other children of similar age could speak fluently, Benito made just this single sound. "What colour is the sky?" his father asked. "Juar," said the baby. "What colour is the sea?" his father asked. "Juar," said the baby. "Juar, juar, juar," he cried, falling through the air.

"Benito Juarez," laughed the father. "The leader of the people and the next revolution." This time he made no move to catch his son.

Benito's mother dove to save her child. "Have I married a murderer?" she demanded, rocking the baby like a rough sea. "I should have known. I should have listened to my mama. It's in your family. There's your sister, after all."

"A saint," averred the father.

"A silent saint," replied the mother, sarcastically. "Those nuns glide about and never make a sound. Even before she took the veil your sister never spoke. She has not said a single word in all her life."

"She was blessed by God," said Benito's father, with fervour. "We are a holy family. God blesses us, and now we have the biggest blessing of all. Our hero, Benito Juarez." The man spat on the floor.

All the children of the town loved the little boy. "Can Benito come out and play?" they called at the door. His mother pushed him outside. "Now don't let him get himself killed," she told the children.

They sang songs and ran in circles around Benito, down the street and to the river. Pushing him into the swampy part of it, they watched Benito try to crawl through the mud. Next the children attempted to pull out all Benito's hair, strand by strand, giving up before they finished only because of boredom. Their favourite amusement was what they called the pinching game. The pinch that made Benito cry determined the winner. If the little boy would not weep, the game ended inconclusively and the children sent him home in disgust. "Why can't you stay neat and clean like all the other children? Is this the thanks I get, ungrateful child?" the boy's mother screamed.

One afternoon the children spied a small punt resting in the reeds of the river's estuary. They put Benito in the boat, then pushed it out to sea. The tide carried it quickly away. Benito sat in the prow, hands folded upon his lap, eyes fixed on the endless expanse of water stretching before him. The children watched the boat until it disappeared from sight. Then they turned and searched for another game to play.

As the afternoon drew on a wind rose from the south, rustling like something shiny through the coconut trees. "The sea is getting quite rough," observed the children, looking up from their fun. "Yes," they said. "Anyone out in a small boat would become very wet, because the waves are so big."

That evening three men brought the little boy in to shore with their day's catch which, owing to the bad weather, was slight. The boy was dripping wet. "A funny fish," the children cried. "A funny fish that can breathe on land." In wonder they looked at the seaweed adorning Benito's head like a crown. "Where did you go and what did you see? Did you float off the edge of the world? Did you sail all the way to China?"

Benito could not answer their questions, and after his journey out to sea he would no longer make even the "juar" sound. He was silent. He became an unsatisfactory playmate and the children tired of him quickly. Their pleasure in the games was ruined because Benito began to participate in them himself. When the children led him down to the river, Benito jumped into the mud before he could be pushed. He pulled

out his hair in great handfuls and pinched himself with extraordinary fierceness, but he never cried. The children stopped
calling for Benito at the door.

For several years he stayed inside the house with his pretty,
nervous young mother. She was driven to tears by his ways.
At the most unexpected moments Benito would fall from his
chair, as though on purpose, banging his head severely on
the cement floor. The various injuries he did himself caused
his mother much unnecessary bother. Worse, there were long
periods of time when Benito remained standing upright in one
position and without the least signs of life, like a statue. His
eyes did not blink and his chest did not sigh with air. He
gathered dust. His mother couldn't stand it. She locked the
boy in the bedroom. Turning on the radio very loudly, she
danced in front of the big living room mirror for hours on end.
When she shut off the music, suddenly, the house was silent,
and the girl looked in fear toward the closed bedroom door.

"You're lucky," said other young matrons of the town. "My
kids just cry and cry. They never stop. I give them the moon
and the stars, but that's not enough. They want more. But
your little Benito, he's quiet as a stone. And such a cute little
thing!"

"He hears everything we say," said Benito's mother, biting
her lip and glancing toward the boy. "The priest told me to
thank God every night for giving me such a pretty baby. He
said Benito was touched by the hand of God. He won't talk
because the Lord is always speaking to him. How can you
listen to God and talk at the same time?"

The young mothers turned silently to look at the little boy.
He was lying on his back on the floor, holding a hand before
his face, and watching it.

When Benito turned six his mother sent him out of the house
in the mornings and allowed him back inside only when evening fell. The townspeople became used to seeing the little boy
as he shuffled down the dusty streets. He seemed to have no
curiosity about what lay beyond the town, and never
wandered off to find himself lost. He liked to circle around
a certain block for one entire day, then around another block
the next day, and so on. People grew so familiar with the sight

of the boy passing at regular intervals before their houses they noticed only his absences. After some time the townspeople recalled the boy's presence only when a stranger to the village wondered about him. "Oh, yes, that's Benito," they said, as if this were all the explanation necessary.

Later his favourite pleasure was to sit in the old, drooping tree in the centre of the plaza all day long. Birds skipped and sang around him. Benito dropped poppies on the heads of everyone who passed beneath him. At first this caused concern, as picking flowers in the plaza was prohibited. "Soon we will have no more pretty blossoms on our poppy tree," the townspeople said. However, it was quickly noticed that for every flower Benito picked and dropped, another grew instantly to replace it. The tree bloomed yellow even out of season. "It's always February, and poppies always fall," was a special saying of the town.

One night, at a late hour when the town was fast asleep, the church bell began ringing with urgency. A house had caught fire! Someone had died! The country had declared war! Something bad had happened, and the people of the town ran anxiously to the church. Inside the dark building the priest was pacing as he puffed nervously on a cigarette. In response to the questioning looks of his flock, he pointed upward, toward heaven.

The small boy was dragged down the stone steps from the bell tower by townspeople angry at having been so unnecessarily alarmed. The boy's parents should look after him better, he wasn't safe wandering alone, something bad might happen.

Chastized, Benito's parents vowed to tend their child more carefully. However, as soon as they fell asleep or turned their backs, Benito ran to the church and rang the bell. Tying him to the bedpost would not stop the boy, for he would undo the most difficult knots, even if it took days. A delegation of irate citizens met with the priest. "I think," he said, "we should neither chain nor lock up this boy. God is speaking to us through the bell. He desires our greater attendance." The priest had long waged an unsuccessful campaign against the town's casual spirit of devotion.

The people deferred to the priest, yet they grew increasingly edgy. At any hour of day or night the church bell rang out, aimlessly, endlessly. The townspeople lay in bed, waiting for the bell to begin ringing; gazing up at ceilings of darkness, they waited for it to stop. Their nights were sleepless, and during daytime they walked with weary steps. At mass the church was filled with sounds of snoring.

After a session of heated debate, the priest agreed the situation could not continue. The church would be locked except when mass was celebrated, thus denying the boy passage to the tower. Still the bell rang. Benito was able to climb the side of the church by means of a ladder of niches carved into it. "He will fall and kill himself," said the townspeople, standing in the plaza with faces turned up to the church tower.

"This is embarrassing the dignity of our town," said the citizens at a special meeting of the junta. "Strangers will think us careless in calling God to hear our prayers and songs." The priest could not argue. "I am becoming the joke of the diocese," he muttered.

It was put forth that Benito be given the task of calling the people to mass. In this way his love for the bell could be expressed in a more suitable fashion. He was taught to ring the bell just so, with five even strokes.

The plan did not succeed. When the moment for mass arrived Benito rang the bell wildly. At other, odd times he gave the correct signal. Many people, not knowing if the boy was entertaining himself or calling them to God, did not attend church. The paltry turnout upset the priest. "I am starting to think," he emoted in his tragic, sorrowful way, "this town does not deserve a priest or church or bell."

Benito was quickly relieved from the job of summoning the town to service. The altar boy rang five steady notes. Yet Benito continued to ring the bell so often it was impossible to know when to heed its call. The townspeople excused their absence from mass with pleas of confusion. "I am sorry, Father. I thought it was just Benito ringing the bell," was a common line. The priest wheeled about and strode up the street, black cloth swirling passionately around his legs.

He began to shut himself in the locked church when the bell

rang. At this proximity, the bell sounded very loud, as though it were ringing inside the priest's head. He was driven to distraction. He harboured suspicions that certain slackers were encouraging Benito to ring the bell, thus providing them with flimsy reasons to miss mass. He felt powerless against the silent stubbornness of the people, and by way of consolation lit large amounts of incense, gulping the sweet smoke as deeply as an opium addict. Simultaneously he conjugated Latin verbs.

In the clearer air outside the townspeople became used to the ringing of the bell. The clouds of smoke and chanted foreign words issuing from the closed church, however, disturbed them. They fretted over their priest like anxious parents.

The day came when Doña Lupita obtained a loudspeaker for her store. Each morning she shouted into the microphone, her words carrying clearly, if somewhat distortedly, through the town: oranges were twenty pesos a kilo; Señor Alemana required men to work his fields; Violetta Valquez was celebrating her sixteenth birthday, and everyone was invited to the party. Now when the ringing bell broke the night and woke the townspeople they knew that any emergency would be broadcast over Doña Lupita's loudspeaker. They knew nothing was wrong.

Often the bell was the last sound the people heard at night and the first sound they heard at morning. On the waves of sound they swam to sleep, and deep, full notes pealed through their dreams. The vibrating air touched the sleepless and soothed them, offering them the comfort of company, telling them they were not alone. Sometimes in the still centre of night it seemed the hushed town was not sleeping, but listening.

On those dull, hot afternoons that like unbroken spells of boredom would not end the sudden sound of the bell caused the townspeople to shrug of sluggishness. The bright patterns of sound formed songs that seemed familiar to them, though they could not recall ever hearing them before. On other days the bell rang slowly, forlorn notes drifting lost through the air, and each person wiped tears that fell from a secret pool of sadness.

The priest turned increasingly moody. When the bell commenced ringing in the midst of his sermon, he threw down the bible and stormed from the church in a fine show of temper. He took to standing on the corner like a beggar, shouting over the noise of the bell in an attempt to drum up some spiritual enthusiasm. His resonant voice deteriorated into a ragged croak. The townspeople would gather around him and listen with care to his words, nodding their heads many times. But when the bell began ringing their faces took on a dreamy look and their eyes glazed. "The bell is pretty," cried the priest, hoarsely. "But the voice of God is beautiful." He knew his only hope was that Benito would tire of the bell: the boy was known to take up and abandon things abruptly and for no clear reason.

However, the boy's love for the bell appeared to deepen as his body grew stronger. With each passing season he was capable of ringing the heavy bell for longer periods of time. It chimed for hours on end without pause. With a cloth Benito polished the bell until it gleamed and shone, and when the townspeople gathered in the plaza at night its light dipped and bobbed above them like a silvery star dancing on a sea. "Look," said mothers to sleepy children, pointing. "We of this town have our own star to watch over us, and we will never come to harm."

The priest knew the bell was drowning out the voice of God, not to mention his own. One day he visited the parents of Benito. "Our Benito has been blessed," he said. "There have been signs. Yet even Jesus was a fisherman. A saint must also earn pesos. Simon was a carpenter. Let us teach our Benito an honest trade. Let him go with his father out in the boats."

Benito's father was dubious. He could not easily envision his son casting out or pulling in the nets. Yet there was no easy way to disregard the priest's advice, as this sensitive man now felt every real or imagined slight against him to be the work of the devil.

So the next day Benito went out to sea. The other men in the boat grumbled. There was no place to put the boy where he was not in the way, and it was immediately obvious that he could not help with the work. The way he seemed to listen to some voice inside his head, raptly, disturbed the men. Having no balance for the sea's motion, Benito fell about with every pitch of the boat until his father tied him to the prow. There he sat still and silent.

When pulled up the nets were heavy, as though a huge mass of seaweed had become entangled in them. They rose dripping from the water, full of dancing, silver fish. The men took in the catch, then flung the nets out again. Time and again they were brought in brimming. The men became tired and the boat became crowded with flapping, squirming fish. With the last of their strength the fishermen got the loaded boat to shore.

The dark beach quickly filled with flaming torchlight. Townspeople crowded around the boat in wonder. Each helped to carry buckets of fish up to the town. It was only after they sat bloated before high plates of clean white bones that the people remembered Benito. He was untied from the prow of the boat, where he was found sleeping beneath stars all arranged in patterns of Pisces.

"Now go and ring the bell," said Benito's mother, shaking him awake. "People have been dropping by all day long, wondering why it has been silent."

As the bell began to ring out with unusual force, the priest licked his fishy fingers and said, "I think it is very clear. God approves of our Benito going out in the boats. He is offering us a gift from the sea, and who are we to turn down divine presents? Listen!" he cried. "Hear how vigorously our Benito rings the bell! He is happy to have found his calling." The priest looked around at his flock with joy, feeling the bad business of the bell was now behind him.

The townspeople were less elated. "What can it mean?" they wondered. The bell tolled in groups of five steady notes, a pattern that was repeated over and over in the most joyless and mechanical of ways. "Is Benito calling us or is he calling God? Can Benito be asking us to hear God or God to hear us? Something is wrong."

For a moment the priest was put out of countenance. Then he beamed too broadly. "Benito is simply thanking God for showing him the way. Nothing more, nothing less. The path to Eden is overgrown and difficult to follow, but the wide, smooth highways to hell are crowded with cars racing a hundred kilometres an hour. Fords, Pontiacs, Chevrolets.'' The priest's voice trailed off vaguely. "Go to bed, good people,'' he said, then abruptly turned away.

The bell chimed all night long, its notes falling like heavy rain upon the town. When dawn broke and the people rose unrested from their beds they said to one another, "Surely the boy will grow tired soon and we will have some peace and quiet.'' As the morning passed and the sound of the bell did not cease, this wonder changed to unease. Hands were held over ears and radios turned up loudly, to little avail.

The priest was devastated by this turn of events. He reminded the people that both church and state would frown on such indiscriminate use of the bell. No president had been newly elected and no holy day had arrived. What was the town celebrating but the overthrow of law and order and decency, plus more? Who could know what might be the consequences upon the outside world hearing of this shameful episode? The priest's words turned the town's uneasiness to fear, and this emotion deepened when the men returned from the sea with empty nets.

The sound of the bell, as it rang through a second night, did nothing to lessen these fears. It pealed in the same monotonous, droning way, seeming to stretch into eternity. With each note that was struck the citizens became more despairing, and soon they could not remember what silence had sounded like. Hope was lost. People ran around clutching their heads, moaning, crying. They believed they had fallen into a semblance of hell, if not the actual place. The group of men that the priest finally led up the twisting stone steps to the tower was quite frantic, and the crowd milling around the church was more so. The devil had come into their midst, and naturally they were alarmed.

The door to the tower was burst through and Benito was found rising and falling with the bell-rope he clung to. Over the clashing noise the priest shouted for him to stop. When he wouldn't, the men tried to pull him away. He clutched at the rope as though it were a lifeline, and was successfully removed from it only after some time and trouble. Then the boy with bleeding hands lay curled in a ball on the floor. Unsure what to do next, the men stood sheepishly around him.

In the town below there was a sigh of relief. Quiet at last! The people breathed in the blessed silence deeply, and it seemed the air was fresher and more fragrant than before. Once again the town was a peaceful place.

To ensure that such a scandal would not recur, the junta agreed to remove the bell from the church tower. A committee was formed to handle the job, and it took an entire day to manoeuvre the bell to the ground with an intricate system of ropes and pulleys. The problem did not rest there: something had to be done with the bell. For lack of a better idea it was set, inverted, in the largest garden of the plaza and used as a kind of fancy planter. No one was surprised that seeds sown in it would not grow.

"I refuse to call people to mass through Doña Lupita's loudspeaker," stated the priest in his usual temperamental way. "Jesus never used a microphone." Thereafter, he preached to a nearly empty church, and his voice echoed in a hollow-sounding style through the dark, gloomy building. "Oh, I can never remember mass without the bell," exclaimed the townspeople, with their old, unconvincing shows of regret.

Those who did sit in the church prayed and sang in a half-hearted manner. They could hear their fellow citizens cavorting in the plaza just beyond the door. With no bell to call Him, they felt God had no way of knowing when to listen to them. Dutifully they closed their eyes and tilted their faces upward. Sometimes it seemed the only person who could hear their prayers was the boy in the tower above.

That Benito continued to haunt the tower after the removal of the bell soothed the consciences of the more delicate-souled citizens. They remarked that the boy did not appear to miss the bell, or even notice it was gone. Perhaps all this time he had been going up to the church tower for reasons other than the bell. Perhaps he enjoyed the fine, panoramic view afforded by the tower, and had rung the bell merely because it had happened to be there.

In fact, Benito spent more time in the tower than ever before.

He often slept there, and gradually made it his home. Twice a day the priest, breathing hard, climbed the spiral staircase, a pot of beans and tortillas in hand. Often in early evening, when talking and playing and romancing in the plaza, the townspeople looked up and saw Benito. The boy leaned against the stone wall which enclosed the tower at the height of his chest, resting his elbows upon it. He gazed down at the plaza, but because of dark and distance the people there could not tell if he looked with longing or curiosity or boredom. Yet the sight of the boy watching over them was reassuring, and when they woke in the middle of silent nights the thought of the boy in the tower was as comforting as the sound of the bell had once been.

One May, when the hills were burned and bananas planted in expectation of rain, a truck-load of goods was brought to the town by the salesman who travelled around the villages of that area. Among the kitchen implements and clothes were a number of small, silver bells. Little children snatched these up. It became the vogue for them to shake the bells constantly as they ran about in their games. The bells were the sort of cheap, inexpensive trinket that breaks as quickly as a child's passion for it dies.

The town was filled with a tinkling sound, as though wind was chiming in the trees. Unlike the heavy, overwhelming sound of the church bell, these small bells rang bright, light notes. The sound was pleasing to the citizens: it was not loud enough to disturb them; yet, except when by a breeze stolen away across the sea, it could always be heard if listened for.

When Benito came running down the steps of the tower and out onto the street the townspeople were surprised to see how big he had grown. He chased the little children and wrenched the toys from their hands, in several instances causing some minor injuries. The children ran screaming and crying to their mothers. After Benito dashed back up to the tower, his arms full of silver bells, a crowd of women gathered angrily around the church. They felt the boy was now a threat to their childrens' safety.

For several days the little bells rang continuously in the tower. Each hour the silver sound became more faint, as though one by one a flock of singing birds was flying from the town, deserting it for some sweeter climate. Without realizing it, the townspeople listened for this dimming sound with increasing attention as they went about their daily chores. Even the priest's voice trailed into silence in the middle of mass, as he too stopped to listen.

In the heart of one night the townspeople awoke as one. No dogs barked and the cocks did not crow. Each person lay in his bed, hearing only the sound of his own heart beating in a void of silence. Very quietly, without lighting candles or switching on electricity, the people left their houses and gathered in the plaza. They met there with no exclamations of fear or wonder or amazement, as though this meeting had been planned long in advance. Crowded around the big, old poppy tree in the square's centre, they looked up to the church tower. It was dark and quiet. "He could be sleeping," whispered one voice. "He could be watching us," whispered another. The townspeople turned to the priest.

Several minutes later a black shadow floated slowly back to them. "He's gone," said the priest.

"Did he jump or did he fall?" cried a woman.

The priest held out his hand. Several little bells rested in it. They were broken, their clappers fallen off because shaken too roughly. With a curious expression the priest shook the little bells. When they made no noise, he smiled. "The sky is empty," said the people of the town, in clear voices of wonder.

There was never any word of Benito after his disappearance. The town junta considered reinstating the big bell to its old place in the tower, but in the end no action was taken. The body supposed the bell was no longer capable of ringing after its months spent filled with dirt. It stayed on the ground, though the priest berated the people for their sinful laziness. "If you cannot lift a bell to a tower, how can you expect to raise your souls to heaven?" was his plaint.

"Bell or no bell, if He takes the trouble God can find us. He knows where we are, and we certainly don't intend to move," remarked the townspeople, carelessly slapping at mosquitoes. The town became known for its lack of a bell, and derided by neighbouring villages because of this fact.

The townspeople were unconcerned. On those early evenings when without end sounds carried through the clear air
they gathered in the plaza, young and old alike, to play or
promenade or just sit. They laughed and shouted, talked and
sang, and how their voices rang like bells! "It's so peaceful,"
they said, with voices full of love for their place of birth and
death. "So tranquil."

In and out of season yellow poppies grew on the old drooping tree in the centre of the square. Sitting on benches beneath
its wide, stretching arms, the townspeople brushed fallen
blossoms off their heads now and then, without thinking.
Yellow poppies fell silently and lay like a carpet of snow on
the ground. "Oh, yes, it's always February, and poppies
always fall," the people of the town remarked, when asked
about the tree.

Mariposo, Butterfly

Fernando was born in a house on the main street of town during the time when this road was not paved. He opened his eyes to find a world where the light seemed too bright and the sun too strong. The baby squinted. Recalling a dimmer place, he crawled into the caves of shadows in the corners of the room. Later he was able to stand at the front window and watch people of the town pass up and down the street. He would not play with other small children in the dirt, and when he saw big boys, wet and dripping from their work in the sea, he took flight, running in fear to his mother. "Mariposo, butterfly," the boys would call after him, their voices floating like bright pools of colour through the air.

Fernando's mother looked at her son as though at something she wanted to forget. She would push away the crying, clinging child, and in a corner of the room he played with scraps of cloth or any odd thing of colour that fell his way. The look and feel of the things he turned over in his hands reminded Fernando of something, and he tried to remember. He learned to sit quietly for long periods of time in order to avoid his mother's notice. But sooner or later she turned from the mirror and saw her son. "Go out and play," she said, sometimes gently, sometimes angrily. "All the other children are playing outside, they don't sit beneath their mothers' feet." But no matter how she pleaded or threatened, Fernando would not go willingly from the house. His mother pushed him outside and locked the door against him. Fernando sat on the steps, trembling with every breath of breeze that brushed by. He waited for the door to open.

His dreams were darker than the nights he slept through. Yet he sensed that just beyond the blackness colours flashed and splashes of sound spoke words which on the day of awakening would tell him what he wanted to know. But when words woke him it was still dark and only his mother's voice could be heard, speaking from across the big bedroom. He could not hear what she said, but only the sound of her voice, angry and biting as the mosquitoes that buzzed in his ears and would not go away. He heard his father's voice, too, deeper and darker and sadder; and though he could not hear his name spoken, Fernando knew it was of himself his mother and father talked.

One morning his father took Fernando by the hand. He led his son from the town and up into the banana fields scattered over the lower hills. While his father worked with other men nearby, Fernando played with sticks and stones at the edge of the clearing. He talked and sang songs, and his voice was the sound of a friend. A white circle of sun was pulled higher into the sky by God.

The jungle that surrounded the clearing was dark green and crowded. Vines and trees clung together in fear and love. Beneath leaves and twigs snakes slipped so secretly and quickly that no one could follow them to learn where they went. Strange birds flapped huge wings close above Fernando, beating air against his face; and he waited for them to swoop down, snatch him in their claws, and carry him through blue sky. The town would appear small beneath him, and he would wave goodbye, so long to everyone below, to his mother leaning on her broom in the doorway. People would turn their faces upward and point to Fernando, watching until the birds carried him out of sight, high above the sea, away forever.

Fernando opened his eyes. His father's glistening back was no longer in sight. He was gone. Machetes rang in the distance like the churchbell, calling. Fernando waited for an answer. Then butterflies danced through the air above his head, just out of reach.

They were big and beautiful and unlike the faded butterflies Fernando had seen in the town. Through the shaded air they floated, in and out of the tangled jungle, feeding from bright blossoms that shone like watching eyes. Fernando bit into a jungle flower and waited for brilliant colours to spread across his dull, brown skin. His arms would become wide and thin, and on paper wings he would fly away. But the flower tasted bitter and ugly, and only pain spread through his body.

When the sun began to fall past the edge of the clearing and into the jungle beyond, the butterflies followed its light and warmth. One by one they vanished through the wall of green, and one by one the ringing machetes fell silent. Shadows stretched into dark, which crept up to Fernando from all sides, then swallowed him. He stayed very still. From the enclosing blackness his father appeared, sudden and near. When father and son returned hand in hand down the hills the town lay pricked with lights before them.

Fernando went up into the hills with his father every day for three years. He never disturbed his father's work and never wandered into the jungle that enclosed the clearings. Time floated by on butterfly wings. Fernando listened to the breathing jungle and watched it grow, and he grew, too. He came to know each butterfly that lived in the hills: their names, the members of their families, the stories of their lives. At night, in his bed in town, Fernando's sleep was no longer black, but full of vividly coloured and flickering dreams.

One day he saw a butterfly unlike any he had ever seen. It was so beautiful. Fernando had to turn his eyes from its blinding colour, for his pounding heart threatened to swoop through his throat and up into the cool blue air, away from him. But he had to look, and he turned back to see the butterfly floating from the clearing and into the jungle. Fernando was seized by a longing to see clearly and closely this thing of beauty, and he yearned to touch it just once, just gently.

He ran from the clearing, following the beautiful butterfly. He stumbled and tripped through thick leaves and beneath hanging vines. As he entered the jungle farther, the light grew green and dark, but not like night. Just at the point where his vision was obscured by dimness and distance, the butterfly shone. Deeper into the jungle it led Fernando; stronger grew his desire to hold within his arms its beating wings, and to know for one moment the reason for his own beating, bursting heart.

When Fernando became too tired to take many more steps the jungle opened into a small clearing. This was not made by man's machetes, but formed by a stream falling over stones and into a small, clear pool. The light in the clearing was silver, as clean as the splashing water.

Above the silver pool the air was thick with butterflies, a glittering, glistening pattern of colour and light and movement. The butterflies merged together, drew apart; they drifted down near the pool to see their beauty reflected in its mirror, they soared high toward the ceiling of jungle to escape this vision of themselves. On jewelled blossoms they fed, and then they slept.

Fernando gazed greedily upon the sight, for the first time hearing the voice he had awaited so long; and this voice said that such a moment would not last and would not be found again, though searched for always.

When his father found Fernando the moon was high in the sky. But it was dark beneath the jungle. The boy was sitting beside the stream, awake. He had heard his father calling him for many minutes: where are you? where are you? But Fernando had not cried out in answer, knowing what his voice would kill besides the sleep of butterflies. And when his father hit him again and again, Fernando saw colours flashing before his eyes, red and blue and purple, scattering through the dark. Then they were gone, and there was only the blackness, the sobbing of the stream, and the sobbing of his father beside it.

Now Fernando stayed down in the dry, faded town that had grown strange to him. He was frightened of the white sun. It sucked the colour from the houses and streets, and from the boy's memories, too. When Fernando began to attend the school across the street the other children did not know him, and between themselves they built high walls of friendship he could not climb over or break through. Still, he remained in the classroom for more years than any boy before, long after the others left the smell of chalk for work in the sea or hills. Fernando grew used to the high, clear voices of girls around him, their freshly washed dresses and skin and hair.

After the school day ended in early afternoon Fernando crossed the street to his house. Within the darkened rooms his mother moved, caught in a trance cast by a gleam of pots and pans, the glow of the fire, the splash of water in the sink. Fernando's presence did not waken her, but when she looked at him there were questions in her eyes: who was this boy? where had he come from? what did he want?

Fernando sat with a book inside the doorway, partly hidden by shadow. He looked at the page before him, then at the street beyond. It was nearly empty during this hottest time of the day, with people away working, or resting on their beds until the air cooled. Now and then a single figure would tread slowly down the baking streets: a man returning early from the plantations, his machete flashing in the sun; a boy coming up from the sea, a bucket of oysters hanging heavily from one arm. "Mariposo, butterfly," the boy would call sleepily, and Fernando would raise his eyes to the hills.

Sometimes butterflies trembled down the street, paler and smaller than those of the hills and jungle. Over hot dust and in harsh sunlight they fluttered weakly, searching without hope for sweet nectar. Fernando's eyes followed them until they moved out of sight. Then he turned down to the book resting on his lap. He fell into worlds of words, lands far away and different from the town, countries to which no one he knew had ever journeyed and which a voice that now spoke more loudly and often inside him said he too would never see. There was always an end to the words, the brilliant lands would drift away like clouds, leaving only the hot white sun, the empty street, the dogs asleep in the shade.

In the hour before dark, when the air softened, a butterfly would infrequently float down from the hills. Large and brilliant, it showed off its beauty, causing the butterflies of the town to look smaller and paler, and the town to look more drab. When Fernando saw such a butterfly he would chase it, run after the colours it recalled to him. But always at the edge of town the butterfly dipped, swirled, then vanished, snatched up by a greedy god. Fernando walked slowly back to his chair inside the doorway, not hearing the voices calling around him: mariposo, butterfly.

While darkness was falling Fernando's father returned from his work on the hills. With eyes glazed from toiling through the hot hours he would walk past his son in the doorway without seeing him. He fell upon the big bed in the back room, and at once deep breaths of sleep spread their sound through the house. Fernando listened, certain that in this way his father was speaking to him. Yet he could never understand what these words might be.

When night and cooling air arrived the main street became crowded with music and people playing beneath streetlamps. Tacos sizzled and dogs barked, and from the noise butterflies fled to the outskirts of town. They folded wings and rested rocking on broad leaves, swayed by breezes that rose up from the sea.

From behind the window Fernando watched bands of boys and tight clusters of girls roam down the street toward the plaza. With his mother he sat near the lamp, listening to the voice of his father's sleep speak into the dark corners of the house. His mother stitched the cloth that rested on her knees. When she pricked her finger and cried out, she remembered Fernando. "Go out and walk with the others," she said, speaking low and fast and fearfully. But Fernando would not often stir. As the hour grew later the groups of boys and girls mixed together, then splintered into pairs of male and female, pressed against a stone wall on the dark end of the street.

On rare occasions some unseen hand or unheard voice would push Fernando outside. He found himself floating above the street, trying and failing to touch his feet to the ground. He could not become familiar with the piece of earth on which he lived; its contours, rough and smooth, did not learn the feeling of his step; and Fernando and the town remained strangers. Sharp eyes of boys and girls pierced through him, their pins drove into him, and in pain and fear of capture he would beat his wings, attempt escape. Yet though his heart raced and leapt, he could not fly away, and with bruised and broken wings he fluttered lamely back to the house. Cries of "mariposo, butterfly" pinned him inside it. He pressed against the window pane.

So Fernando lived until the age of seventeen, and as the

seasons passed one by one the boys and girls his age married, set up house, and new babies played in the dirt. The time came for Fernando to leave school, for there was nothing more the teacher could tell him, and already he was full of knowledge that had no place in the town.

His father died, a body worn and scratched as an old record, and the house became a silent place. There were no more sleeping breaths of words, and Fernando knew he would never learn what his father could have told him. Fernando and his mother did not grow closer, but in separate, widening orbits moved around the house.

Fernando's mother was advised to turn the large front room of the house into a store: its location on the main street, just across from the school and three doors down from the movie house, was excellent. She was indifferent to the details of business, and from the start her son ran the place. He stocked a little of everything, so supplying the small, daily needs of the townspeople. But the greatest part of the trade was in candy.

From the capital city Fernando ordered a variety of candy the like of which the town had never seen before. Bright colours shone in the dim store. Gazing into the rising steam, Fernando's mother stirred bubbling pans of caramel and fudge in the back room, and the rich smell drifted across the street to the children in the classroom. They skipped over at recess to fill themselves with coloured candy, they buzzed like flies around the sugar. The store was always crowded with little children clutching flat, dull pesos that could be exchanged for something sweet and rainbow coloured. The kids sometimes stood frozen in awe and indecision, mouths open wide, fingers pointing. "I want," they said, losing themselves in long moments of complete desire. Fernando moved quietly amid the vivid sounds and colours of the children, giving them what they wanted, and watching them place the red and blue and purple candies upon their tongues. Inside their mouths the colours melted, and then the children flew from Fernando and through the afternoon. At night their parents stopped in and bought treats to savour secretly in the darkness of the movie house. The store did good business, yes, and Fernando and his mother prospered.

One afternoon Fernando was drowsing before the store when he heard the clopping of a horse's hooves approach down the main street, which was now paved. Both horse and rider looked hot and tired; and the animal's hair was matted and stiff, showing it had sweated then dried many times, as on the course of a long, hard journey. The rider's hair was blonde, an unusual colour in the town, and one found more often in Jalisco, a southern state. It was said those people were so blessed because God looked upon them with special favour, touching them with a smile that turned their heads to gold. Fernando stared at the locks of the rider, glinting and dazzling in the sun, obscuring the features of the face beneath them.

The rider dismounted in front of the store and asked for water. Fernando fetched a bucket, and horse and rider drank deeply. The stranger did not say from where he had come or what had brought him to the town. He was silent. As horse and rider moved off, Fernando stared after them, one hand touching his own thick, black hair.

That evening Fernando did not appear his usual inexpressive self. His attention seemed troubled: often he did not hear what customers demanded of him; several times he gave back incorrect change, a very rare mistake. He sat up late, long after the movie ended and the street emptied. In the darkest hour his mother woke to the sound of weeping. She touched her cheeks, and found them dry. Stealing from her room, she discovered Fernando pressed against the front window. He turned once toward his mother behind him, then looked again at what he saw out in the deserted street. Down near the end of the block yellow light clung around a lamp post. The mother returned to sleep, and when she woke at morning her son was gone.

Fernando climbed the trail that led up into the hills, the same path he had followed with his father, when a child. He walked quickly and steadily, not pausing to look at the jungle and blossoms and birds around him, the sights he had been without for so many years. He brushed impatiently past vines that hung in his way, and snakes slid from the noise of his footsteps.

He climbed higher, and the air turned cooler and clearer.

Earth and plants smelled rich and damp. Suddenly the colours surrounding Fernando splashed against his face, like a slap of cold water that wakens a sleeper. Look! Look! called the birds; the boy's steps slowed. In wonder he gazed at the jungle, trying to remember when he had seen it before, and what it had meant to him then. He began to breathe quickly, not only from exertion.

In the years of his absence the butterflies had grown more large and beautiful, and they were more numerous, too. As Fernando climbed they came to fill the air; and God was shaking heavenly trees, sending blossoms to float and flutter down, red and purple and blue. Three times a butterfly brushed its wings against Fernando's face, and the youth gasped. A powder clung to his skin, like the tattoo of a touch. Dazzled by the swirl of colour, Fernando climbed on, not noticing when he left the trail to enter the jungle.

A singing voice flowed on and on. When the jungle fell away to clearing Fernando halted, but the silver song drew him forward. Then another sound, louder, filled his ears.

All around him wings beat against cocoons. New wings unfolded and stretched in sighs of pleasure, feeling for the first time their strength and grace. From all sides they reached toward Fernando and merged as one, enfolding him. At their touch his clothes melted away, and wings quivered against bare skin, trembling with contained power. Fernando closed his eyes, the dull ache of long years dissolving into a sharper pain. The movement of the wings grew stronger; they beat against the young man's body with a strength that would surely rip and tear, and then they beat harder. Caught within the long, loving embrace, Fernando could no longer breathe.

The butterfly arms dropped him and Fernando fell to the ground beside the silver pool. In the moment before he fell asleep he saw his reflection shining in the water. Behind his red and blue and purple image was mirrored one figure of gold.

Later, the air was cold; then the light in the clearing was dimming fast. Fernando roused his aching body, found in a nearby place his crumpled clothes, and covered the coloured bruises with them. He walked over a carpet of fallen, torn, and mangled butterfly wings, which rustled like dead leaves as they were crushed beneath his step. Through the ceiling of thick jungle no light of moon or stars could penetrate, and Fernando went in darkness. Despite this lack of light he made his way surely and steadily down the hills. He walked heavily, treading unaware on worms that slowly crawled over the earth they were imprisoned upon.

Years passed secretly, and Fernando was known as a steady young man, a hard worker, a good son. As his mother grew older she spent more of her days in the rooms behind the store, and was so infrequently seen that when she died Fernando did not appear to be left more alone.

Upon his mother's passing Fernando altered the large front room that housed the store, installing a long, low counter before which a number of stools were placed. Behind the bar he built a small kitchen consisting of cupboards, a two-burner gas stove, and a cooler. In one corner of the room there was a jukebox, and scattered around it were chairs and a few small tables. Fernando strung coloured lights along the ceiling above the bar, and also crepe paper streamers, which dropped listlessly, waiting for a breeze to flutter them.

The candy store was gone. From the start, though for no discernible reason, small children and young girls and adults did not frequent the changed place. It became a meeting spot for the town's teenaged boys, a kind of club. At the counter the boys sat with tortas and chocomilk, which Fernando sold to them at prices lower than were common in town. Often the boys neither ate not drank, but just lounged in the chairs, listening to the jukebox and smoking cigarettes. They would lean against the doorway of the place, calling out to girls who passed down the main street.

The place was not nearly as profitable as the store had been; but although some people wondered at the change, they did not question the silent, solitary man. It was good that the boys, when too old and restless to remain in their mothers' kitchens, had a place to go. People were used to the quiet man, and they did not ask themselves why he did not take a wife, why he remained alone.

No, the townspeople did not remark upon Fernando until the first Sunday he locked the door of his place and ventured through the early morning streets with a wicker basket in one hand, a new straw hat upon his head, and a blue scarf around his neck. "I am going up into the hills," he replied to those who questioned him; and all that day people wondered. Fernando is going to meet his love, they told one another at once, then proceeded to envision who this might be. When their imaginations failed them, people remembered the voices which sometimes called down from the western slopes, those familiar voices of loved ones long passed from the town. Fernando is going to meet the ones who have gone from us, some people said, and when he returns he will tell us news of them.

By evening Fernando had been forgotten as the townspeople busily prepared themselves for church and the dance that would follow. The bell rang and rang at dusk, calling for evening mass, and the sound floated up the hills, drawing Fernando back down. He returned to town when night was dark and lights were lit. The band was tuning up for the dance, and down the main street Fernando passed through crowds of people dressed in their Sunday finest. No one noticed him enough to ask what old ghosts he had seen upon the hills.

In his room Fernando opened the picnic basket and drew out butterflies, tenderly, as though in death they could still feel the touch of hands. The next day a truck arrived from the capital city, and many glass cases were unloaded from it and placed in Fernando's front room. Each Sunday during the following months Fernando went up into the hills to fetch more butterflies. Slowly he filled the glass cases on his walls with images of frozen flight, while outside the Sunday cries grew louder, drunker, wilder. No matter how brilliant the specimens he had captured that day, Fernando's eyes were always most still at this time. One Sunday he did not go up into the hills. Whether he had lost interest in his butterfly collection or felt it complete, no one asked; but Fernando did not climb the western slopes again.

For a time, when passing Fernando's place, people would look through the doorway at the butterflies arranged neatly upon the walls, and shining there. They thought it very wonderful and curious that someone would trouble to catch such things, offer them death without flurried struggles of wings, then display them as if they were each a Virgin. He has every one in the world! marvelled the people; and it was true that from this time all butterflies seemed vanished from the air. Then the townspeople no longer paused in Fernando's doorway. He is the butterfly man, they shrugged.

Beneath the butterflies sat sullen boys, the bright beach shorts they wore more splashes of colour in the dark. Their skin glowed, their teeth shone like moonlight. They laughed and made jokes which carried only between themselves before dying. Sometimes they carved their initials into the tabletops, carefully scarring those surfaces. But the boys took little notice of the man whose features slowly blurred with something more than fat.

With time the butterfly man left his place less frequently, finally venturing out into the streets only to buy food or other necessities. Days in the dim room made his eyes narrow when confronted by sunlight. Through cracks he saw women, whom he remembered as little girls standing in trances before his candy, now pulled and pinched by their circles of greedy children. The butterfly man! cried the little children, catching sight of Fernando. The butterfly man can fly! they cried, waiting for him to soar into the air and dance above their heads, then lead them away to some place of colour. Fly! Fly! the children pleaded, and Fernando walked quickly from their voices, trying not to run.

Every year the world turned more slowly. The records on the jukebox became outdated and scratched, and played less often. Faded, wilted, the crepe paper streamers hung like cobwebs from the ceiling. The boys who came to Fernando's place were sons of boys who long ago had called after him down the street: mariposo, butterfly. Fernando still tended the place both day and night, though more and more he seemed to be dozing in his chair. The place was mostly empty and quiet during daytime, for through these hours the boys dove for oysters in the sea. At night, too, there was little business after the town went to its early bed. But during those late, lonely hours Fernando still waited in his chair inside the doorway, even after midnight when the door was closed.

Sometimes at three or four in the morning, when all the town was dark except for the flickering light in his window, Fernando would be awakened by hammering. The wings of his heart beat wildly for one moment. He unlocked the door and let in a pair of boys come up from the beach. Their hair was dripping and their eyes dazed with spent love. While the boys dozed at a table, their heads resting on pillows of arms, Fernando moved quickly over the stove. Without a word he fixed them something to eat, and he was bathed in the changing colours of the strings of lights: red and purple and blue.

As Fernando placed tortas and Cokes on the table, the two boys wakened. Reaching for the food, one boy seemed to brush against the aging man. Fernando blinked, the way people do when a bright light is switched on suddenly in darkness. His body trembled, almost imperceptibly, only for a moment. The boy's sharp eyes caught this movement he had caused, and he whispered softly, gently to the man. Mariposo, butterfly. Then with the other boy he laughed.

Fernando stood still behind his counter, beneath his cages of glass. Sometimes, in the blinking of the coloured lights above, the nearby butterflies seemed to move, though pinned.

Heaven, Hell, and
Some Points Inbetween

Chileno searched the town high and low, but he could not find his brother. "Have you seen Tomás?" he asked children playing jacks in the plaza. "I don't know where he's gone," he explained to men gathered beneath acacias blooming beside the church. "Tomás might be in trouble," he told women lounging in doorways. "Where can he be?"

Several boys stood on the corner at the end of the street. Chileno's pulse quickened at the sight of their black heads and brown backs. But as he neared the boys his blood slowed in sadness. He stared silently at this group that did not include his brother, as though hoping a boy would be transformed before his eyes into the shape he longed to see.

The townspeople watched Chileno comb the burning afternoon streets as carefully as a mother searches her child's head for lice. "Since it's hot as hell right here, that devil Tomás must be close by," they told each other. Every day thick black clouds pushed in from the sea and rested against the hills above the town, pressing down on the earth parched by a long season of sun. Though the clouds promised rain, the heavens would not open. The heavy air held the townspeople in place like a firm hand, and they fidgeted restlessly, their irritation increased by the invisible nature of the bonds upon them.

People advised Chileno to relax in a hammock with some cold beer. "Blood is thicker than water, but less refreshing," they pointed out. "This April heat is trying enough without the presence of bad brothers. Don't waste your prayers on that terrible Tomás. Hope for rain instead. Tomás will never come to harm. His kind never do, and they always come back, too."

Aside from his unrelenting concern for his brother, Chileno was thought to be a fine young man. He was tall and strong, and a hard worker besides. "What a waste," sighed mothers of unmarried daughters. "He would make any girl a handsome husband. Save for his one little quirk, Chileno is a model young man." Women spent idle hours puzzling how they could erase the picture of Tomás from his brother's heart and replace it with a portrait of a lonely daughter.

It was only too well known that Tomás often hid in some nook or cranny, then laughed himself all the way to heaven at the sight of his brother's fruitless searching. Young devils, friends of Tomás, sometimes ran to Chileno with tragic tales: Tomás has had his throat slit by a switchblade; Tomás has been run over by a truck; Tomás is drowning in the sea. Then the boys rolled upon the ground in delight of Chileno's foolish fear.

Screams rang nightly through the late, lonely streets. "Help me! Help me!" Tomás would cry, and Chileno stumbled sleepily to his brother's aid. Chileno would take his brother's side in losing battles which he didn't understand, while Tomás deserted the fights, laughing and leaving Chileno outnumbered. Later, his lip split and his cheek bruised, Chileno would find Tomás nestled with a bottle or a girl beneath a tree. Still breathing heavily from the fight, Chileno gazed with love into his brother's dancing eyes. Dark leaves, shining in the moonlight, fell between the two brothers.

After all the afternoon streets had been searched and Tomás not found, Chileno called his brother's name. "Tomás! Tomás!" he called in a persistent, hopeless way. Feeling a kind of shame, the people of the town went inside their houses and turned on radios to drown out the young man's cries. But Chileno shouted loudly, as if trying to call to heaven. "Where is my brother?" he called, and this question echoed in the hearts of all who heard it.

The priest dashed out from the church, glancing fearfully at the black sky above. The street was dark, though night was yet far away. "I have heard your cry, and so has God," he told Chileno. The priest looked with pity at the young man, whose face was lined before its time by overwork and worry. "You are sad when you look for your brother and sadder when you find him. Listen, my son: if you must carry a heavy cross, at least choose one made from strong, sweet-smelling wood. Jesus didn't burden himself with a rotten board teeming with termites, did he?" The priest leaned confidentially toward Chileno. "Of course we don't like to admit it," he whispered. "But let's face facts. We cannot all be saved. Some of us go up and some go down. Put down your crooked cross. Remember, the fires of hell require fuel just like any other flames."

The sky rumbled and grumbled, and the priest ran back into the shelter of the church. "Tomás is my brother," Chileno said slowly to himself, as though in explanation. He passed down the empty street toward his mother's house.

This was a shabby four-room place across from the school. The large front room served as a store, and Señora Lizama's family was crowded uncomfortably into three small rooms behind. Though she fancied herself a devoted businesswoman and worshipped commerce, Señora Lizama ran her store in a careless, profit-draining style. Also, being highly strung and nervous, she often offended her fellow townspeople and potential customers, causing them to take their trade elsewhere. A subsequent lack of capital prevented Señora Lizama from acquiring a stock of any size at all, and the shelves of her store were more empty than full. The few goods on hand were old, stale, and covered with dust.

Señora Lizama was sweeping the floor in a fiery fashion. It seemed she was more intent upon disturbing the dirt than ridding the room of it. Dust flew like a desert sandstorm, swirling over a figure crouched in one corner. Upon observing her oldest son, Señora Lizama continued sweeping as though immersed in her life's main passion. "My accounts," she suddenly said in a theatrical way. She bustled over to the counter and sat on a little stool. With short-sighted intentness she squinted at a piece of paper covered with a muddled array of marks and symbols. Muttering numbers beneath her breath, Señora Lizama frowned with businesslike concern.

"Have you seen Tomás?" asked Chileno at last.

Señora Lizama looked up, feigning surprise. "My favourite son!" she cried maternally. "What is wrong? You look so tired."

His sharp, shining machete hung forgotten in Chileno's hand. "We were working in Ramirez's fields, cutting the last of the cane. We swung our machetes and our arms ached. It was hot, and sweat turned the dust on our faces to mud. We were working side by side."

"Who is we?" asked Señora Lizama, a note of fear entering her voice.

"I could see by my brother's eyes how tired he was, how much he longed to sleep on sheets or play in the sea. He is less strong than I. Don't lose heart, little brother, I told him. The day of work is almost done, and as long as we are together it is not so bad. But I'm thirsty, he said. I'll go down to the creek for a drink of water, then I'll come back and work some more. Tomás went away, but he didn't come back."

"Rest," commanded Señora Lizama, jumping up and pushing her son into one of the little chairs that littered the room. She fanned Chileno briskly with a comic book. "We're both tired, you and me. We work too hard. Tomás is like his father there, he thinks if he rests long enough he'll have the strength to fly to heaven. Count your blessings that your father was different than this old man." Señora Lizama shouted at the figure in the corner: "Wake up, old fool! Ramón! Jesus has come to carry you away!" However, the figure did not stir.

Señora Lizama observed the sadness in her son's eyes with irritation. Quelling this emotion, she spoke soothingly to him. "You work like a slave and save all your money in that box beneath your bed. But your money doesn't make you happy. Investments bring joy. My store is just crying out for some snappy investor with sense enough to sink some pesos into a going concern. I'll make you a partner. Put some cash into this business and you'll receive a high return of happiness. Think! We'll have the largest store in town. We'll sell cameras, cake mixes, and TV trays. People will stand in line to buy our fancy goods. We'll be the envy of our neighbours. We'll vacation in Puerto Vallarta when we're not too busy flying around on airplanes and cheering at bullfights. We'll eat oysters by the sea."

Señora Lizama chattered on with her most engaging airs. Chileno gazed searchingly into the dark corners of the room. His eyes came to rest upon the figure of his stepfather, who still crouched against the wall. The old man's clothes were shabby and stained, and his bare feet crusted with dirt and scars. His head rested on his thin knees.

Señora Lizama followed her son's gaze. "Oh," she exclaimed. "Ramón knows enough to stay out of my way and to keep quiet. What else is he good for? He's too old to work and too tired to laugh. The only things he's ever given me have been Tomás and trouble. Look how skinny he is! He's sick, he's dying, but he's taking his sweet time, hanging around as long as he can because he likes to spoil my ambitions. But your father! Oh, Chileno, your father was young and so handsome. He was never tired. He worked all day, then took me dancing all night. And always laughing!"

"Tomás?" mumbled Ramón, peering at Chileno.

"If I knew he was free from danger that would be enough," Chileno said slowly. "I don't need to be with him or talk with him, but only know he's safe."

Señora Lizama's patience failed her. "Actually, I saw Tomás myself just an hour ago. He burst in here, changed his clothes, then flew back out the door. Said he was going to the sinful city. Who knows when he'll be back? When he needs more money, that's when!"

"I must find him." Chileno went into the back rooms and pulled a box from beneath a bed. He took several banknotes from his pocket to add to the ones already inside the box. However, upon opening it, he found his box empty.

Señora Lizama ran to her son and threw her arms around him. "Don't go," she begged. "Stay. Stay with me. Be my partner. Let Tomás lose himself far from home. We don't need him. We'll put gay curtains on the windows and grow flowers by the door. You'll see. You'll be so happy you'll think you're in heaven. Chileno, you'll laugh even when you're sleeping."

"Our little house," said her son, looking into the empty box. "I was saving that money to buy a little house for us."

"Don't be silly," trilled Señora Lizama. "Enough jokes, my precious son. What do we need a little house for? If you invest in my store, we'll be rich enough to buy a castle in Spain. Big house, big drinks, big laughs. Everything big, and nothing little."

"Our little house," repeated Chileno dreamily. "We would live together, Tomás and me. Just us two. We would never be apart. I'd take care of Tomás and he would never want to wander out into the wide, wide world again. He'd stay at home forever."

"Fool!" sneered Señora Lizama. "Your money's gone, isn't it? Take two guesses who's eloped with it. I'll tell you. Tomás stole it. I saw him take it and I never said a word. I don't need your money. There are plenty of financiers who beg daily for the chance to sink their silver into my store. You can kiss your chance goodbye. Find yourself another place to sleep while you're at it. I'm turning these rooms into offices and storage spaces. There'll be no more sons sleeping in my house. And take that old man with you. One fool deserves another!"

Señora Lizama ran to her bed and fell crying upon it. She heard her son's footsteps fade away. Shortly, she rose and retrieved a movie magazine from beneath her pillow. Opening its pages, she looked at the banknotes cached between them.

Señora Lizama started, dropping the magazine. The banknotes fluttered to the floor like falling leaves. "Ignacio!" she cried to her first husband above. "Why did you die and leave me? You weren't sick and you weren't old. Did you fly away just to leave me here alone with shadows? Oh, how can you laugh in heaven, seeing my sorrow here?"

Señora Lizama stared at the empty beds of her sons, which were jammed together in a small space between the cramped kitchen and the bathroom. She went out into the front room and looked around it unhappily. Old Ramón was still leaning against the wall, and though his mouth opened and closed, no sounds issued from it.

"This is the last straw!" screamed Señora Lizama, swooping down upon the old man. She herded him toward the door, speeding his progress with pokes and jabs of her broom. "Out!

Out! All of you, out!" she cried. Then she sat down at the counter and formed plans, her hands pressed tightly against her ears, against the mocking laughter which now seemed to issue from beneath her feet.

Several weeks later Chileno returned to the town. He did not appear rested by his holiday from the hot fields; on the contrary, his face looked more lined and drawn. "Did you find Tomás?" people cried to him as he walked the streets. "Where is your brother?" Chileno answered only with a grim, forced laugh that sounded more painful than any of his sad calls ever had.

Chileno took up with the town's young idlers, pulling pranks and wreaking havoc. He drank and caroused at all hours in the most joyless and disturbing way. "Where has our sweet, sad young man gone?" wondered the people of the town, when woken late at night by Chileno yelling and swearing in the street. "Chileno is now worse than Tomás ever was." He became involved in fights, deliberately placing himself at poor odds against other young men of the town; and only when beaten upon the ground did he seem released from the grasp of an evil spirit. He did not go to his mother's house, but slept where he fell on the street.

During daytime Chileno no longer worked on the hills, but continued his drinking and swearing, weaving like a sick snake over the hot dust. Often he would stagger by his stepfather, who was also homeless now. After being driven from his corner by Señora Lizama, Ramón had wandered lost through the town for several days. In pity distant relations had taken the old man in and passed him among themselves, sharing a family duty. However, Ramón preferred to sleep on a bench in the plaza and eat how he could than to curl up in a cousin's kindness. He stumbled through the streets morning, noon, and night, searching for his old corner in his old house, not seeming to notice he passed the place twenty times a day.

It was no wonder Ramón could not recognize his former home. The business had been transformed almost overnight into an impressive, modern affair, complete with all the most expensive goods and elegant fittings. Señora Lizama hired a girl to keep the place immaculate and to handle the actual sales; as owner, she contented herself with keeping accounts and talking constantly of mergers, stocks, and quarterly interest. When asked the reason for her swift success, Señora Lizama offered intimations of silent partners, government holdings, and company boards. Plus more.

The townspeople were fascinated by Señora Lizama's store, but unfortunately few of them had means to buy its costly wares. Yet they thronged the aisles for hours on end, oohing and aahing and touching the goods. The store was more entertaining than a circus. There was always a crowd on the sidewalk before it, pressing faces against the glass windows, pointing to what they vowed to have the day their ships came in. As days passed and the air turned hotter, people stopped praying for rain and hoped instead for things inside Señora Lizama's store to fall into their hands.

Attired in a smart suit, heels, and several strings of beads, Señora Lizama would not deign to discuss fully the scandal of her family situation, which was the talk of the town and, in fact, one reason for the large interest in her store. "Though I follow the commercial course of life, my heart is not for sale," was all the businesswoman would allow. Observant eyes, however, noticed her mouth curl cruelly whenever Ramón or Chileno wandered into the throng outside the store. Only once when pressed by the inquisitive townspeople did Señora Lizama lose her composure. "I wash my hands entirely of the whole lot of them!" she cried, nervously jingling the large collection of keys she always carried.

"Blood does not always rinse away so easily," muttered old people who remembered a time when a woman's only business had been her man and children. The tide of feeling in the town turned against Señora Lizama and toward Ramón and Chileno.

That young man persisted in his mean and muddled ways. As he acted more and more like his brother, it was noticed that his eyes looked increasingly frightened and lonely. "It's just the heat that makes Chileno act this way," decided certain ladies, patting their damp faces with cloths.

"I see it differently," said one wise woman. "Chileno is being bad because he wants to feel that Tomás is near to him and not lost far away somewhere. If Tomás returned, then our old Chileno would return also."

Another woman, just as smart but more practical, saw Chileno's wounded wandering as a chance that should not be missed. "Chileno is good. All he needs is a strong harness and bridle to be as hard a worker as before. The time has come for some girl to cure him of his fraternal fevers."

Striking while the iron was hot, the female relations of a certain señorita arranged the matter. Necessary details were settled with surprising ease, as Chileno offered no resistance; he seemed uninterested how his fate was decided for him, and actually appeared relieved to be freed from his present state. Giving up his wild ways at once, he trudged to the hills each morning, worked hard all day long, then returned tired to the town at evening. The bride's mother bragged of her wily wisdom.

The month of May arrived, and the hills were set ablaze with brushfires in anticipation of the coming of the rainy season and planting of new crops. The men of the town took shifts controlling the flames. In the evenings women and children sat before houses, watching the red and orange light in the darkness above. "Why is heaven burning like hell?" asked little children, and they ran crying in the streets, fearful that the flames would float down and scorch the town. "Silly babies," crooned their mothers. "The fires will stay away. Your fathers fight the flames to keep them from you." But the children sobbed more loudly when the men returned to town, covered with soot and ash, faces black and strange.

The heat from the fires turned the town into a furnace. Violent acts of love and hate flared up, quickly died, smouldered. Smoke drifted down the western slopes, causing tears to stream from the irritated eyes of the townspeople, and it seemed a spell of sorrow had fallen over them. The smoke billowed and wavered, forming into shifting shapes which sometimes seemed familiar. A man would stumble toward a cloud of smoke, calling the name of a wife long dead and gone, and he would fall into an empty, acrid embrace.

Mothers would cry when children stepped behind curtains of smoke, perhaps vanishing forever.

Señora Lizama stood in the doorway of her store, snorting and sneering at the folly of her fellow citizens. Ramón shuffled by, his face glowing orange as the flames above. From a shape of smoke her two sons emerged. His arm around Tomás's shoulder, Chileno gazed down into the laughing eyes of his younger brother. The two young men walked together, and then a blanket of smoke fell upon them.

Wheeling about, Señora Lizama entered her store. The place was empty, for customers had become extinct and people had wearied of gazing at what they knew would never belong to them. Bright electric lights flooded the room, denying the corners their concealing darkness. For some minutes Señora Lizama punched frantically the keys of her modern cash register, seeking comfort in the sound of the ringing bells. "I don't need to wait for rain to cool the air," she suddenly thought, turning on newly installed electric ceiling fans. A strong wind arose, papers flew about, and Señora Lizama clutched her head, holding her hairdo in place. "I need no rain. Save your stingy tears, Ignacio," she told her first husband in heaven. "Lord don't cry for me."

Worry had recently furrowed deep lines upon Señora Lizama's brow. The pages of her movie magazine contained no more money, and she did not know how she would be able to meet certain bills which had fallen due. Señora Lizama sat in her office, frowning and scribbling numbers on paper. Picking up a gilt-edged handmirror, she gazed deeply into it. "Where have all my riches gone?" she sighed.

A noise startled her. Fearing a thief, she jumped up. Tomás strolled into the store, pawing the goods in a careless manner. "You've come back home," said Señora Lizama with breathless fear. "You've seen the wide world and learned it isn't much. It doesn't compare with my modern store, does it?"

Tomás brazenly slipped a shiny silver watch, the most expensive one in stock, into his pocket. "I've been waiting for you to return," Señora Lizama said quickly. "Ramón and

Chileno have no business sense, they are no help to me. But you are quick and smart, Tomás. You and I know there's no profit to be made by saving for a rainy day. Pesos don't fall from the sky. We can make a fortune, Tomás. Join me. I'll make you a full partner, I promise."

Without looking at his mother, Tomás turned and left the store. Señora Lizama ran to the doorway. Lightning began to strike at that moment, not in thin threads, but in great flashes which flooded all the sky to the east. Moments of darkness followed moments of light, as though someone in heaven were playing with a switch. When revealed for an instant people in the street appeared frozen like statues, caught like animals in traps. Each time thunder cracked the sky they started fearfully, jerking as if bullets exploded inside them.

That night Señora Lizama lay awake, listening to the whoops and hollers of her second son and the companions who welcomed him back to town. Chileno also lay sleepless, trembling beside his wife. She curled her arms around him and held him tightly. The room was dark.

"Help me! Help me!" Chileno freed himself from his wife's clasp, dressed, and ran outside. Though the streets appeared empty, the cry for help still sounded in Chileno's ears, and with every passing moment it rang more urgently. Panic burned inside Chileno and he ran after his brother's voice. He passed from the town and climbed the western slopes. There brush exploded in showers of sparks which flew upward into the darkness, then fell dying upon the earth.

The next morning the town awoke to the sound of rain beating on the tin rooftops of the houses, like a drum calling. The heat had broken. People rushed outside and stood in the rain, laughing with relief as cooling water fell from heaven, streamed down their faces, washed them clean. Children screamed in excitement and played in puddles already forming, and their mothers did not scold them for the mud they splashed upon their clothes.

A figure approached down the main street. One by one the townspeople fell silent, laughter dying on their lips. Chileno was covered with ash and soot the rain had not yet succeeded in washing away. A silver object gleamed in one hand.

Chileno's wife started forward from the crowd and stood alone, separated from it. Chileno passed her with the dreamy eyes of a sleepwalker. Lifting their eyes to the hills, the people of the town saw the fires still burning in the rain.

For three days the fires continued to burn, and then they went out. The hills looked black and ruined. Every afternoon thunder and lightning crashed and flashed across the angry heavens. Toward evening the rain would begin again, and it would fall heavily through the night, stopping at dawn. Though this wet season settled into the same pattern as those of years gone by, it seemed different and new. The people walked with bowed heads down the drenched streets of their town, and they felt themselves lost in an unknown time and place. From within the shelter of their houses they looked out through windows. Often they would gather and attempt to tell stories to pass the dark, tedious nights. "When the governor's daughter came to town," they would begin. Then they would falter and look at each other with blank faces. "Next year I hope," they would fumble, their words trailing into silence, and they were also unable to attach meaning to the future. They quickly tired of the rain and soon could not remember they had ever longed for it.

Relief in the cooling freshness slowly turned to puzzlement. "Why is the rain still falling?" they would wonder through those dark, dripping nights. "The ground is wet and the fires have gone out. The rain has done its work," they said, and then they saw smoke still rising from the charred earth, ascending from some hidden fire below. It puffed in signals, which gathered around the tops of the western slopes, obscuring those peaks. No matter how long and hard the heavens poured, the smoke still rose, and it seemed even to become more hot and thick with each night of streaming skies. The townspeople began to avoid looking at the smoking hills. "The rain will stop one day, it always does," they said, uncertainly.

Señora Lizama turned desperately sentimental. She wore a silver watch around her wrist, despite the fact that it was a man's model and much too large for her. She was always slipping through the wet streets, bursting into her neighbours' houses, shaking raindrops from her hair. "I've brought the tickets for this week's raffle," she would say. "This time the prize is that deluxe electric blender you've all admired in my window," and the household would crowd around Señora Lizama with excitement.

She was raffling off the goods in her store, one article per week, to meet certain outstanding bills. The townspeople eagerly paid twenty pesos for a ticket, and then they hoped and prayed for luck to fall on them. The announcement of the winner was made every Friday evening in the Casino, rain or shine, and this central social event of the week possessed a delirious quality. The losers wept, cursed heaven, cried foul play, while the winner could not believe his good fortune. Already many houses in town contained one handsome object that was not used, but displayed like an offering beneath the burning candle and icon.

Señora Lizama would beam tearfully at the families cooped restlessly together under strong roofs. Twisting her fingers, she would feverishly say, "I can't stay still. Yesterday I climbed a mountain. Tomorrow I'll row a boat across the bay. Oh, it's so warm and snug and dry in here, and you all seem so contented." The families would shrug their shoulders and Señora Lizama would grasp her timepiece excitedly. "Of course, my watch is waterproof. And it's all I have left of my darling Tomás." For a moment she would seem to listen to the song of the rain on the roof. Then she would shake her head. "What time is it?" she would suddenly ask, making a fuss of holding her watch up to the silver light that streamed through the window. Like a palmreader she studied its hands. "Three o'clock!" she would say in the triumphant voice of someone discovering the secret of the universe. "I'm late. Time flies, and so must I. Now where is my beloved? Have you seen him?" And off she rushed out into the rain, jumping over puddles like a young girl, calling her man's name.

With pity the townspeople watched through windows as Señora Lizama found Ramón and by the arm led him home. "You're just like a stray dog," she scolded, "always wandering off and never knowing where your home is. But even a stray dog knows where to find his food." Arm in arm they walked to the store, which was as bare and dark and dusty as it had ever been.

One day the townspeople noticed that the rain had brought all the smells of the earth alive, and they saw that smoke no longer rose from the hills. The blackened slopes turned pale green as new shoots sprung up through ashes. However, the townspeople felt no excitement at these changes. They had become used to the voice of the rain, and they felt both day and night a drugged sleepiness that almost seemed a kind of peace. In the evenings they would be lulled gently to sleep by the rain, and when a voice cried in the midnight streets they would only stir, turn over, then melt back into dreams.

"Help me! Help me!" called the voice, and children crowded together in beds sat up and hugged each other. "The ghost!" they exclaimed with excited, joyful fear. "The ghost is right outside our door," and their eyes were wide and full of wonder. "Go back to sleep," their parents would murmur from adjoining rooms. "It's just Chileno."

Señora Lizama hurried through the rain, a shawl wrapped around her shoulders. The two figures met in the wet shining street that ran between rows of dark houses. "Go home," said Señora Lizama, pushing back damp curls that fell upon her brow. "You'll catch the chills and fevers walking in this rain. Why do you call for help when nothing is wrong? Nothing is wrong!" she cried, turning her face to the sky, to the sweet, soft rain. It seeped into the earth and dripped through dark caves that lay a thousand miles beneath the surface of the globe.

Flowers of Love

"Have you any news? Have you any news?"

Petra de Lizama stood alone in her house, listening to the women of her neighbourhood call to one another from doorways: Eduardo is up in Fresno and he's making out all right; Alfredo is working in the Napa vineyards and earning many American dollars every day; Miguel sent money in the mail and today we're eating meat instead of beans. Listen! Felipe writes that he may be home in time for Christmas.

There was never enough space in this house, thought Petra. She turned from the window and the sight of women waving letters like white banners of hope. There were always too many people crowded too closely together: six beds jammed into two small rooms; nightly battles between the rhythms of seven sleepers' sighs; syncopated snores. And now this: Petra extended her arms wide, stretching into empty space.

Beautiful shrimp, beautiful shrimp, and chicken tamales, too! cried street vendors. Food for joy! they called, winding their way through the town. "Oh," said women, their flags of letters drooping in suddenly stilled breaths of promise. "Oh," they said, turning into houses and closing doors against the watching street. "I've lost my appetite since my children went away."

Petra went to the counter and read the letter again: Mama, I hopped on the train first, and as it gathered speed my brother ran beside it. Jump, I shouted. Hop on. I held out my hand. But the train was moving too fast, he waited too long, and when he leaped my little brother fell and now I'm feeling too bad and don't know when I'm ever coming home.

Home. Petra wandered from room to room, among objects that had lain before her eyes for years. She touched them gently, as if she might stroke some meaning from them. I'll come back some day, she had called over her shoulder upon leaving her first home all those years ago. Now where did it go? Petra wondered, rummaging through a drawer of old momentos. Where is that picture of a twelve-year-old girl carrying buckets beneath the cold white peaks of the Sierra Madres? Those buckets were always so heavy when full, and as she carried them down the hills half the water spilled along the way. The winding trail led to her mother's garden. There her mother would feed the flowers carefully, dividing the water evenly between the plots, as though there were some just way to meet the endless thirst of the earth. Very early in the morning her mother would cut the stems with a sharp knife, and drops of dew fell like tears from the blossoms. The man already dead, her mother went out into the mean city streets. Flowers of love, her mother would call, winding through the throngs of buyers and sellers. Fresh flowers of love. Her mother would return home drooping and tired with the unsold red and yellow roses. The world could never buy enough flowers of love to feed fifteen hungry children.

As the vendors' cries faded, Petra sifted through the clutter of broken toys and clothes that no longer fit. Children grow so quickly, she thought, reaching past the letter and making an effort to sweep worn out shoes and babies' baubles beneath beds. I could sell these empty beds. I could buy a brand new sofa, a coffee table, and a little blue carpet for the floor. A vase of flowers would look pretty in that corner, she thought, trying to place a picture of a clean, neat parlour over that of a train speeding and clanking upon steel tracks. I could sit still like a statue in the afternoons, drinking coffee like a rich lady. Now that all my children have gone away and won't be coming back. Why? she wondered.

For two years the oysters in the bay had been too small, and the government would not buy them. The surface of the sea had changed, turned blank and no longer broken by boys emerging from the depths, gasping for breath, knives in one hand and crusted shells of oysters in the other. The boys had

left the sea, and for one whole season they sat restlessly in
their mothers' kitchens, stood idle on the corners of the streets.
There is work on the hills, their elders told them; but when
the men returned to town from long, hard labour for too little
money, the boys looked away. They turned from these ghosts
of fathers who were tired and old as grandfathers, whose
machetes hung heavily in their hands, like weapons of battles lost daily. The boys raised their eyes to the plantations
where their young, strong fathers had vanished, and they saw
the moon rising above the western slopes.

One by one the boys had left town, secretly, without saying goodbye. Dawns were torn in two by screams of women
standing over empty beds, and sympathetic wails of other
mothers spread through the town, rose over the hills above.
The boys had crossed the hills and made their way north by
hitch-hiking and hopping trains. They travelled over the burning deserts and reached the River. Stealing across it, they were
delivered upon the other side.

Now the town was emptier, and quiet except for the roar
of the sullen, abandoned sea below. The movie house closed
down. Girls no longer paraded around and around the plaza
at evening, their finest dresses fluttering in a Pacific breeze,
their calls soft as doves'. Women no longer sat in little chairs
on sidewalks, peering sharply down dark streets for the sight
of a boy walking with a girl, the promise of a marriage. Late
at night the plaza was deserted, haunted only by bats and owls
and ghostly cries of boys itching to go far away. Sometimes
at midnight dogs would bark at what seemed like silence, their
ears tuned to a higher pitch, to the sound of remembered
footsteps falling drunkenly down the sleeping streets.

As the rooms darkened with evening, Petra went into her
kitchen. She turned on the radio, letting signals from far away
fill the empty space and silence. Singing, she moved over the
stove. The pain is not worth it, she sang, stirring the contents
of pots. No se vale la pena.

"Ramón!"she called in a little while. "Come and eat!
Ramón!" she called, more loudly. But still silence answered
her. From the kitchen she passed into the larger room at the
front of the house, which served as a store. "Ramón?" she
asked the dimming light.

"I'm not hungry," came her husband's voice from one dark corner.

"That's no excuse," said Petra quickly and loudly. "After I've made the meal you can't say you're not hungry. You're so thin! I might as well be living with a skeleton. I might as well be buried in a tomb. Come, I can't eat alone."

He shuffled after her, coughing, "We have a letter from Chileno," she said, standing over the stove again.

"I can't read," Ramón said in the thin, high voice of a child. "I never learned how."

"Chileno says he's doing fine and taking good care of Tomás. They're both working in the bakery at Coalingua. They can eat as much fresh bread as they want." Petra stared into the bubbling pots. "How can we eat all this?" she asked at last. "I've made too much. There's enough here to feed fifteen."

She stood helplessly there, the strong aroma of tomatoes and onions and potatoes streaming past her out the window. It drifted through the sky and travelled a thousand miles to the north.

The night was black with mourning. Suppers sat uneaten on kitchen tables. Men slunk to smoke and squat on street corners. Women sat limply inside with barely enough strength to fan themselves. Also as usual, Petra Lizama dropped in on her friends with news of Ramón's lastest escapade. The town ladies listened dully to their neighbour relate what was but one more variation on an endless theme; the trouble caused her by her husband had been a great and continuous source of joy for Petra for eighteen years.

"He went off to the capital city in a taxi cab," she said that evening. "He primped himself before the mirror for one entire hour like the vain peacock he is, trying his big white sombrero a dozen ways on his little head. He dreams those city sluts will fall for him. I've got business in the capital, he told me, just like that. Then he stepped into a thousand peso taxi with that jaunty air of his. Business! What kind of business can involve a man who needs a diaper changed and a spoon held to his mouth?"

The neighbourhood ladies sat spilled into their chairs, idle hands fiddling in their laps. The news they had received earlier that day had already grown stale and the ladies listened somewhat enviously to Petra's account of the lively life her man led her. "How do you do it?" they roused themselves to ask. "How can you keep so peppy with both your sons vanished somewhere across the other side? Since my boys went away, I haven't been able to take interest in a single thing. I can't fill my days."

Petra paused and looked distractedly around. Then she rushed on, speaking feverishly. "My Ramón! Can you believe it? The older he gets, the worse he gets. He's one child I'll never be free of, unless I cross the Pope and get one of those godless divorces."

"My man is out all day," lamented the ladies. "He's busy gossiping and smoking with his cronies in the plaza. He's no trouble, I hardly see him. He comes home only to eat and sleep," they sadly said. "He's quiet as a lamb."

After spreading her complaints across town, Petra went to her house to await the return of Ramón. Shortly after seven o'clock, seeking to buy sugar to soothe their sweet teeth, a number of women discovered the door of Petra's store to be locked from the inside. "The poor thing is probably lying lonely in bed, crying for her lost children and missing man," they said. However, very gay music issued clearly from inside the bolted house. "Are you all right?" the neighbourhood ladies called through the door, becoming anxious after a while. "Have you fallen and hurt yourself? Are you sick?" A small crowd of señoras gathered on the sidewalk, and there was some talk of trying to force entry. However, in the end no action was taken; weighted beneath their own sorrows, the women went home.

During those evenings of mourning for missing sons the townspeople turned indoors early. By eight o'clock the streets were quite empty. Still, lights burned in most houses, like beacons to guide boys safely back into their beds. Comforted somewhat by the sound of husbands breathing in sleep, women sat framed in the windows against backgrounds of yellow light. They gazed out at the stirring palms and the rising moon above. Usually it would be long past midnight before the windows emptied, the lights vanished, and the women settled into uneasy, sleepless vigils.

On that night, however, the dreaming women in windows were stirred unexpectedly from their trances. When they first noticed the figure flash down the street, most women crossed themselves against evil spirits, then continued combing out their hair and saying prayers. The figure passed again, and this time the women heard a padding of bare feet on rough cobblestones, a panting of exerted lungs.

Doors opened a cautious inch. Through cracks the ladies peered at the figure that continued to race up and down the road. As it passed beneath streetlamps, the shape was revealed quite clearly to be their neighbour of many years, Petra de Lizama. She was completely naked. For some minutes the women watched this spectacle in silence, a mixture of curiosity and horror playing upon their faces. Soon they began to call in whispers from doorway to doorway.

"She's naked," said Olivia Ramirez, unnecessarily.

"As bare as a baby," said Beatriz Alamana.

"It looks as though she doesn't know where she wants to go," remarked Carmela Cervantes.

"When you run naked in the street it is with the intention of going nowhere except straight to hell," replied Consuela Lupita grimly.

Dressed in odd, old-fashioned nightgowns, their hair falling loosely on their shoulders or hanging in long braids down their backs, these old friends looked unfamiliar to one another and disturbingly different from their daytime aspects. They conferred quietly amidst the shrill screams of crickets. Something had to be done. "Petra, Petra, go back home," the women softly called. "You're having a bad dream." Their nude neighbour did not seem to hear them; she continued running up and down the street. A blanket was fetched and several of the bravest ladies attempted to grab the bare woman as she ran past. Petra eluded capture for some minutes. At last a throng of ladies succeeded in backing her against a wall. They advanced slowly with the blanket, like a group of inexperienced hunters faced with a wild beast.

Petra would later have been forgiven much more quickly if at that moment she had not begun to laugh loudly, wildly, shamelessly. "Look, I've become a little fat," she laughed, pointing down at the belly which swelled above her thickened waist. "Look," she giggled raucously; and she placed her hands tenderly upon the rising flesh, holding it like a last child she would never let go.

In the end capture was achieved without struggle. The unclothed woman seemed to have become very tired all at once, and she let herself be led peaceably back to her empty house. The ladies thanked God that no men had been awake to witness such a scene, and they blessed fate for taking Petra Lizama's children from her, thus sparing them the sight of their mother gone mad.

After that night Petra was not seen in the streets for some weeks. Several women had stayed by her bed, watching over her until morning and the return of Ramón from the capital city. "She had a slight dizzy spell," they told him; and at that moment the women tacitly agreed to keep full details of the incident from their men.

Despite these conspiratorial efforts, one way or another news of the disgraceful episode spread through the town. The concensus of opinion was that Petra was ashamed, and that by staying out of sight she followed the only proper course of action open to her. There was, initially, some sympathy for poor Petra. "It's understandable. None of us are quite ourselves with our sons so far away," commented women; and some could even imagine themselves also falling from decency through despair. "Ramón has led her a hard life for all these years," it was noted, too. "Petra was perhaps suffering from a nightmare, perhaps wandering in her sleep. She was unlucky, such a thing could happen to any of us."

Sometimes customers in the Lizama store glimpsed Petra passing like a ghost through the back rooms. Ramón had taken charge of the business, and when asked about his wife he stated with unusual firmness that she was not feeling well and so was unable to receive visitors. The longer the disgraced woman remained hidden in her house the stronger grew the curiosity of the townspeople.

As time passed this curiosity turned into bitterness. Old grudges, slight and long forgotten, were now recalled and held against the hussy. Certain señoras stated that Petra had always liked to be the centre of attention and that this naked running in the street was only her latest effort to hog the spotlight. Others accused the shamed woman of flaunting her wares, of trying to seduce safely married men with the sight of her flesh. There were whispers that the woman had lost her mind completely and was raving in her rooms. A small delegation of concerned ladies advised Ramón to persuade his wife to re-enter the natural course of town life through a decorous appearance at an evening mass. "Petra has done her penance," they said. "We are a forgiving people. But you must know, Ramón, that there is talk."

Speculation and scandal passed from house to house, filling minutes and minds and mouths. The town women were enlivened as they had not been since their sons had left them, and letters from boys on the other side were tossed unread into the backs of drawers. Only when excitement over Petra's condition began to die did mothers anxiously open envelopes once more.

The news was not happy. "My Miguel must have already forgotten how to write his mother tongue," a woman would mutter, frowning in puzzlement at a sheet of paper. "These words must be that fancy American kind. I can't make head or tail of what he's saying." One or two phrases in each letter would be understood, but by themselves they only added to a general sense of mystery. "On the road to Stockton," a mother would say wonderingly. "Hot dogs and hamburgers on the beach at Santa Monica," she would read, clucking her tongue. The women murmured these small phrases again and again, hoping some clearer vision of their sons would emerge; but through repetition the words lost the little sense they once possessed, and evolved into mere sounds. They were chanted like prayers which might evoke the image of an invisible god. But no deities appeared, and soon the women no longer stood on doorsteps waving letters and calling out glad tidings.

By implicit agreement mothers ceased speaking of these messages from the other side. They fell silent about their sons, and the letters were once more put aside unread.

Cries of street vendors rang more frequently through the town. Beautiful shrimp! beautiful shrimp! and sweet tamales, too! came calls floating through the air, entering Petra's house. Through a crack between two shutters she saw her neighbours run out into the street, clutching pesos, swarming around the sellers. Food for joy! the vendors cried, and the town ladies returned to their houses with arms overflowing with delicacies. Petra noticed that her neighbours, formerly thin with anxiety over missing children, had recently gained weight. She saw them sitting before their houses, eating one tamale after another, ravenously, intently, greedily. Then they sat looking full and heavy and unhappy, and they seemed hardly able to rise from their little chairs.

Her mother had not risen from bed for three days, and she had looked scornfully at her worried daughter. Don't stand there staring down at me like that, can't you hear the children crying? You must sell flowers to buy food, you are the oldest, quick, go. Petra cut the stems in the garden. She walked through the hard paved streets of the city, the flowers filling her arms and feeling strangely heavy. The strong scent blurred her eyes and she walked blindly through the crowds. Flowers of love, she cried up and down the streets. Fresh flowers of love. Afterward, she hurried home with food for the hungry children. Mama, she cried, rushing into the house. Mama? Where has she gone? The children stood around the empty bed. They did not answer her question, but only stared at the food she held in her arms. Petra dropped the unsold flowers onto the grey sheets of her mother's bed. The red and yellow roses fell slowly, they drifted down as though through a great, empty space of air.

Now the wind tore them from her hands, and the blossoms flew like birds through the sky. They fell upon the grey, wrinkled sheets of the sea. Standing on the shore, Petra looked at a world that seemed forgotten and now recalled, new, changed. She tossed the petals upon the water and saw them carried away. They vanished from sight, slipping past the horizon, sinking beneath the waves like drowning children, or simply obscured by falling darkness.

Having heard of Petra's sudden ascension from her bed, the women of the town hurried across the rocky beach stumbling frequently in the darkness. The figure of the small woman by the sea loomed abruptly before them, blacker than the night. Upon nearing Petra, the ladies halted, all at once unsure what they wanted to say. They could hear the woman speaking, but the roaring of the sea obscured the meaning of her words. Flora Paez believed Petra was calling the names of her own sons; Consuela Lupita thought the names of other missing children were being evoked. It was Celeste Ortiz who finally said, uncertainly, "There's no point in shouting at the sea. You're calling to the west, and our children are in the north."

Petra turned her face slowly toward the ladies. "Matilda Marquez," she said. "Your son has just married a tall, blonde American girl who possesses green eyes and a great fortune. Your son and new daughter are at this moment sailing toward this spot on a large, luxurious yacht. They will arrive in three days. Wait for them. They will take you to Acapulco for a long holiday.

"Carmela Cervantes," the strong, squat woman said, turning to that lady. "Your son has bought for you a very large white house in California. You will live there amidst the most modern conveniences for the rest of your life without a care in the world and with a staff of servants to attend your every want. Right now a passport, which your successful son obtained for you at great cost, is travelling toward you through the mail."

Petra spoke at considerable length to each woman, explaining clearly the present and future fortunes of their sons. All her news was good. Following these proclamations, the women danced like children back across the beach. They scampered to their houses to prepare for new and better lives.

After that day Señora Lizama was the most important personage in town. At once the scandal surrounding her was forgotten. The seer stayed at some distance from her neighbours, neither dropping in to visit former friends nor receiving callers at her house. "She is resting," Ramón would explain in hushed tones to any ladies who inquired after her. "Her visions tire her and she must save her strength."

Petra would remain in bed for a period of three days, then she would rise and make her way slowly to the shore. News of her resurrection spread more quickly than that of any birth or death. Young girls would run up to the visionary and ask if they would grow more beautiful with the passing of years. Old men would ask if the pains in their legs would some day go away. However, Señora Lizama would not respond to any questions which did not in some way concern the boys missing on the other side, and she would reveal her special sight only when down upon the shore.

There was but a slight delay between the seer's ascension and the appearance of vendors in the streets. As Señora Lizama drew down the dusty road toward the beach, the vendors' cries began to ring through the town. Flowers of love, they cried, happy with the certainty of many large sales. Fresh flowers of love, called these vendors who had once sold beautiful shrimp and sweet tamales, too. Big baskets of red and yellow roses bobbed through the town, their colours splashed and their scent spilled upon the streets.

The town ladies clustered around the vendors, paying high prices for the flowers. Then they rushed to the shore, their arms laden with blossoms, their hands clutching latest letters from sons. "Have you any news?" they called, as they approached the seer.

They found her by the sea and offered her both flowers and letters. The latter she did not open; after allowing them to rest briefly in her hands, she tore the letters and scattered their pieces on the wind. The flowers she held more tenderly and at greater length. She pressed the blossoms to her face, inhaling their aroma greedily, as though it were oxygen or some other essential substance. Then, empowered by the scent, she pronounced. She often spoke quickly and with distraction, words dropping like pearls from her mouth, falling upon old oyster shells once discarded by diving boys and now scattered on the shore. Each week the tidings had less to do with the missing children and more to do with the ladies who listened so attentively. Although the promises did not immediately come to pass, Señora Lizama's manner and bearing left no doubt as to their absolute accuracy.

In fact, the women became increasingly excited by the seer's sights, which grew more grandiose and marvellous as time went by. "I see a castle," she would say, staring out to sea. "This castle has fifty rooms and is in Spain. It stands on the top of a hill which rises from green sisal fields. Small white houses cling to the sides of the hill. From the windows and terraces of the castle you can see far across the Mediterranean and all the way to Africa. You will live in the castle, which was once the home of a Spanish Princess, and this will happen soon."

After promising the women the world, the visionary would turn her face abruptly from them, clearly desiring to be left alone with the flowers. Once, at this moment, Carmela Cervantes asked the wise woman: "And what about you? What great piece of fortune will be placed in your hands by your sons?" Señora Lizama gazed at the ladies with a soft, tender smile, and they felt themselves falling into her dark eyes, sinking into a darker place on the other side. The seer turned back to the sea, and she was not asked about her own fortune again.

The ladies hurried back to their cramped, crumbling houses, full of hope and anxious to lose no time preparing for lives in Spanish castles and Californian condominiums. The town was thrown into a happy turmoil by the excited women, and each week was filled with the giving of goodbye gifts and farewell fiestas. "Yes, I will be leaving directly for Japan," the guest of honour at one of these lavish affairs would say. "They sit on the floor to eat and live in' paper houses there, you know," she would drawl, affecting a world-weary way. The hopes of the ladies grew and grew, and lost in their delirious dreaming they forgot completely the sons who would be the cause of these sudden, splendid fortunes.

After the sound of the ladies' footsteps faded, Petra stood

alone with the song of the sea. Sometimes she turned her face to the sky, where first stars were appearing, and she saw Victor Aquino's boat sailing around the moon. But she looked mostly at the stretching sea, staring intently at it, anxious not to miss the sudden sight of a child's head breaking above the cresting waves. She stood there, listening to the cries of Isabela Inocence and Emilia Estavez and all the other sons and daughters vanished without warning. Their calls sounded forlorn and high, and buffeted by the heaving wind and waves. They struggled upon the eternal expanse of the sea, then sank beneath its surface.

Flowers of love, cried Petra, answering the call of the hungry children. Fresh flowers of love, she sang to the sea and to all the drowning children beneath it. Red and yellow blossoms floated through the darkness like illuminated butterflies, then fell to rest upon the swirling, starving sea.

Beneath the Western Slopes

During the time when the town beneath the western slopes was mad with mourning for its lost children, Chonita chose to turn her house into a hotel. The townspeople were appalled. "While we grieve for our drowned daughters and disappeared sons, the old lady is busy scheming to acquire more pesos," they said. "While we hope without hope for our missing children to return to us, she prepares to welcome strangers to our town." Chonita seemed oblivious to the mood of hysterical heartache which possessed her neighbours, and she oversaw the transformation of her house with a clarity and precision that impressed the contractors she had hired. This was despite the fact that among the missing children were a number of her first cousins' nephews and nieces, as well as more distant relations.

Nearly every family in town had lost a child. Girls had thrown themselves into the sea and boys had vanished across the hills, never to be seen again. Children disappeared right and left before their parents' eyes, and the fact that no bodies were recovered added to the forlorn quality of this time. "If only there were something to put into the ground," was a common lament. Bereaved parents could not believe God was deliberately and cruelly robbing them of their offspring. "We are not wealthy people," they cried in anguish. "Our children are our only treasures." Deranged in desolation, parents wildly searched for some cause for their losses. Many believed Chonita was in some way to blame, though if asked they would have been unable to explain this suspicion. "All I know is that if that old woman had not returned to town, my Miguel would still be by my side,'' a mother would stubbornly insist.

Chonita and her husband had left the small town several decades before, as poor as all their neighbours. One year before the children began to disappear, they had suddenly returned in possession of more money than honest people had a right to. They were unwilling to say where they had been for so long and how they had acquired their wealth. Upon her return, the old woman had not made the slightest effort to resume acquaintance with former friends and neighbours, and snubbed town ladies said she gave herself airs. They hinted that Chonita had made her fortune by pressing her reluctant husband to steal land and money from various innocent, hardworking people, including blood relatives. It was noticed that Chonita's husband had become strangely frightened of her. The town whispered that she threatened to go to the police with certain proof of the countless crimes he had unwillingly committed. The price of her silence, it was said, was one large, white house.

While mothers wailed and fathers drank themselves into sorrowful stupors and children disappeared strangely, mysteriously, tragically, Chonita oversaw the construction of her grand residence. She sat in the shade of an avocado tree, sipping iced orange juice from a crystal goblet. She would point and call commands to her husband, who toiled in the burning sun, building the house brick by heavy brick. "Work more quickly!" she would call, fanning herself with one of the many movie magazines she devoured during this time. "She is killing the poor man," said the townspeople, watching through their tears. "He is building his own tomb."

It surprised no one when Chonita's husband died several minutes after laying the last tile on the roof. The old woman seemed as untouched by this death as she had been by all the others in town. On the morning of her husband's funeral she was occupied with the arrangement of many handsome furnishings which had just arrived by truck from the capital city and points farther beyond. Three drunks were hired to throw the corpse into a hole and only one raven, perched on the wall that surrounded the graveyard, observed the burial.

As though not satisfied with owning the largest and newest

and whitest house in town, Chonita lost no time having walls torn down and seven small rooms constructed around the main body of the building. "Instead of mourning her man, she desecrates his grave," the townspeople said, watching with horror through eyes made red with weeping. They were particularly offended by a tall red iron fence the old woman had built around her property; this seemed to indicate she felt her neighbours to be thieves she could not trust or spies from whom she needed to hide her sins. It was at this point that the town's sadness for its stolen children began to turn into resentment toward the old woman. "Pride comes before a fall," the townspeople said hopefully, and Chonita's planned hotel was seen by all as a grand folly. "Why would anyone want to visit our little town?" asked the realistic citizens. "This place is neither an Acapulco nor a Puerto Vallarta, and it never will be." However, the old woman pressed on steadily with the renovations, and she did not rest until the final touch was set in place. A sign, imprinted with the words Holiday Hotel, was hung before her gate.

To the amazement of the townspeople, a steady stream of strangers began to flow through the hotel almost at once. The seven guest rooms were always filled. "Why, they're hardly more than children!" exclaimed the townspeople when they saw the first foreigners in their streets, and it was true that all the visitors were young. "They should be home with their mamas," town ladies said, and wiping tears from their cheeks they wondered if the mothers of these strangers also cried for missing children. Despite the pride they had always taken in their boundless hospitality, the citizens only stared stonily through windows at these unknown boys and girls. When at night the children from far away appeared in the plaza dressed in strange rainbow-coloured clothes, the townspeople affected ignorance of their presence. Anxious mothers warned children not yet taken from them to have nothing to do with these gringos. "Oh, no," the mothers moaned. "These foreign youths will fill our surviving children with dreams of California and places farther away. Our boys and girls will disappear like their brothers and sisters did. Our town will become empty of its young, no more babies will be born, when we die our memories will die with us. Only ghosts will walk our streets and sleep in our houses, and our town will crumble into dust, then vanish.''

The people bitterly believed that Chonita had in effect invited these unwanted children to disturb their already troubled hearts. "If there were no hotel, then there would be no strangers," declared the townspeople with the force of logic. Indeed, these foreign children did not seem to have any specific purpose in their visits. They appeared interested in neither the surrounding scenery nor the daily life of the people. They did not swim in the sea or climb the hills. "Why don't they go back to where they've come from?" was one question the baffled people asked themselves. The town ladies wept with rage to see the young strangers flock around the large white house. "That witch surrounds herself with children only to remind us of our lost babies. Look at her pretend she is the mother of the universe! Everyone knows that her only son, to whose existence she will not admit, lives as a stranger one thousand miles to the north. If he landed dying on her doorstep, Chonita would only sue him for trespassing.''

One day the old woman's house turned suddenly silent and empty. She lived alone inside it, rarely venturing outside the red iron gate. The young strangers seemed to have vanished into thin air, and they left no visible trace upon the town. The people felt relieved at their disappearance, and they did not express a large amount of sympathy for the old woman's sudden solitude. "Let her have a taste of the lonely life," they said. "Let her know how it feels when children melt off the face of the earth. Let her drown in empty hours and eat the bitter fruits of her sins.''

They were blown in from the sea, carried upon Pacific breezes like red and yellow flowers. They fell gently into the seven beds of the seven waiting rooms, which were small and furnished as barely as cells. "Haven't I seen you before?" Chonita asked the first sad, silent children who materialized on her doorstep. She squinted at them as though at dazzling suns. "I remember your face.''

As in a dream the drifting children appeared then vanished, passing suddenly and silently without names or histories through Chonita's hotel. They seemed lost. They did not say where they had been or where they were going, and the strange children did not explain why they had come to the town. Pictures of faces swirled in the old woman's mind, like memories.

In their seven rooms they surrounded her like another layer of breathing skin. She heard their voices through the walls. In the womb of her parlour Chonita listened to the drifting children bump around their rooms late at night, searching for things they could not find. Bottles fell over onto floors with hollow sounds. Matches flared and sweet, heavy smoke drifted from the outer rooms to curl in a cocoon around the house. Sometimes the seven beds creaked sadly, and the rusted hinges of Chonita's heart groaned with disuse.

Awoken, she paced away the nights. She appeared greatly excited, striding to and fro amid her fine new furnishings, her arms clasped tightly around herself, her lips silently speaking. Pausing before the mirror, she was surprised by the sight of her own eyes glittering like two Persian rubies.

"Every child who has left his home has died," Chonita thought, staring searchingly into the mirror on the day her house turned quiet. She listened for their voices, but heard only the pounding of her newly aching heart, and one loose shutter banging in the empty wind. The lost children no longer came to Chonita, though breezes still blew in from the Pacific and red and yellow poppies still fell from the old amapa tree in the centre of the plaza.

Seven nights after her house turned empty Chonita heard the lost children crying and the streets of San Miguel appeared in the sky. Two long paths of light rose straight from the horizon and disappeared into the heavens far above. San Miguel galloped his horse along these streets of light, and he was so busy carrying messages between heaven and earth that he could not stop to help the children lost between these two places.

The lost children wandered up from the sea along the road that ran before Chonita's house. They sobbed with longing for heaven. They cried for San Miguel to lift them onto his horse and carry them quickly through the sky. They would wrap their arms tightly around his waist, stars would fly by, and winds of distant galaxies would whip their hair into flags. San Miguel would loosen the reins and the white horse would stretch his head forward like an arrow.

But though they cried and cried no horseman lifted them upon his flying steed, and the children wrung their hands in despair. They wailed before Chonita's house until they saw the hills rising above the town. The lost children ran along the path that climbed the western slopes, and when they reached the summit they cried for joy. They were so close to heaven. The stars were so near above, and the children pulled them down. They carried the stars like candles and lights bobbed in the darkness. Their faces glowing in circles of light, their voices rising high and clear, in unison the children sang of their desire for heaven, and they waited for God to hear them.

But the children were as young as any children, and soon they leaped up from their songs to play games. They played hide and seek in the dark dips and hollows of the hills. "We'll get to heaven when we're older," they carelessly called, chasing each other around and around. "It's not so far away." Close to the sky the children laughed and laughed, and their happy voices spilled down upon the deaf, silent globe that spun below.

Chonita ran to the windows and doors and flung them open wide. She switched on all the electric lights until her house shone as brilliantly as a star. She opened the red iron gate, but she could see no figures on the dark, dirt road. The children had passed by. Chonita shivered in a breeze that brushed against her heart, that blew the children away from her. She looked up at the starless night and saw the hills that sloped toward her dancing with light. Straining to hear childrens' voices, she heard only the sound of pounding hooves fading in the sky, like dying heartbeats.

At first she kept the seven rooms unlocked. Each morning she made up the seven beds with new sheets and by the windows placed fresh flowers in glass jars filled with cold, clear water. She swept away the gathering dust. But as time passed it cost more and more strength to keep the rooms clean and ready, and Chonita would suddenly feel overcome with weariness in the midst of the work. She would fall into one of the empty beds, fall into a deep, dark sleep.

She awoke with a start and looked around in surprise. The rooms appeared as unfamiliar as any place returned to after long absence. Her house had decayed. Cobwebs hung like curtains in the corners and grime covered the windows like shutters. One day Chonita sealed the seven empty rooms and left them to their loneliness.

She waited through nights that passed each as slowly and darkly as one long lifetime. Before the mirror Chonita sat with things boys and girls leave behind when they drift lightly and unburdened from the world: bright, rainbow-coloured clothes; paperback novels in foreign languages with wild dried flowers pressed between their leaves; torn and tear-stained pages of letters never sent. She looked at unspent coins, and at keys that did not unlock the closed chambers of her heart.

Through her rooms at the centre of the house she wandered, searching for a way out but unable to find a door. On the carpet she wore trails that crossed each other and led nowwhere except back to their beginnings. The candle flame rose from her hand, gasping for breath and exhaling great shifting shadows on the walls. The rooms around her were silent but for the scratching rats who built nests in abandoned beds, bore babies in feathers of torn pillows. The gardens around the house grew wild, and blossoms tumbled from vines, strained from stems. Their strong scent encircled the house, and inside Chonita waited.

The red iron fence around her property grew taller. The town above and the sea below moved farther from the large white house, beyond the boundaries of Chonita's thoughts. But sometimes at dusk the sea heaved with unusual force upon the shore, and Chonita heard it calling. Sometimes high, clear voices of children growing and playing in the plaza floated out from the darkness around her, like fireflies. In these points of light Chonita saw the children who had vanished from this small town and from all the other small towns dotted upon the globe, and she knew that a mother whose children had left her had died.

Once or twice a week she emerged from her gate and walked quickly through the town, a blue milk pail swinging on one arm. Concealing the ill-feeling they still harboured, people greeted the old woman respectfully, and her failure to respond seemed more the result of abstraction than rudeness. She was tall and big-boned, and she carried herself very erectly. Her white hair was carved into sharp waves and the features of her face were harsh. "She looks more like a man than a woman," people thought, and this impression was furthered by the plain, simple clothes the old woman wore, which had once belonged to her husband. "She drinks like a man, too," town ladies said, smelling the spirits that trailed like a shadow after Chonita.

A number of town ladies felt compelled by conscience and curiosity to visit the old woman once a week. Every Sunday they knocked upon the gate, and upon hearing no answer tentatively entered the yard. They viewed the overgrown gardens with dismay. The sight of the old woman's parlour, filled with expensive possessions left to rot, made the ladies heartsick. "You've done enough housekeeping for one lifetime," they nervously said. "You have earned your rest, doña. And here are a few small delicacies you might enjoy."

Chonita sat on a red velvet chair before her large dressing table, which was covered with an assortment of glass bottles containing perfumes and oils and creams. She looked into her mirror intently, turning only occasionally to the town ladies. "Is that you, Consuela Lupita?" she asked. "And can this be you, Flora Paez? What happened to you? Your faces are all lined and your hair is turning grey."

The town ladies glanced at one another. "We're all growing old," they said, placing gifts of food on the round table upon which spoiled and untouched presents from the previous week still stood. They began to pound great clouds of dust from the drapes and to scour clinging mould from the walls. However, each week the old woman would turn irritably toward them before they could make a dent in the decay of the house. "Leave it exactly the way it is," she would say, her voice all at once turned weary.

She gazed through her large window of a mirror once more, seeing a young girl wading in a shady stream. The girl held up a skirt with one hand so it would not trail in the quickly flowing water. This was clear and cold, and little minnows darted between her toes.

Years passed, and the town beneath the western slopes grew peaceful. It did not suffer from poverty and it did not enjoy prosperity. Quiet nights and undisturbed days slowly unfolded, and each one was the same. "We have a right to this calm after all the storms we've lived through," the people said, though they could not remember clearly the time when children had been taken from them. Still, sometimes a mother would waken in the middle of the night and wonder: "Didn't I once have a daughter named Naomi?" She would slip from bed and hover over her sleeping children, counting them. "They're all here," she would say, then shrug her shoulders, perplexed. On the Days of the Dead the townspeople felt in their hearts a hollowness as empty as graves in which no children lay soundly sleeping, for they had no places on earth to put big wreaths of plastic or paper flowers.

Parents maintained instinctively the habit of jealously watching over those children still with them, and they contrived never to let them out of sight. At bedtime mothers told babies about the old woman who lived alone in the large white house. "Wicked! If she looks a child in the eyes, the child will disappear. Mean! She kidnaps children and holds them prisoners inside her red iron fence, and no matter how sadly they cry for their mothers she will not let them go. Greedy! She made a fortune selling children to the rich Americans, and now those children must starve and slave all their lives in a foreign country."

The townspeople became complacent in their peace. "We don't ask for much," they were fond of saying. "All we want is to see our children grow." Yet even when their streets were most quiet and the skies above most clear, the people felt a nagging sense of unease. Sometimes the sign before the old woman's house, suspended from a pole by two chains, swayed and creaked though no breeze stole up from the sea. Sometimes a group of men, emboldened by drink, would gather on the dirt road before her house and serenade Chonita with obscene songs all night long.

The children on the western slopes grew weary of waiting for heaven. The songs they sang to God in the evenings echoed sadly in the air around them. "We must be old enough for heaven now," the children would say. Every day they carefully studied each other, trying to discern signs of age. "Haven't I grown taller since yesterday?" one child would ask another. "Can you see lines around my eyes?" But the children on the western slopes did not grow older.

At first they enjoyed the clear, sweeping vision afforded them by their point of vantage. They would look down upon the Pacific stretching to the west, and they saw all the way to China. Looking toward the east and across the breathing land, they saw the Gulf of Mexico and all the other gulfs which separate the pieces of the world. They watched foreign lands and lives with interest.

But with time they became frightened of endless visions appearing through empty air, of sights too large for children's eyes. They gazed with longing at the town beneath them, so far away and silent, no more than tiny black dots of pepper sprinkled along the sea. In the evenings the children grew homesick for small houses, the sound of breathing between four walls, the smell of supper cooking on the stove. Sometimes they jumped up, silent and spellbound, and tumbled down the hills, rolling over and over through the long grass until they landed dizzy at the bottom. They would rise to reel like drunks, unsure which way was up and which way was down.

At midnight they slipped into town. They gambolled down the silent streets and knocked on windows. "We've come back!" they cried. But though the lost children pounded their small fists on the locked doors, the townspeople would not waken. The children sobbed on empty corners of the streets. Then they saw the large white house with candles burning in every window, and they ran joyfully toward it.

Chonita paced her rooms and waited. Candles spat and flared in the corners. The bottle of brandy stood on the dressing table before the mirror. "Where did you go?" Chonita asked the glass, leaning into it. "Where are you now?" she asked aloud, as though thinking were too lonely. She traced the curves of her face with the searching fingers of the blind, looking for a lost child. "Eugenia?" she asked the glass, waiting for a vanished version of herself to appear reflected behind her. "Eugenia?" she called softly to the other side. "Will you come back to me?"

Suddenly she turned and sat breathless. She heard the lost children calling to her. "Come and play in the garden," they implored. "The flowers have unfolded."

Chonita slipped out the back door and sat very still in the ruined gazebo, a small contented smile on her face. The lost children scrambled and tumbled upon her, they danced in circles of joined hands around her. Songs were sung and garlands of flowers were woven for her hair. Out from the masses of dark shrubbery children came running to show her some queer insect or blossom they had found. "Look," they said.

An hour before dawn, when the leaves were dripping with dew, the lost children darted off to bathe in the red water of the sun rising across the far side of the western slopes. "We'll come and play another night," they called over their shoulders, waving goodbye.

Chonita re-entered her house. The candles burned low, drowning in pools of hot tears. Brandy glowed inside the bottle. The world seemed to spin beneath Chonita as quickly as the passing of a thousand brief lives.

Though the children of the town were warned to stay away from the white house, they were attracted by the forbidden, and on nights when the moon was full and laughing they climbed over the red iron fence. They would trample through the gardens gone wild, pull up exotic plants by their roots, and pluck hundreds of blossoms for no other reason than to scatter them like falling stars through the dark. Often in the midst of their mischief they would be startled by the sight of the old woman standing like a statue beside the pond in which red and yellow tropical fish had once swum. She appeared white in the moonlight.

The lost, ghostly children, come down from the western slopes to play in Chonita's garden, laughed merrily at the sight of the town's sturdy Marias and Miguels. They ran laughing and skipping around their new companions. They climbed trees and dropped showers of avocados upon the town children, and with ghostly fingers they tickled their dark skin. "It's haunted!" cried Marias and Miguels, running from Chonita's garden. They fled back to their parents' houses, trembling with fear, excitement, and also a kind of longing.

One Sunday the town ladies who still visited Chonita each week found the white house and its wild gardens empty. The door was ajar. "Well, the old woman has run away because she knows the devil will be around here looking for her," the people said. Shrugging their shoulders, they did not think it necessary to raise a search party.

From that day the town was disturbed as it had not been since its children had disappeared all those years ago. Long, gloomy shadows were cast upon it both morning and afternoon by the hills above. Women woke at dawn to find earth from the graveyard thrown inside their doorways. They noticed salt sprinkled in circles around their houses. Every mirror in town fell from its wall. Water flowed blue from taps. "It's that old woman," ladies said. "She'll spend eternity cursing us."

The people suddenly observed various long-forgotten features peculiar to their town: a poppy tree that dropped showers of red and yellow blossoms day and night, in and out of season; a large hopscotch game painted in disturbingly bright colours on their plaza; a shore upon which were washed jewels made from coloured glass.

To make matters worse, the townspeople were at this time upset by voices calling in their streets after midnight. At once they recognized these as belonging to their long lost children, whom they had by this time completely forgotten. They heard drowned girls calling from the sea. Boys cried from the north. The churchbell pealed at odd, late hours, though rung by no visible person. "It's Benito," the people said, recalling a vanished boy who had once driven them crazy with his fondness for ringing the bell. Showers of stars fell upon the town every night, smashing into slivers of glass in the streets and requiring the people to walk with care to spare their feet. "Victor Aquino is throwing pieces of the sky at us," it was remarked, and a boy who had once sailed his boat through the stars was remembered. The townspeople took to staying up through the nights, waiting to hear the voices of their dead children. As a result, the town fell into disorder. The school and stores closed, work in the fields and sea halted. Abandoning housework and babies, mothers with glazed eyes sat upon little chairs. Often they would silently rise and walk like dreamers toward the edge of town. Husbands were continually chasing after wives who seemed intent upon wandering from the world. Shaken from trances by their men, mothers would be startled to find themselves at the bottom of the path that climbed the western slopes. "We are going mad," they said in their lucid moments. "We're letting our precious babies die of neglect."

However, they could not stop themselves from packing trunks and planning journeys. "Our missing children are calling for us to fetch them home," wives explained to husbands. "I have no doubt at all," they said, quickly throwing clothes into suitcases. "My Marcelino isn't dead. He's working as a lawyer in the capital city. I'll bring him home where he belongs. We need a good lawyer in this town." Convinced of the need to retrieve children from the unknown world at all costs, some women prepared to travel to California or even across the seas toward this end. "Little Luis is living in the snows of Siberia. He eats snow, he lives in a snow house, he bathes in snow. He is turning pale in the snow. God meant our children to live in the sun, eat tortillas and beans, and bathe in the river."

The men of the town tried in vain to dissuade their wives from undertaking these rash journeys. "We have a child living alone in the wicked world!" countered town ladies with emotion. "He is far from a home he cannot remember and someone must bring him back. I will go and you can stay behind to look after the babies."

Soon the town was deserted of women. At first the men had difficulties keeping the houses clean, the babies fed, the streets swept. After several months, however, they became very adept at their domestic duties, and in fact performed them with the avidity and thoroughness of new disciples. The children grew healthy with good food and obedient with firm, fair discipline. In the afternoons the men liked to sit in doorways and embroider white cloths. They compared stitches and boasted of babies.

When the women returned some months later without the missing children, they had changed. They had turned modern. "I saw Vicente and he's doing fine in San Diego. He's become an American in every sense of the word. You know, there are more ways of living than the ones we have known in this town." The ladies smoked in the streets and gathered together one night a week to play cards and drink. "You seem to be doing fine with the housework and the babies," they told their husbands. They dyed their hair red and took an interest in business. Soon the streets were lined with modern stores and cafes which the ladies ran efficiently and prosperously.

Because they were so fully occupied away from home, mothers became strangers to their children. They would call a daughter by her sister's name. "Who are you?" they sometimes asked a forgotten child who strayed into view. Although at first very serious, the women began to fall into spells of playfulness, in which they acted as foolishly as young girls with no knowledge of the world. They dressed in bright fashionable clothes they had brought back from the outer world, and their appearances were so drastically altered that husbands fell in love with them all over again. Rejuvenated by their youthful wives, middle-aged men began to court as romantically as young boys.

As their parents became lost in the intrigues of young love, the children of the town were left much to their own devices. They learned at remarkably early ages to take care of themselves, and they turned precociously practical and serious. Sighing at foolish parents, the children took over the domestic and commercial affairs of the town. They felt obliged to watch over their mothers and fathers, who liked to dress up in fancy clothes and promenade around the plaza at evening, flirting and falling in love. "Be home before midnight," strict children would say. The adults behaved as though every day were a holiday and the moon were made of honey. They would take picnic baskets and play in the wild gardens of Chonita's yard through the afternoons. Among the whistling birds and dancing butterflies they sang songs in unison. They played tag amid the overgrown shrubbery.

One day the playing parents noticed the old woman sitting in her parlour, which was now reduced to rubble. They fled through town, shouting that they had seen a ghost. The practical children went to see for themselves. "It's no ghost," they firmly said at once. "Spirits do not smoke Partytime cigarettes and drink Presidente brandy. Old Chonita has come back from wherever she's been."

The old woman had changed. She had a new pair of eyes, and they were very bright. She was now more sociable and invited old and long-forgotten neighbours into her ruined rooms. While their elders drank and laughed and mamboed obliviously in Chonita's tattered parlour, parties of children worked around them, restoring the white house to some semblance of its former grandeur. They patched the roof and swept the rooms, aired furnishings and scoured walls. "If we let one house decay, our entire town will fall apart," the children said.

When the white house was mended, the children remembered the existence of Chonita's son a thousand miles to the north. They wrote to him, explaining that his mother had turned into a baby and both she and her house needed care.

A short while later Guillermo turned up with a truckload of possessions, a wife named Beatriz, and three small children. Beatriz took one look at the town and said, "This place is crazy." She and her husband were practical, hardworking people, and they quickly raised the white house and its gardens to a state of immaculate order. Various notices stating dos and don'ts were placed in six of the guest rooms. The Holiday Hotel sign was freshly painted. Almost at once travellers of all ages and nationalities began to arrive in the town, and six of the spare rooms were always full.

Chonita lived in the seventh guest room, banished from the centre of the house by Beatriz, Guillermo, and the three children. She took her exile in good grace, and actually seemed to believe she had been elevated in status. Her small room was stuffed to the point of bursting with a long lifetime's momentos, knick-knacks, and prizes. A guitar and a sombrero hung upon the wall. The largest mirror in town and an extra big double bed dominated the decor.

The old woman took no interest in the life her son's family led in the centre of the house. She lived apart on cigarettes and brandy, declining the more substantial meals which Beatriz dutifully brought her. "Tortillas and beans do not nourish the soul," she would say, waving one arm with an air of regal rejection. "Go away, please," she would command when her daughter-in-law tried to disturb her possessions with duster and polish. "There's nothing wrong with my treasures. They're only old."

Chonita was not especially fond of her grandchildren. When they came dancing to her room in search of games and songs she would push them out the door, preferring to listen to fast music on her record machine. Often other older ladies stopped by for a drink and a chat. However, Chonita spent the greatest part of her time lying on her bed, with a French or English novel propped upon her stomach. She would look out the window, now and then turning a page.

She seemed largely unaware of the passing presence of the travellers who occupied the other rooms of the hotel. Dedicated tourists, they explored the hills with maps and swam religiously in the sea. They walked around with cameras, taking pictures of everything they saw. Sometimes Chonita would graciously pose for their photographs, dressed in the costume of a pirate queen.

There was one boy from far away who remained in the house while other tourists came and went. During the afternoons, when shadows of leaves waved in the window, Chonita held court from her big bed. Sometimes she would smile to herself and vaguely say, "Oh, you American boys." Yet for the most part she seemed to think this boy an anonymous member of a vast audience. "The gypsy life," she would sigh nostalgically, exhaling puffs of smoke from the fires burning inside her. "Travelling from town to town with the circus, that was a rough and tumbling life. The smell of sawdust and the dancing bears! Every night I performed bareback tricks on Arabian horses in the centre ring, and the crowds always cheered."

The old woman leaped from her bed and executed a few shuffling dance steps before the mirror. She waved an arm before her eyes, clearing her vision. "A girlhood spent in a shadowy palace beside a Venetian canal is always sentimental. I was locked in the tower room because all the young men were wild with love for me. In the evenings the gondoliers would serenade me with sad songs from the purple water below. I would hang out the window, my long hair trailing down like a ladder."

The old woman's eyes glittered. "We lived in a Spanish castle on the top of the hill. From the terrace I could see the blue Mediterranean melting all the way to Africa. Little white houses clung to the slopes of the hill. Every Sunday the women whitewashed their houses so they would always sparkle in the sun. All I ever wanted was to live in a white house." Chonita paused, and then with one hand she gently patted the air, as though it were a precious child.

The town beneath the western slopes settled down. The people expressed no more wonder at the stars still falling from the sky, the red and yellow poppies dropping from the trees, the coloured glass washing upon the shore. They did not remark upon the voices which called out at night. The serious children grew older, and with age they began to take on some of the childish ways they had previously disdained.

The older generation remained as happy children, and they spent the afternoons jumping rope in the main street. Sometimes they climbed the hills above the town simply for the pleasure of rolling over and over down through the long grass. They fell limp and dizzy at the bottom, then rose to sway and stumble. "Which way is forward and which way is backward?" they shrieked with laughter.

Once a week there was a large party given by the old woman in her gardens, which everyone in town attended but herself. On these nights she put aside the clothes of her dead husband, that she had been wearing for years, and dressed herself in the rainbow-coloured costumes left behind by the lost children from far away. Wearing in layers these clothes which had aged into tattered ribbons, Chonita looked like a very exotic flower. She ate oysters in bed, licking oil from her fingers with the grace and dignity of a woman who might have been a queen. She sat in her room listening to the young and old children who played in her garden.

A band played in the gazebo and Japanese lanterns burned red and blue and green. Their light shone on stone statues of gods scattered through the yard. Soft breezes blew in from the Pacific, and beneath the glittering stars the people drank and sang and told stories. Babies played tag with fireflies. Children danced in rings around the pond in which red and yellow fish swam once more. There was kissing and hugging in the shadows. The town beneath the western slopes laughed.